DUKE WITH A LIE
WICKED DUKES SOCIETY
BOOK FOUR

SCARLETT SCOTT

Duke with a Lie

Wicked Dukes Society Book 4

All rights reserved.

Copyright © 2025 by Scarlett Scott™

Published by Happily Ever After Books, LLC

Edited by Grace Bradley and Lisa Hollett, Silently Correcting Your Grammar

Cover Design by Wicked Smart Designs

This book or any portion thereof may not be reproduced or used in any manner whatsoever without the express written permission of the publisher except for the use of brief quotations in a book review.

The unauthorized reproduction or distribution of this copyrighted work is illegal. No part of this book may be scanned, uploaded, or distributed via the Internet or any other means, electronic or print, without the publisher's permission. Criminal copyright infringement, including infringement without monetary gain, is punishable by law.

This book is a work of fiction and any resemblance to persons, living or dead, or places, events, or locales, is purely coincidental. The characters are productions of the author's imagination and used fictitiously.

Scarlett Scott™ is a registered trademark of Happily Ever After Books, LLC.

For more information, contact author Scarlett Scott™.

https://scarlettscottauthor.com/

For Steve ~
I'll gladly be your grasshopper.

For my readers~
Thank you for making it possible for me to live my dream every day and for loving historical romance as much as I do.

CHAPTER 1

*A*ubrey Villiers, seventh Duke of Richford, had committed an untold number of sins in his life, all of which would be responsible for one day sending him to Hades where he belonged. It was glaringly apparent, given the most unfortunate and present state of his cock, that he was about to add one more to the ever-growing compendium—lusting after his close friend's virginal younger sister.

Lady Rhiannon Northwick was a gorgeous, annoying hellion, and one day, some man would have the colossal fortune of bedding her. But that man would not be—could not be—Aubrey. There seemed no better occasion for reminding himself of that than as he dragged the troublesome minx from a game of naughty charades at a country house party to which she decidedly had *not* been invited.

"What do you think you are doing, sirrah?" she growled at him *sotto voce*, tugging at her arm in an effort to escape.

She wasn't going to escape him, however. He was stronger than she was. Wiser than she was. Far more jaded than she was. And he was more determined than she was too.

Aubrey pulled her down the hall in search of an empty private salon. "Rescuing you, little naïf."

As much as the villain in him would have dearly loved to continue watching her parade her saucy curves about whilst she pretended to be a wanton shepherdess in desperate need of a sound shag, he knew better.

He very much doubted she even understood what the phrase *in need of a sound shag* meant. The urge to show her was strong, which was more proof of just how bloody evil he was. Depraved to his core.

Aubrey paused at a closed door and knocked loudly, issuing a stern rap of his knuckles on the paneled mahogany. When no answer came, he turned the latch, only to find a couple within, the woman bent over a settee, skirts and petticoats up to her waist, whilst her gentleman friend rammed his cock into her from behind with furious abandon.

"Damn it," he muttered, slamming the door and turning to scowl at his unwilling companion. "You didn't see that, did you?"

"See what?" she asked, pouting. "This is outrageous. You must unhand me and allow me to return to the games at once. I demand it."

"Oh, you *demand* it, do you?" Chuckling darkly, he found the next room blessedly empty and crossed the threshold, pulling her with him.

"Yes, I do." She tossed her head in defiance, and her unbound golden curls shook with indignation, emphasizing the unparalleled beauty of her hair. "You are treating me as if I'm a piece of furniture, and I do not appreciate it."

"A piece of furniture wouldn't find a way of stealing into a house party for which she received no invite, my lady." He snapped the door closed and locked it, pocketing the key before he turned back to her, releasing his hold on her arm at last.

Which was just as well, for he was far too tempted to jerk her luscious form into his chest and kiss that sulking mouth of hers.

"Of course I was invited," she lied, blue eyes blazing from behind her mask. "Why else would I be here?"

"Because you are a wayward hoyden." He crossed his arms over his chest, unimpressed.

The hellion had found herself in many scrapes over the years since she'd made her debut in society. But sneaking into an impending orgy was rather bold, even by her astounding standards.

"You do not know me," Rhiannon huffed. "I am masked."

Of course he knew her. God, how well he knew her. And how he wished he knew her better, but that was a damned stupid thought his puerile prick wanted him to entertain. Aubrey's half-cockstand didn't know that touching Lady Rhiannon Northwick was the rough equivalent of consuming a platter of poisonous wild mushrooms. The rest of him, however, was too intelligent for such tomfoolery.

He tilted his head now, considering her, trying to keep his gaze from the lush breasts her scandalously cut gown put on proud display. "How charmingly innocent. You truly supposed that donning a scrap of silk would shield you well enough, didn't you?"

A flush crept up her throat, giving her away. "Everyone else is masked as well."

"The illusion of anonymity pleases some more than it does others," he offered with a careless shrug.

"What does that mean?"

"It means that a mask cannot hide anyone. It means that the members of this club wear masks at gatherings such as this for titillation as much as preserving privacy."

That much was true. Oh, he had no doubt some of the lords and ladies in attendance—all members of the highly secret Wicked Dukes Society, over which he presided with his five friends, the dukes of Brandon, Camden, Whitby, Riverdale, and Kingham—were either too obtuse or too deep in their cups to recognize one another. But for anyone with a discerning eye or ear, a mask provided no barrier at all.

Aubrey was reasonably certain Rhiannon could walk about with a sack over her head and he would still know her. She could hide in another room, and the faintest strain of her husky voice would give her away. Even her scent lingering after she had gone would be sufficient—jasmine and bergamot with a hint of rose. He had taken note of everything where she was concerned.

Far too much.

But Aubrey didn't dally with innocents. And he didn't bed his good chum's virgin sister. Not even a golden goddess who put Venus to shame and possessed a tendency to stare at him as if she wanted to devour him. *Especially* not her.

Wilt, cock, he inwardly urged that unruly appendage. *Wilt.*

"For...titillation," she repeated, her eyes narrowing, as if she didn't believe him.

Christ. He should not explain himself to Whit's little sister. And Aubrey most assuredly should not allow his gaze to slip to her décolletage or to wonder if a hasty tug of her pink silk bodice would release her equally pink nipples.

He clenched his jaw, fighting for inner composure for a moment. "Yes, titillation, my lady. You see, some prefer the pretense they do not know their lovers. For them, it heightens the pleasure. Others may fear repercussions with husbands, wives, or polite society should word of their transgressions reach the gossipmongers. They cling to their masks for fear of discovery. Either way, no one is fooling anyone else. Least of all, you."

Rhiannon blinked, her full lips parting, the lower caught by white, even teeth. "Me? Forgive me if I fail to believe your bluster, sir. You claim to know who I am, but you have yet to say my name. Perhaps you've mistaken me for another. Either way, I can assure you that you haven't the right to pull me bodily from the drawing room and lock me up inside this room with you."

She had the audacity to punctuate her diatribe by holding out her hand, palm up. "The key, if you please."

Aubrey reached up to his own mask, untying it and pulling it away from his face. "On that, I fear we must disagree, Lady Rhiannon. I have *every* right to keep you here, safe, in this room. Your brother would expect no less from me, and when I inform him of your presence here, I have no doubt he'll send you back to London and your mama where you belong. The reckoning for you will be harsh, I'm sure."

Her shoulders sagged, and the defeat in her jaw and eyes made something within him clench. "How did you know?"

I would know you anywhere, he thought before tamping down all such ridiculous notions.

Aubrey shrugged again, one shoulder only this time. "As I said, minx. Masks mean nothing. Did you not recognize me?"

"Of course I did."

He raised an imperious brow. "Well, then. Why should the reverse be any different?"

"Because you don't notice me. You never have. You don't even know I'm *alive*, and now you have seized my one and only adventure and seek to ruin it utterly."

How wrong she was. He *did* notice her. From the moment she'd become a woman, making her curtsy, flitting about ballrooms, he had been irritatingly aware of her. Not just her beauty, but her stubborn nature, her ludicrous bravado, her laughter, her smile.

Fucking hell. He had to stop this maudlin nonsense at once.

"I notice what happens here, within these walls," he said

smoothly, because lying was far more comfortable than speaking plain truth. "As one of the founding members of the society, doing so is my duty. And as your brother's close and enduring friend, it is also my obligation to take note when his naïve, wayward sister somehow manages to all but ruin herself. To step in before it's too late."

She scowled, the pink mask she wore that matched her gown so perfectly still in place and obstructing his view of her lovely face.

Which was for the best, really.

The mask was silly.

Lady Rhiannon Northwick was anything but. Therein lay the danger. To him, to her, to everyone who mattered.

"I am not your obligation or anyone else's," she snapped at him, planting her hands on her nipped waist. "Nor am I naïve or wayward. I am simply in search of a bearable future for myself. I want to experience life as I choose."

A bitter laugh tore from him. "My dear little naïf, there is no future at all to be found at these fêtes. Not for you. Nor for anyone else. These house parties are intended for sin the likes of which a virginal miss such as yourself cannot possibly fathom."

It was the wrong thing to say to a stubborn hoyden, as it turned out. Lady Rhiannon Northwick couldn't resist a challenge. He recognized that in her—so much of himself when he had been a lad, before darkness had consumed him.

Her irresistible, dented chin went up. "I can fathom a great deal, Your Grace."

"Not what happens within these walls, I can assure you of that."

"I've read books."

"No book could aptly describe pleasure. Not truly."

Renewed color appeared over her pale throat and chest,

almost reaching the tempting swells of her breasts. "I do know about it."

He moved toward her, some impulse he could neither define nor deny rising. "You know about what, little naïf?"

"Don't call me that."

"It's what you are, is it not?"

"No!"

He stopped before her, and dear God, the headiness of her scent and nearness was an intoxicating combination that not even opium could rival. "Then tell me. What do you read about in your books?"

It was a question he should not ask.

Just as lingering here with her was a foolish risk he should not take.

And yet Aubrey stayed, awaiting her response. Needing it more than his next breath.

"About…about lovemaking and what happens between a man and a woman," she said breathlessly.

And his stupid cock, which had begun to settle, twitched back to life.

Such words alone were paltry. They meant nothing. Issued in her sultry voice, however? They meant everything.

Aubrey cleared his throat. "You've been reading vulgar books?"

"*Books*, yes," she corrected with a prim air that had no place coupled with what she had just said. "*Not* vulgar, however."

Damn it all, *why*? Why did she have to make such an inappropriate admission, and why did it have to affect him so?

He had to get her out of this bloody house party.

Out of this room.

Out of his reach.

"Ah, yes. Not vulgar at all. Would you care to repeat what you just explained to your brother?" he asked cruelly.

"It is none of Whitby's concern what I read," she snapped.

"Because you know he wouldn't approve."

Her nostrils flared. "Because I am a woman grown."

He raised a brow and raked her over with a wilting gaze. "Are you? Because I do confess, you look rather like a girl playing at being a woman just now."

For a moment, he thought she might slap him.

But instead, she did the opposite.

Lady Rhiannon Northwick took one step forward, her pink evening gown slamming into his trousers, billowing outward, and then she grabbed his necktie and tugged him toward her. In the next second, her lips were on his.

And Aubrey?

He was bloody *lost*.

Lost in her hot, silken lips. Lost in her curves melding into his hard frame, lost in her scent, in her breasts crushing into his chest, in the way she fit against him, as perfectly as if she'd been made to do so. Aubrey had no choice but to kiss her back with all the suppressed desire within him…

Fuck.

This wasn't going to end well.

∽

Rhiannon could scarcely believe that she was *kissing* the Duke of Richford.

The beautiful, cruel rake. The gentleman every woman threw herself at, be she wife or widow or debutante. The most beautiful man she'd ever met and the most confounding man she knew too.

Because he had called her a girl playing at being a woman. Because she had been harboring a secret *tendre* for him ever since she'd first set eyes upon him at sixteen, and he never looked at her with the same melting gaze he settled upon every other lady. Because she wanted him to notice her, to flirt with her, to bestow his disarming smiles and wicked sallies upon her. To lead her into darkened alcoves at balls and kiss her breathless.

To desire her.

And yet, he had never paid her any more notice than he would a fly winging past his head. Not in all this time. No matter how hard she tried to draw his gaze or earn his approval. He never strayed from his icy mask of impassivity for her. He had scarcely ever spoken more than a handful of words to Rhiannon.

To her shame, she had come here in the hope that she would cross paths with him. That she might woo him from behind the haven of her mask and anonymity. That she could give herself to him before she settled into a predictable, staid life as another man's wife.

But he had dashed all her hopes with his cutting words.

She would show him that there was nothing at all girlish about her.

She was three-and-twenty, damn him. And he was being high-handed and condescending and…

Oh.

He kissed quite well.

She shouldn't be surprised. He had likely seduced half the ladies in London by now. But as his lips moved over hers, lightly at first and then with greater, almost ravenous insistence, she quite forgot her reason for kissing him.

Damn him twice.

He had humiliated her, and Rhiannon had intended to filch that blasted key from his pocket. Instead, she was savoring his skilled seducer's mouth. She was supposed to thwart him at his own game, to best him, to show him she was as unaffected as he was, although that was a dreadful lie.

And yet, her knees were going weak. Because how could

she resist the only man she'd ever truly wanted, the Duke of Richford? Her every breath was of his maddening scent, like a forest tinged with musk and amber. The center of her being became her lips, and then just as suddenly, it changed to the small of her back, where his palm gently pressed, bringing her body into his.

A liquid heat slid through her, settling in her core and dampening her drawers.

This wouldn't do.

Rhiannon released his necktie, slowly moving her hand between their bodies.

His tongue plundered her mouth and simultaneously wiped all thoughts from her mind. He tasted like wine and sin. No man had ever dared to kiss her like this, carnally, deeply, in a way that made her feel as if he had plumbed the depths of her. The handful of suitors she'd had—before the Earl of Carnis—who had been bold enough to make an overture had given her nothing more than a chaste press of their lips to hers. She had never been consumed as if she were a decadent dish laid before a starving man.

Rhiannon opened for the duke, surrendering. Giving him everything he wanted, everything he would take. She thought she could kiss him like this forever and never grow weary of it.

But then she reminded herself with firm determination that he was only kissing her because she had initiated the contact. He didn't see her as a woman, and she needed to get that blasted key and restore her pride and sanity both.

His stomach was lean and firm beneath her slowly questing touch. She didn't dare linger overly long or take her time. Her fingers simply crept into the pocket of his waistcoat and slid against the cool metal of the key.

She almost had it.

Just one small move, and the key would be entirely free...

Richford tore his mouth from hers and moved away with such hasty force that Rhiannon nearly fell onto her rump. She stumbled, blinking, lips tingling with the aftereffects of his kiss, cheeks going hot.

The key was still in his pocket.

Curse him. She had failed at her task.

And to make matters worse, he appeared utterly unmoved by what had just happened between them. His green gaze was cold and unreadable, his bearded jaw hard, his expression smug. Whilst Rhiannon was breathless, face flaming, feeling like the gauche naïf he had accused her of being.

"You see?" he asked softly, his tone pitying. "You are naught but a girl, playing a woman's games."

"Let me out of this room," she commanded through gritted teeth.

"Not a chance." He raised a golden brow, leaning a hip indolently into a settee at his side while he studied her. "You claim to know what these house parties are about, and yet your ignorance shows."

"Of course I know what they're about," she brazened.

"Oh? Enlighten me."

More heat washed over her cheeks, but she held his stare, determined not to allow him to embarrass her. "Do you think I'm unaware of what your secret society truly is? I can assure you I'm not. The ladies and gentlemen who belong to your club convene at the house parties you host because they wish to indulge in congress beyond the bounds of their marriages."

"Congress," he repeated in a silken tone.

One that made her nipples tighten into hard points within her bodice.

She licked her lips, which proved a mistake because she tasted him. And good, sweet heavens, she wanted more. She wanted this man on her lips first thing every morning and before she went to bed each night.

That wasn't meant to be, she reminded herself sternly. She was almost promised to wed another.

"Yes," she bit out. "As I said, what happens between a man and a woman."

"Such as?" He began prowling toward her.

Rhiannon didn't want to take a step in retreat. Even if he was like a beast stalking its prey.

She tipped up her chin. "I needn't elaborate. I'm sure you already know the answer."

He chuckled softly, stopping before her once more. "How knowledgeable you are for a girl who has just had her first kiss."

"That was hardly my first kiss."

Richford stilled, a strange, intent expression on his face. "Who?"

She blinked, confused. "I beg your pardon?"

"Give me names, minx. I want to know who to tell your brother to beat to within an inch of their miserable lives."

"Perhaps you ought to begin with your own name," she countered archly, crossing her arms over her chest in a defensive pose.

"What just happened is scarcely anything of note."

If his tongue in her mouth hadn't been *anything of note*, then the sky wasn't blue. Rhiannon was still breathless, her knees still weak, her body still flushed, every part of her still intensely aware of him. But perhaps for such an experienced, wicked rake, their heated kisses had been commonplace. It was a sobering thought indeed.

"Of course you're right," she forced herself to agree, trying with all her might to conceal her umbrage and the hurt lurking close beneath the surface. "My beaus have all been far bolder. But that's neither here nor there. All I want is for you to give me the key so that I can carry on."

His jaw tightened. "Carry on with what? Surely you aren't foolish enough to imagine I'd allow you to return to the house party."

"Yes, that is precisely what I imagine. I came here for a reason."

"To ruin yourself?" Richford shook his head. "I won't allow it. As one of your brother's closest friends, I could never in good conscience keep your presence here a secret from him."

The notion of her brother discovering that she had stolen her way into this wicked house party and unraveling the sculpture of lies she had so carefully constructed made her throat seize.

"Whitby cannot know I'm here."

But the duke was unrelenting. "He has to know. You need to go back to London. Posthaste."

"I'm staying at this house party, and my brother has nothing to do with my presence here," she countered.

"Wrong, little naïf." A small smile curved his sensual lips.

Lips she had felt on hers, coaxing and knowing.

But she couldn't think about his mouth now, or how moved she'd been by his skilled kisses. Finally, after all these years of longing and yearning, of watching him from across the room, she had felt those wicked lips on hers.

Stop thinking about it, Rhiannon, she urged herself sternly.

No, she had to do something.

Anything to keep him from immediately seeking out her older brother and making certain that she would be sent back to London. This had been her one chance for adventure. To make the Duke of Richford notice her at last before she became a wife and mother. Mater was determined to see her married to the Earl of Carnis, a man who was handsome but staid and boring and unfailingly proper.

He was also kindhearted almost to a fault and had confessed he was in love with her. Mater had vowed that Carnis would make the perfect husband. He would worship Rhiannon, and she would never want for anything, from the finest gowns to the wealthiest estates. Carnis was rich as Croesus. He had asked for her hand in marriage, and Rhiannon had begged him to give her time to consider his offer. He hadn't even tried to hold her hand, let alone steal a kiss, and she had hoped for more...for at least a spark of passion, a hint that he found her irresistible.

Anything other than his bland patience and insistence upon propriety.

Still, she knew Carnis would make an excellent and loyal husband and father. She would marry him.

Eventually.

When she had learned that her brother was again hosting one of his forbidden house parties, a thought had risen in her mind, one that had proven unshakable. It had seemed her last opportunity to find herself alone with the man who had occupied all her secret, heated longings from the moment they'd first been introduced, and she had leapt at the opportunity. Mater was so caught up in her own concerns that she had been easily fooled. Whitby—Rhys—had been too busy organizing the house party to even bid Rhiannon a farewell before he'd gone. She had orchestrated her escape, found a room in which to stay in the wing of the house that was largely unoccupied. Everything had been unfolding according to plan.

Until Richford had realized who she was on the very first night, ruining her improbable dream. She wasn't certain which was worse, that he had known her at once, that he was intent upon sending her immediately back to London, or that he very plainly still considered her nothing but a mere girl. Either way, she couldn't allow him to cut her adventure short before it had even begun. Being here was all she had left before she capitulated to a boring, staid future. She was desperate to remain for the house party's duration.

"If you tell Whit about me, then I'll have no choice but to tell him you kissed me," she blurted, grasping at anything she might use against him.

"There's just one small problem with your machinations, my dear," he drawled, his gaze lingering on her lips. "You were the aggressor in our tête-à-tête."

He was so assured of his success. So calm and arrogant. She wanted to slap his handsome face. But she also wanted to kiss him again in equal measure. Of all the men in London, why had she lost her heart to this one? Why couldn't she shake the way he made her feel?

"Do you think he would believe that?" she demanded. "I'm his innocent sister, whereas you are a rake of the worst order. If I told Whitby you had led me into a private room and ravished me, which of us do you think he would trust more?"

His emerald gaze narrowed. "What a bold liar you've proven to be. I confess, I didn't think you had such heartless manipulation in you."

She wasn't heartless, nor was she a liar. She was, however, desperate. And willing to deceive Richford into thinking she would go to her brother with such a ruse when, in fact, she would never dream of uttering such a shameless falsehood. He had left her no choice.

Rhiannon held his stare defiantly. "How do you think Whitby would react to learn you had dishonored his sister?"

Richford passed a hand along his bearded jaw, his expression hard. "Fair enough." He extracted the key from his pocket and extended it to her. "You're free to go for now, minx. But don't say I didn't warn you. And don't look to me when you need saving."

She accepted the key, ignoring the frisson that went through her as their fingers brushed. Richford had made his opinion of her more than clear, and her pride was still smarting.

"I can assure you that I won't require saving," she tossed flippantly over her shoulder as she hastened to the door. "Not from you."

Rhiannon slipped the key into the lock, turned it, and then fled the room, resisting the urge to glance back at him over her shoulder.

CHAPTER 2

Aubrey's cock was harder than an anvil as he watched Rhiannon flounce from the room, slamming the door closed at her back. She was brazen. She was beautiful. She was cunning.

Damn, but she was glorious.

Full fucking stop.

He had wanted nothing more than to pin her to that bloody door instead of allowing her to flee through it. To take her lips and kiss her again. To lift her skirts and find the slit in her drawers. To see if she was as wet as he hoped after all but bringing him to his knees with those innocent but ardent kisses.

And then to sink inside her. To fuck her until they were both spent. To fill her with his seed. To make her his in every way and obliterate any memory she had of the bastards who had dared to kiss her before him.

With a low groan, he adjusted the fall of his trousers.

Thank Christ she had gone.

He couldn't do any of those things. Not with her. He

shouldn't even be thinking such vile, traitorous thoughts. He couldn't bed Whit's sister. His friend's not-as-innocent-as-he-had-supposed sister.

There were facets to Lady Rhiannon Northwick that Aubrey hadn't begun to imagine existed. He wanted to hunt down every man who had tasted her lips and beat him to within an inch of oblivion. But he couldn't do that either.

No.

He inhaled slowly, trying to summon any notion that would wilt his rampaging prick. What he needed to do was exit this chamber and return to naughty charades. He could find an experienced woman for the evening. One who would be more than happy to exchange mutual pleasure with him, sans consequences. He could bury his cock inside her, fuck her until they were both satisfied, and forget Rhiannon was even in attendance at this house party.

Except he couldn't very well do that. For one thing, he needed to know where she was sleeping so that he could at least watch over her on his friend's behalf. Her threat to go to Whit and tell him that Aubrey had been the one to initiate their scorching kisses was still echoing in his mind. He didn't doubt the minx would be bold enough to do it, should sacrificing his friendship with her brother suit her purposes.

Whit was like a brother to him, as were Brandon, Riverdale, Camden, and Kingham. Hell, the five of them were all he had. He couldn't afford to lose Whit's friendship. And he damned well should have thought of that before putting his tongue in his friend's sister's mouth.

Blast.

He scrubbed a hand over his face, relieved that his whirling ruminations had at least served to wilt his cock. There was no hope for it. He was going to have to be the one to look after Rhiannon and make certain no harm came to her at this cursed house party. He owed that much, if not far more, to his friend.

Aubrey started after her. She'd had sufficient time to disappear whilst he'd been arguing with himself and willing his cockstand to abate. Fortunately, the servants were the soul of discretion. He found a chambermaid and, after a circumspect inquiry, discovered that a masked woman meeting Rhiannon's description had been headed in the direction of the wing of the manor house that wasn't presently in use for most guests.

Wise girl. It was an excellent hiding place, as Whit had made certain to keep the revelers contained in the opposite wing.

Aubrey stalked after her, the benefit of his long legs not lost upon him. It didn't take much time to discover which room she had claimed, catching sight of her pink skirts disappearing just as a door closed.

It happened to cleverly and helpfully possess the same locks Brandon had ordered installed on each room, both outside and inside the doors, the better for their guests to make use of the chambers as they saw fit. With a grin, Aubrey closed the distance to Rhiannon's door. Slowly and taking care to avoid making any sound that would alert her to his presence, he settled the key she'd left in the door of the salon into the lock and turned the latch.

At least for this evening, he could be certain the minx would stay out of trouble.

~

THE MORNING SUN was rising fast.

Rhiannon was starving and incredibly irritable as she cast a final glance in the looking glass. Unaccustomed to dressing herself without the aid of her efficient lady's maid, she had struggled into her underpinnings and morning gown. She'd scarcely been able to sleep last night, restless in her bed as the memory of the sinful kisses she had shared with Richford had turned over and over in her mind, haunting her.

At least she had managed to plait her hair into a passable braid, which she had coiled on her crown with tendrils free to frame her face. All she had to do was continue avoiding her brother and the Duke of Richford, and today would hopefully prove more entertaining than the evening before had been.

That disaster had been *his* fault, of course.

He had hauled her from charades, locked her in a room, and proceeded to be an insufferable, arrogant arse. He wouldn't have an opportunity to do so today. She vowed it. She would banish all the unwanted, pent-up feelings she had for him until there wasn't so much as a crumb left.

Beginning today.

With a deep breath, Rhiannon turned and crossed the chamber she had commandeered for the house party. It was a pleasant room with windows that faced the gardens. But best of all, it was entirely removed from the wing that was housing most of the other guests, which had proven a boon for her ability to hide in plain sight.

Rhiannon's hand landed on the latch.

But it didn't budge.

She frowned.

Locked?

Surely not.

She tried again, but the latch was firm and immobile.

It was definitely, without a doubt, locked. But how? And most importantly, *who*?

"Richford," she snarled, instantly knowing who would be behind such a thing.

He had *locked her* inside her bedchamber.

And it was time for breakfast.

Furious, she tried to open the door with greater strength. Then she threw her shoulder into it, attempting to force it open with her body weight until pain radiated from her shoulder and down her spine. Nothing worked. She was trapped in this room.

There was a bellpull, of course.

Rhiannon spun from the door, intent upon ringing it. She was halfway across the Axminster when she heard a click of the latch, followed by the slight creak of the door swinging open.

"Good morning, my dear," drawled a familiar voice.

Rhiannon whirled about, facing her enemy directly. There, on the threshold, looking smug and despicably handsome, was the Duke of Richford. He was dressed for riding, his trousers hugging his muscled thighs and lean legs, his boots shined. She hated herself for being affected by him, for the way her stomach flipped as she drank in the sight of him. He was in shirtsleeves and a waistcoat, his golden hair tousled as if he had run a hand through it.

Or perhaps a lover had, she thought sourly before she could stop herself.

He was also grinning.

She hated him. She loved him. She couldn't have him.

Rhiannon reached for the nearest available missile, which happened to be her hairbrush, and launched it at his beautiful face. Sadly, her aim was incorrect. The brush sailed toward his chest instead, but Richford caught it with ease, using only one hand.

"Whatever is amiss, minx? I confess, I'm not accustomed to a woman throwing objects at me when she's not my lover."

"You are a scoundrel," she accused, looking for something else she might hurl in his direction.

"I pride myself upon it," he said, unmoved by her insult.

Rhiannon thought about the women who had tossed objects at him in anger. His lovers. She refused to consider that the sharp twinge of emotion inside her was jealousy. Why would she be envious of the legions of women who had warmed his bed? The villain had locked her in a room on no fewer than two separate occasions. He had called her a girl. Had kissed her and then acted as if he found her as desirable as a spider in the corner. He didn't want her, and he had made that abundantly, painfully, humiliatingly clear.

She found a book she'd thieved from the library and whipped it toward his head.

To her vast disappointment, he caught the leather-bound tome as well.

"Are you going to continue throwing bric-a-brac at me?" he asked, sounding bored. "Because if so, I'd like to set these things down so that I may catch future projectiles. I'd dearly hate to suffer a perfume bottle to my pretty nose or something infinitely worse."

"I'm glad you find it so amusing to lock me inside rooms against my will," she countered sharply. "You're lucky I haven't a pistol in my possession."

He raised a brow, still looking utterly unruffled by both her anger and her threats. "Never say you would think of shooting me, little naïf."

"I dreamt of it all last night," she lied.

"How delightfully bloodthirsty of you." He sauntered forward, placing the book and brush down on a nearby Louis Quinze table. "Tell me, did you shoot to maim, or did you shoot to kill in this charming reverie of yours?"

He was still smiling, the knave.

How dare he lock her inside a room and then make light of her ire? How dare he break her heart? She looked around and discovered a boot lying on the floor. In the absence of a lady's maid, the chamber was rather in a state. Rhiannon bent and retrieved it, flinging it at his gorgeous head.

He caught it, looking about the room with renewed interest. "Sweet God, was there a house cracksman in here last night?"

She sniffed. "Of course not. How would anyone else get within when you locked me in here?"

"It certainly looks as if a thief has ransacked the room. But then, I reckon it would have to be a thief who was searching for the family silver in your drawers."

To her utter horror, she spied a pair of drawers draped over the arm of one of the chairs by the cold hearth. Why had she not taken note of it before? And why had she flung her garments about with complete disregard for who might later enter and spy them? Not that she could have suspected Richford himself would come here.

Heat skated through her before she could tamp it down.

Rhiannon stalked across the room and snatched up her drawers, wadding them into a ball and holding them behind her back. "Why are you here, Richford?"

"To check on you, of course," he said in a tone that suggested he was affronted she hadn't already considered it. "Surely you didn't think I would leave you here indefinitely to further plot my murder, did you?"

She glared at him. "Get out of my bedchamber."

He pressed a hand to his heart. "Grant me a moment to collect myself, won't you? This is the first time in my life that a lady has demanded I leave her bedroom."

Rhiannon gritted her teeth, grinding her molars so hard they ached, and issued a low, infuriated sound. "Do you never cease?"

"Did you just *growl* at me, minx?" He looked intrigued.

"Of course not."

"Hmm, I think you did."

"I'm going to breakfast," she announced, nettled beyond measure by his charm and his handsome face and his smug grin and his failure to react as she wanted him to.

Why was he so cursed *entertained* by all this? Why did she still want to kiss him? Why couldn't her broken heart simply accept that he was a callous rake who would never, ever return her feelings?

But as she made her way past him, he caught her elbow, staying her. "Not yet, I don't think. At least, not whilst carrying yesterday's drawers behind your back. This *is* a house party for the depraved, but even I must caution you against bringing your soiled undergarments to the dining room."

Drat the man. She was still holding her drawers behind her back. She'd been in such high dudgeon that she hadn't realized it.

She surreptitiously tossed the garment beneath the bed. She would retrieve it later when she didn't have an audience.

"You're still not going to breakfast quite yet, even if you have just thrown your dirty knickers under your bed," he cautioned, sounding like a governess who had just caught her charge doing something for which a punishment would be forthcoming.

Except that he was talking about her *drawers*. Whilst standing in her bedroom. And the Duke of Richford didn't resemble the grim-looking Miss Sharp, who had served as her own governess. Not in any way.

"Do stop talking about my undergarments, if you please," she snapped, annoyed with herself for the heat that prickled her cheeks.

Good heavens, he had *seen* them.

He had *spoken* about them.

And now she had as well.

Was that worse than his tongue having been in her mouth? Rhiannon wasn't sure.

"As you wish, my dear," he said, as politely as if they had been facing each other in a ballroom instead of her private chamber.

Where she slept and dressed and bathed.

How mortifying.

If anyone were to find him here…

"If you're done enjoying your levity at my expense, then I will fetch my mask and excuse myself to the dining room. I find that I'm famished."

"You don't think I'm allowing you to go about this house party unescorted, do you?"

"Yes, I do. Because I haven't gone to great lengths to secret myself within these walls so that you could hover over me like a mother hen watching her chicks. Did you forget that only last night, you agreed to let me carry on as I wish?"

He shook his head slowly, cocking his head as he considered her. "Oh no, sweet girl. In this instance, I am afraid that I am rather the fox who has stolen into the proverbial henhouse, all the better to feast upon the chicks. And I only agreed because I had every intention of locking you in your room for the night."

Heat slid down her spine.

She straightened, ignoring it. "I am no chick, so you shall have to have your feast elsewhere."

His smug smile returned. "You needn't fear on that account. I'm already quite sated at the moment."

Was he speaking about the kisses they had shared? Or had he returned to naughty charades? Had he taken one of the ladies in attendance to his bed?

Rhiannon told herself she didn't care if he had. It mattered not one whit to her. He had made it more than apparent that her unfortunate feelings for him were not returned.

"Good, then there is also no need for you to accompany me to breakfast," she retorted, moving to skirt around him for the second time.

"On the contrary. There is every need." He offered her his arm. "You have two choices. Accept my escort, or I'll lock you in this room again and have a servant bring you a tray to break your fast."

She eyed his elbow as if it were a snake poised to strike. "I daresay you'll have a far more difficult time locking me in this room when I'm aware you are doing it. I'll fight you every step of the way."

"Don't be tedious, minx. I would so hate to have to tell your brother about your propensity for kissing gentlemen."

"Then I shall have to tell him about *your* propensity for kissing *me*."

"It only happened the once, my dear, and quite against my will if you will but recall."

Fresh shame washed over her. That had been badly done of her, she knew. She had been so desperate to get the key from him that she hadn't given a thought to whether he had wanted her lips on his. And, well, she couldn't lie. She had dreamed of kissing the Duke of Richford for years. In the end, it had simply happened.

"You needn't fear that particular folly shall be repeated," she told him curtly.

"Excellent," he purred. "I do believe we're at a stalemate, which means I'll accompany you to the breakfast table."

She glared at him, thoroughly vexed. How had he managed to back her into this corner? All she wanted was to fill her stomach and to investigate the house party now that everyone had settled in, and yet here he was, attempting to thwart her at every turn.

"Do hurry and make up your mind," he prodded when she hesitated. "I haven't all day."

"Very well," she grumbled, settling her hand in the crook of his elbow. "You may escort me to breakfast."

"As I thought." He placed a large hand over hers. "Come along, minx. I should like to eat before luncheon."

Grudgingly, she allowed him to guide her from the room.

∼

Breakfast was an informal affair, with the guests coming and going as they pleased. The sideboard was laden with eggs, bacon, fresh fruit, and Bayonne ham. Rhiannon had eaten little thus far, despite her hunger. She had been too preoccupied with finding a way she might escape Richford's clutches.

Fortunately, she had been saved from having to implement her plan of leaving the breakfast table under the guise of going to the withdrawing room. She had been determined to slip away into the gardens where he would have a difficult time indeed finding her. But a servant suddenly arrived at his side with a note on a salver. Rhiannon recognized her brother's penmanship instantly. Her heart leapt as Richford took the missive and read it, keeping it carefully averted from her gaze.

"Is something amiss?" she asked him quietly, fearful she had been discovered.

"I've been summoned," he said, his expression and voice carefully neutral.

"By my—by Whitby?" she guessed, correcting herself before she revealed too much information in front of the other revelers who were moving about the large dining room, breaking their fasts.

"Indeed." Richford nodded toward her plate, which was still mostly filled with food.

His, in turn, was empty. The duke had eaten with the unrepentant gusto of a man who hadn't partaken of a meal in days. She had watched him with fascination as he had made short work of rashers of bacon, two poached eggs, and a mountain of hothouse pineapple, thinking it a miracle he was as trim and lean as he was, given his appetite.

More than once, she had given in to the urge to look at his lips. What a mistake that had been, for each time, a spark of longing had burst into undeniable flame. She shook her head, reminding herself she must forget all about the Duke of Richford's mouth on hers and the sinful joy it had brought her. To say nothing of his wicked tongue.

"I must take my leave," Richford added to her in an aside, keeping his voice low so that it wouldn't travel to the others. "But I will return for you. Pray see that you don't get yourself into any trouble whilst I'm gone."

He was leaving her.

Disappointment sliced through Rhiannon despite herself.

"Trouble?" she repeated, batting her lashes at him, feeling like an entirely different woman beneath the shelter of her silk mask. "Me? Never, Your Grace."

"No naughty charades."

"Of course not." She took a sip of her tea, trying not to smile.

Did he truly care, or was he watching over her solely for her brother's benefit? Rhiannon knew it was foolish indeed, but she couldn't seem to help herself. When would she ever learn?

"No wandering off with gentlemen," he added sternly.

"Yes, Father," she mocked.

He bared his teeth. "Someone ought to swat you on your misbehaving rump."

She lifted her fork toward him as if it were a weapon, tines pointing evilly in his direction. "*En garde.*"

"Christ," he muttered, shaking his head. "I must take my leave before I go mad."

"I shall miss your company most dreadfully," she said with a dramatic flair. "Perhaps you might grant me a lock of your hair to hold on to in your absence, o fair knight."

"Minx." He rose and offered her a mocking bow. "I meant what I said."

She smiled. "As did I."

As she watched him stride from the room, she couldn't help but to admire his long legs and broad shoulders. He moved with the self-assured gait of a man who knew how attractive he was and wasn't ashamed to flaunt his looks. It seemed criminal that he was so beautiful.

Curse the man. Unfortunately, it would seem that her feelings for him couldn't be extinguished by his poor behavior alone.

A sigh interrupted her thoughts.

"Quite the handsome devil, isn't he?"

Rhiannon turned to find a lady in a blue mask hovering over her. The woman's eyes were warm. Her voice wasn't familiar, which filled Rhiannon with relief. One of her greatest fears had been that she would come across someone who knew her and would easily see through her ruse.

Aside from Richford, who was busy attempting to ruin everything.

"You mustn't say so in his vicinity," she told her newfound companion. "He's already intolerable enough."

The woman chuckled. "Do you mind if I sit with you?"

"Of course not," she said, smiling. "In fact, I'd be delighted."

Her companion settled her repast on the table and then

seated herself. "It is lovely to find a friend here. At least, I hope we shall be friends."

Rhiannon's need for an ally was even more obvious, given Richford's campaign to continue locking her away in rooms.

"Nothing would make me happier," she said sincerely. "It is going to be a dreadfully tedious house party if I only have Richford to speak with for the duration."

Unlike most of the other guests, Richford hadn't been masked this morning, so there was no need to shield his identity from her fellow revelers. Perhaps he only bothered with the pretense on the first night. She couldn't be sure, and she hadn't spied any of his fellow hosts yet either to determine whether he was alone in eschewing a disguise.

This was a new, dangerous world in which she found herself. It was thrilling to be a part of it, even if her chance was to be short-lived and even if Richford refused to see her as a woman.

The notion left a bitter taste in her mouth.

"The two of you are well acquainted, then?" her new friend asked at Rhiannon's side.

"He is a friend of my family's," she answered, taking care to keep her response politic. "Do you have any acquaintances in attendance?"

"Yes, unfortunately, I do." The woman's lips pinched with distaste. "Only one, however."

Rhiannon cut a delicate bite of pineapple. "Oh?"

She didn't wish to pry, instead allowing her companion to reveal as much or as little as she preferred. This was a game they were all playing. One of secrecy and scandal.

"My husband," the woman elaborated, bitterness tingeing her voice.

Sympathy swept over Rhiannon. Perhaps her friend was trapped in an unhappy marriage and both she and her spouse had come in search of comfort in the arms of another. Such arrangements were commonplace enough in polite society.

"Did the two of you arrive together, then?" she asked carefully.

"No." The woman sliced her Bayonne ham with vigor. "He hasn't even the slightest inkling that I am here."

That certainly added another layer of mystery to their conversation.

"I see," she offered, though, in truth, she didn't see at all.

It wasn't her place to pry, however. Heavens, they had only just met, and Rhiannon had a host of secrets of her own to protect. Starting with who she was and why she was in attendance.

"If we are to be friends, then we ought to call each other by name, do you not think?" her companion asked. "Not our true names, mind you, as I expect that given your mask, you'd like to remain anonymous, as would I for now. But a *nom de plume*, if you like."

"Lady Blue?" Rhiannon suggested, considering that the woman was wearing a mask of that color which matched her silk morning gown.

"And Lady Pink," her friend countered with a wry grin. "Perfect. But I do think we ought not to be so formal. You may call me Blue."

"And you must also call me Pink," she agreed, smiling at their silly game and grateful to have met someone who at least seemed friendly.

They shared a chuckle at the foolish names.

It would have been a long and lonely house party indeed if she'd been forced to rely on Richford for company. He had already proven himself an annoyance rather than a boon.

The two ate together for a few moments, their fellow houseguests moving about, gathering food from the sideboard and sitting in various seats a convenient distance away, affording them privacy.

"May I be bold enough to ask why you've come?" she asked Blue.

Her new friend sighed. "I'm not certain I know the answer to that. Why are you here, my dear?"

"I'm about to be betrothed," Rhiannon answered quietly, making certain that no one else overheard. "I wanted...I don't know...perhaps to understand what I shall be missing."

And if she were brutally honest with herself, she would admit that she had come because she had known *he* would be in attendance. The Duke of Richford.

"You are not in love with your future husband, then?" her companion asked softly.

"He is a kind man. He has professed his love for me." She paused, thinking about the earl and feeling none of the flames sparking to life that happened whenever she was within proximity to Richford. Even when she was furious with him, and even after he had locked her in a room twice, her attraction to him was as magnetic as ever.

"You do not return the sentiment?" Blue asked shrewdly.

"I'm not certain I do. But perhaps, I hope, in time..."

"My dear, you mustn't marry anyone thinking that your love will grow. Pray, trust me on this matter. The only thing that *will* grow is your resentment of him, until one day you're choking on it, and by then, it shall be too late. You'll be saddled with him until death do you part."

Poor Blue had a very grim notion of marriage. Rhiannon wondered what had transpired between the woman and her husband to make her feel thus.

"Yours is not a love match?"

Blue laughed, but there was no humor in the sound. "I'm not certain my husband is capable of that finer emotion."

"He sounds perfectly dreadful," Rhiannon said, feeling

sorry for her new friend. "I scarcely think I would have come to this house party in search of the villain if I were you."

"I'm not here to seek him out, my dear," Blue said serenely. "I'm here to commit adultery so I can persuade the rotten man to divorce me."

She finished her words with a beaming smile.

The woman's husband was about to have a rather unpleasant surprise, Rhiannon decided. But whoever he was, it would serve him right.

They continued on with breakfast in a companionable silence.

CHAPTER 3

*A*ubrey wasn't certain which ached more as he searched for Rhiannon later that afternoon, his knuckles or his head. The minx was the source of his throbbing temples. Because she was missing, curse her.

He had returned from beating the vile Lord Roberts to a pulp for harassing an unaccompanied female—the reason for his aching knuckles—only to discover that she was nowhere to be found. Not in the bedchamber she had commandeered for her secret use. Not in the breakfast room. Not in the main hall, the stables, the gardens, or anywhere else he'd attempted to locate her thus far.

He stalked into the music room, thinking he might find her within, but all he saw was a woman's legs wrapped around a man's waist as he pumped into her on the piano bench. The position looked deuced uncomfortable. Fortunately, the skirts gathered about the woman's waist didn't match Rhiannon's.

Aubrey took his hasty leave, giving the couple their privacy.

If it had been her, he didn't know what he would have done.

Bloodied his other knuckles for a start.

He knew he shouldn't have answered Whit's summons, leaving Rhiannon alone at the breakfast table. She was a bloody menace, capable of anything. Christ knew what manner of mischief she was making. But answering his friend's note had proven a necessity, an obligation thanks to his duty as one of the founding members of the Wicked Dukes Society.

The ladies in attendance had to be protected at all costs. The men and women of their club paid hefty fees to ensure not just silence but the protection that their little coterie would bring them. Instead of finding their pleasure in brothels, they came here to Wingfield Hall. It was imperative that no man attempt to force unwanted attentions upon a lady, which had been Roberts's sin.

The beating he'd received at the hands of Aubrey, Whitby, Riverdale, and Kingham had been well deserved. They had also turned the bastard out on his arse, sending him back to London.

One piece of rubbish gone.

One crafty minx left to be discovered.

Right.

Perhaps it was time to make a few inquiries with the servants, he decided. This wasn't how he had intended to spend the house party, chasing after a vexing female whom he couldn't even bed. But so be it.

His friendship with Whit was too important to allow Rhiannon to go flitting about unsupervised. God only knew what manner of trouble she would find herself in. A sharp stab of guilt pierced him as he thought about the kisses he had shared with her yesterday. Whit would bloody well murder him if he knew, and Aubrey wouldn't blame him in the slightest. He hated himself for giving in to her soft, lush lips on his. For kissing her back instead of pushing her away.

It wouldn't happen again.

Aubrey strode toward the library, lured by the sound of raucous masculine and feminine laughter. He hadn't thought to check that room yet. Perhaps the minx was within. He stopped at the threshold to quietly observe. No fewer than a dozen men and women occupied the room, most of the players masked.

"It's my turn for a question next," said a familiar voice.

His gaze swung to her at once. Rhiannon was seated primly on a Grecian couch next to a man who had stripped down to the waist. Aubrey was going to kill the bastard.

"On what part of the body do you prefer to be kissed?" asked another man who appeared to be at the helm of the festivities, seated on a makeshift dais, also masked.

Aubrey had played such games before. It was a version of Questions and Commands that had been corrupted so that all the queries were carnal in nature, as were the resulting commands if the Commander issuing the questions wasn't satisfied by the answer.

"The lips, I should think," Rhiannon was answering. "Although I daresay I haven't tried many other places just yet."

Her innocent response made his groin tighten. There were so many other places and ways he might kiss her. So many sensual delights he could show her. If only she weren't his closest chum's sister.

"Allow me to be the first to volunteer for research," said the man at her side, who Aubrey now recognized as Lord Chattingham.

The company tittered.

"What a selfless offer," drawled the chap who had asked the ribald question.

And something inside Aubrey broke.

He stalked into the room, scarcely aware of his surroundings. If that half-dressed arsehole had even thought about touching Rhiannon, Aubrey would thrash him senseless. He was dimly aware of eyes on him as he moved toward Rhiannon. Even a shocked exclamation.

"Well, if it isn't Richford, come to join us," purred a feminine voice he recognized as belonging to Viscountess Heathcote.

Perdita had been trying to get into his bed for the last month. She was a beauty—voluptuous, golden-haired, big-breasted, and notoriously adventurous in the bedchamber, with dark appetites to rival his own. But he hadn't yet accepted her offer. He glanced in her direction now with disinterest despite the remarkable display of her breasts bursting forth from her immodest décolletage. Christ, if she sneezed, her nipples would spring free.

"I'm not joining you," he bit out, stopping before Rhiannon. "You. Come with me. Now."

"I'm afraid you aren't the Commander, Richford," Perdita said, a hard edge to her voice. "You cannot waltz in here and spoil our fun."

Aubrey didn't bother to glance in the viscountess's direction. All his attention was upon the minx before him. Rhiannon stared up at him, her blue eyes wide behind her silken mask. No doubt she hadn't expected him to find her and demand that she leave her sordid game.

Chattingham puffed up his chest. "I say, Richford. You're being a bit too heavy-handed. Lady Pink and I were just beginning to become better acquainted."

Lady Pink, was she now? At least she wasn't going about telling everyone that she was Lady Rhiannon Northwick. Small mercies and all that bloody folderol.

Aubrey pinned the irksome man with a warning glare. "If

you don't leave the lady alone, the only thing you'll become better acquainted with is my fist."

Rhiannon gasped. "Richford!"

As if *he* were the one who was sitting about sans shirt, waistcoat, and neckcloth, leering at her.

He turned back to her, extending his hand. "Come, my lady. You are needed elsewhere."

"But I am currently here," she said, her eyes snapping with stubborn fire.

"Richford, you're quite ruining Questions and Commands," complained the man who had been leading this little farce. "This is most unlike you."

"I'd be more than happy to ruin your face instead," he returned politely.

The man made a huff of annoyance but wisely said nothing else. Which was just as well, because Aubrey would have entirely crushed him in a physical challenge.

"Richford, you cannot sweep in here and begin threatening everyone," Rhiannon chastised him in a low voice.

"You have five seconds to come with me before I toss you over my shoulder and carry you out of here," he warned her calmly, meaning every word.

His already limited patience was gone. He needed to figure out a means of getting her back to London with her reputation intact and without Whit discovering she'd ever been here at this cursed house party. Christ, why had the meddlesome chit insisted upon sneaking into Wingfield Hall in the first place? And why had he been the one with the grave misfortune of discovering her deceit?

"I'm not finished playing just yet," she informed him coolly. "I'll speak with you later, after our game is complete."

"Why don't you stay and play with us?" Perdita asked coyly. "Come and have a seat by me."

He didn't miss the way Rhiannon's gaze went to the

viscountess, narrowing as she took in Perdita's bountiful curves and lack of modesty, before flitting back to him.

"Yes, why don't you stay and play?" Rhiannon asked, her tone mocking.

It was more than apparent she disapproved of Perdita. Perhaps the minx was even a bit jealous. She needn't have been. There was only one woman in this library he longed to kiss breathless and spank until she was moaning and wet for him, and that wasn't Viscountess Heathcote. Sadly, he couldn't indulge in that particular fantasy.

"Would you have me make a scene?" he asked Rhiannon quietly, ignoring Perdita entirely.

"You have already made one," Rhiannon gritted, pinning him with a pouty glare.

He met her glare with one of his own, warning her without words that he was utterly serious about his threat and intended to follow it through. He would haul her from the damned Grecian couch and cart her out of this library if she refused to accompany him. He had no intention of allowing her to remain here for more lewd rounds of Questions and Commands. He shuddered to think of what the forfeit required of her would be.

"Now, my lady," was all he said.

She sighed, sulking some more, but reluctantly accepted his hand.

He pulled her to her feet before turning to address the occupants of the room, who were all watching their drama unfold as if it were a riveting comedy at the theater. "Carry on. Forgive me for the interruption."

Sliding Rhiannon's hand into the crook of his elbow, he escorted her from the library. When they had reached the hall and he'd closed the door behind them, she spun on him, eyes blazing with fury.

"How dare you embarrass me like that?"

"You were sitting next to a half-naked man," he countered sharply. "What the devil did you think you were doing? In ten minutes, it's likely to become an orgy."

Damn. He shouldn't have said something like that in front of Whit's sister. Did she even know what an orgy was? He sure as bloody hell hoped not.

"What is an orgy?" she asked breathlessly as he all but dragged her down the hall, confirming his suspicions.

She didn't know.

He wasn't going to be the one to tell her either.

"Never mind," he bit out. "Have you had your belongings packed?"

"Packed? Of course not. Whyever would I do that?"

"Because you're leaving," he growled. "You're going back to London where you belong before you do something foolish and ruin your reputation beyond repair."

The truth of it was, she had already ruined her reputation merely by being in attendance. But fortunately, no one else was the wiser, save him, and he would go to his grave keeping the secret if it meant protecting her.

"I'm not returning to London until this house party is over, Richford." She yanked her arm away, her lips compressed at a mulish angle that told him she was ready to go to battle with him yet again.

His cock twitched to life.

Was it wrong that he liked sparring with her? Yes, it was. Did that stop his prick from stiffening the moment she started glaring at him with indignant fury? Not at all.

"This isn't an argument to have here in the midst of the hall, minx," he said. "Come with me."

He would find an empty salon and attempt to reason with her, all whilst keeping his hands, lips, and unrepentant cockstand to himself. Aubrey could exercise restraint, even if the sorts of restraints he preferred were the kinds he applied to his lovers in bed.

"So that you can lock me inside a room again?" she demanded, sounding indignant. "Ha! I think not, Richford. Go find someone else to torment. Leave me alone."

"Unfortunately for both of us, I'm obliged to look after your welfare," he countered, annoyed with her as much as himself for the never-ceasing lust that prevailed whenever he was around her.

And when he wasn't.

He had come twice with his own hand wrapped around his cock, once last night and once this morning, to thoughts of plundering her sweet mouth while he drove inside her wet heat and claimed her for himself. He wasn't proud of that, but he also was more than aware that he was likely to do it again until he could get the poison of wanting her out of his blood.

"I'm not *your* sister," she snapped.

"Trust me, minx, I'm more than aware of that," he drawled, unable to keep the irony from his voice.

"You have no obligations where I'm concerned," she countered.

"That's where you're wrong." He took her arm in a gentle hold and pulled her to an empty salon. "Believe it or not, I have a conscience, and allowing my friend's innocent sister to remain at a debauched house party is more than it can allow."

He became aware of another couple at the far end of the hall. They were arm in arm, caught up in each other, but Rhiannon was hell-bent upon making a scene, and the last thing he wanted was for anyone to guess who she was.

"Damn you, someone is coming," he muttered. "Get into the room."

Rhiannon, however, was stubborn.

"I've already told you, I'll go to my brother with what has happened," she protested. "What do you think he will say when he learns you were kissing his—"

Aubrey interrupted her by hauling her into his chest. He stopped her babbling the only way he knew how, with his mouth. As he kissed her, he backed her into the room, kicking the door closed behind them. She broke away from him at the sound of the thudding portal.

"You overbearing, arrogant, irritating, ridiculous scyrant. Toundrel!" She was spitting mad.

And she was making no sense.

It was actually quite adorable.

"Calm down, minx," he urged with deliberate sangfroid. "You aren't even using proper words."

"Oh! You know what I mean. I was trying to say tyrant and scoundrel at the same time. You have me so furious that I can't even speak."

He grinned at her, vastly amused. "And yet, here you are. Speaking."

She growled. "It's a figure of speech, you…you…"

"Do go on," he said. "I'm hoping you create yet another new word. The last two were so deuced entertaining."

Rhiannon launched herself at him and began pummeling his chest with her fists. It was rather like watching a mouse taunt a lion. He almost took pity on her.

But not quite.

She was causing quite a bit of trouble for him and putting herself in danger. He'd intended to spend this house party lost in pleasure, and instead, he'd been fucking his hand like a green lad of eighteen who was too afraid to speak to the fairer sex.

Aubrey caught her flying fists in his hands. "Are you this much of a brat at all times? It's a miracle Whit hasn't married you off to the first unsuspecting bastard he could find by now."

She stared at him, chest heaving, eyes glistening with outrage, fury emanating from her body in almost tangible waves. He was being rather a bit cruel, and he knew it. The fault was his—he was so damn drawn to her, and he had to push her away in any capacity possible. One couldn't shag one's best friend's virgin sister after all.

Aubrey opened his mouth, intending to offer an apology, but Rhiannon acted first. She moved swiftly, bringing her knee into his groin with an unexpected and impressive amount of force. Pain radiated through him, the breath leaving him as black stars speckled his vision. With a groan, he released her, doubling over, the agony almost unbearable.

Rhiannon didn't waste a moment, of course. She fled the room, leaving him there trying to catch his breath, pain searing him as he vowed he would find the minx and have his revenge.

$\sim$

RHIANNON TAMPED down the guilt that assailed her as she rushed from the salon where she'd left Richford, bent at the waist and howling in pain. Perhaps she had used a bit too much force when she had kneed him in that particularly vulnerable place.

But the fault was his as much as hers. She wouldn't have kneed him if he hadn't yet again hunted her down and dragged her into a salon to deliver a withering assessment of her maturity and character. All Richford had to do was keep his distance, and there would be no problem. Why, oh why, did he insist that she must return to London? What did it matter to him if she remained here? It wasn't as if she was his betrothed.

For now, where to hide that he wouldn't find her?

She couldn't flee to her bedchamber.

Nor could she return to the library to finish the edifying game of Questions and Commands she had been in the midst of playing when Richford had unceremoniously shown up and made a spectacle of them. Perhaps she could go for a nice, long ride.

Rhiannon changed direction and made her way to the doors leading to the stables.

"Where are you running off to so soon, my darling Lady Pink?"

The question brought her to a surprised halt as she turned to see the half-dressed man who had been seated on the couch with her in the library approaching. He had shrugged back into his shirt, but the twain ends remained scandalously apart, revealing a solid swath of his muscled chest. Earlier, she had been aghast when he had been commanded to remove the upper portion of his garments after a failed response to a question. It had been the first bare male chest she had seen, and she had to admit, she'd been fascinated.

Beneath the cut of his half mask, he appeared quite handsome.

Pity that her heart didn't leap when she saw him, and when he had used his low, pleasant-enough voice to whisper naughty things to her during the game, she hadn't even felt so much as a flicker of interest.

"I was..." Her words trailed off as she sought an explanation that would suffice.

"Waiting for me?" he asked swiftly, offering her his arm. "I was hoping you would say so. How did you manage to slip away from that hound, Richford?"

Rhiannon wasn't certain she should accept his offer of escort. The man was likely every bit as much of a rakehell as

Richford was. The only advantage was that this particular rake didn't know who she was, nor was he bothered by any so-called obligation or fits of conscience. Then again, perhaps she ought to go with him.

He might be just the gentleman with whom she could seize a bit of adventure and distraction from Richford's rejection of her.

And a kiss.

Even if the only man she currently longed to kiss was the same one she had just left sputtering in pain over his high-handedness.

With a smile, Rhiannon settled her hand on his proffered arm. "He's not a hound, sir. You are his guest, are you not?"

It seemed wrong to allow the man to insult Richford, despite how frustrated and angry with him she was.

"Forgive me," the man said smoothly. "Tell me, where shall we go so the two of us can have a tête-à-tête in private? Would you care to join me in my bedchamber?"

Her eyebrows rose. My heavens, she hadn't expected such a forward invitation.

"Perhaps a salon instead," she hedged, not wanting to be alone in a bedroom with someone she had only just met.

It seemed a dangerous plan indeed.

"Where do you think you're going?"

Rhiannon stiffened at the duke's familiar voice at her back. Curse the man! How had he found her already? She hadn't made good on her escape, thanks to the gentleman at her side.

She and her escort turned to face Richford, who looked a trifle pale but none the worse for wear as he stalked toward them in menacing fashion. His emerald gaze was locked upon the man at her side, and there was no denying the quiet fury emanating from him.

"This one is mine," he told the man. "Find another lady to your liking."

For a stupid moment, her heart rejoiced at the notion of the Duke of Richford calling her his. But then she recalled why he was chasing after her. He was angry with her and likely intent on punishment, before he chased her from the house party.

He wanted nothing to do with her. This was all about his pride and sense of duty to her brother.

Outrage shot through Rhiannon. "I am not—"

The look Richford suddenly gave her had her words dying in her throat.

"Mine," he repeated. "And I'm not sharing, Chattingham."

"The lady has a mind of her own," protested the man at her side—presumably Lord Chattingham—who was indeed a notorious Lothario. "I should think that if she wished to be with you, she would have been with you instead of you chasing after her like a mongrel nipping at her heels."

Richford's nostrils flared. "Insult me again, and I'll see your arse thrown not just from this club but from this house. You'll never again attend another house party at Wingfield Hall."

Chattingham stepped away from Rhiannon, clearly not wanting to be banished from the pleasure soirees hosted by the club. It would seem his interest in her had easily waned in the face of Richford's threats.

"Forgive me," Chattingham said coolly. "I didn't realize Lady Pink was yours." He gave her a speculative look as he performed a dramatic bow. "If the two of you will excuse me, I'm off in search of other entertainments."

Richford's lip curled. "See that you are."

When Chattingham had taken his leave and disappeared down the hall, Richford's hand clamped firmly on Rhiannon's upper arm.

"Unhand me," she snapped instantly, struggling to free herself, to no avail.

"I think not. You're coming with me, and you're not leaving until we're through having our talk, even if I have to tie you to a bloody chair."

At his words, a frisson of something went through her. There were many whispers about the Duke of Richford, some of them more salacious than others. One of them concerned his preferences in the bedchamber. It was said he liked to tie his women up.

Rhiannon found the very thought horrifying and yet also strangely intriguing at the same time. Just as with the books she secreted filled with wicked scenes and sinful words, she was at once ashamed by her interest and disgusted with herself for it, yet unable to deny the way it made her feel.

She hadn't given the rumors a thought during their heated arguments, however. Not until now.

Unbidden, thoughts of his lovers filled her mind. All the women he had kissed and taken to his bed, the ones who had spread those rumors.

"I suppose you are skilled with a knot and rope," she said unkindly.

His bearded jaw hardened. "Don't test me, little naïf."

The air between them was suddenly simmering and heavy. She was potently aware of him as a man in a way she hadn't been of Chattingham or any other gentleman in her acquaintance. Why, of all the gentlemen at this cursed house party, did she have to harbor a secret *tendre* for this one? He had made his disdain for her lack of experience more than clear. Had called her a girl. Had never spared her a second glance before yesterday. He was intent upon sending her to London.

But was he also attracted to her?

She licked her lips, thinking of the kisses they had shared, of the taste of him, of his tongue wicked and slick and demanding in her mouth.

His gaze dipped to her lips. "I ought to turn you over my knee for what you did to me in that salon. You're fortunate indeed that your aim is slightly off and I was able to recover. Christ knows what that arse Chattingham had in store for you. Tell me, how would you explain to your brother if you went home with a babe in your belly?"

His words were tinged with anger.

They shocked her.

Richford bent his head toward hers. "You didn't think about that, did you, brat? Nor, I'll wager, did you think about what might happen if a man pressed you to do more than you wished."

Her brow furrowed, the heat in her veins turning to ice. "What are you saying?"

"I'm saying that while we do our utmost to protect all the members who attend our house parties, anything can happen here. We are but a few pairs of eyes, and we cannot be everywhere at once. An innocent lamb like you would be no match for any of the jaded voluptuaries here."

Someone else was approaching them now, two women and a man, all three of them singing a bawdy song. It appeared as if they were deep in their cups. The women's arms were around each other's waists, and the one of them had an arm around the gentleman's hips, her hand on the fall of his trousers.

"Greedy wench," the man growled loudly. "Can't wait for my cock, can you?"

Richford muttered something unintelligible under his breath and began propelling her down the hall. "Don't listen to a word they're saying," he cautioned, his voice low.

Too late. She had ears. Did Richford think she was a

child? Rhiannon made a disagreeable face at the back of his golden head while he plowed on down the hall.

"Richford, is that you?" asked the man as they neared each other. "I say, would you like to join us? You can bring your luscious lady friend along."

"Not a bloody chance," the duke bit out, continuing on.

"Shy, is she? She can watch," the man suggested.

"Go to the devil," Richford snapped.

"Suit yourselves," the man called after them.

Richford rushed her through the great hall next, forcing her to hasten after him and nearly trip over her hems in the process.

"Where are you taking me?" she demanded, breathless.

"To your bloody room where we won't have an interruption every two minutes."

"I'll not be locked within again," she warned him. "My aim won't be so poor next time if you try it. I'll render you a eunuch."

"Christ," he muttered. "You are the most maddening bit of baggage I've ever met. I ought to turn you over to your brother this second."

"Why don't you, then?" she taunted.

They both knew the answer. He didn't want her to tell Rhys about the kisses they'd shared.

The remainder of her forced march back to her bedroom was conducted in a tense silence. She was too aware of Richford at her side, her body painfully attentive to his. By the time they were once more closeted in her bedroom, away from prying eyes and ears behind a closed door, she was all but breathless. And not just from struggling to keep up with his long-limbed strides either.

Richford turned to face her, his expression a stern and impassive mask. "Now, then. First, you will apologize for your vicious attack upon my person."

He was speaking about her knee in his groin.

She tipped up her chin, feeling defiant. "I'm only sorry you caught me."

His eyes narrowed. "Wrong answer, minx. Try again, and the next place I'll take you is directly to your brother."

"So that I can tell him you kissed me?"

"If it comes to that, yes. He can hate me all he likes. I'm more than happy for you to go back to being his problem instead of mine."

Rhiannon sighed, resisting the urge to throw something else at him. There was nothing sufficiently close at hand. Her hairbrush was too far away, on the dresser where he'd left it earlier.

"Fine. I'm sorry for attempting to escape from you in such a fashion. Are you happy?"

Richford cocked a golden brow. "I'll also require your promise you won't try anything like that again."

"Then I'll also have your promise that you'll stop making disparaging comments about me," she countered, still stung by his continued treatment of her.

It was difficult enough to accept that he would never see her as a woman. That despite the kisses they'd shared, he felt no more for her than he had for anyone else. Her pride wasn't just wounded; it had been decimated, and her fragile heart along with it.

He chuckled darkly, crossing his arms over his broad chest. "I don't think you're in a position to be making demands of me, little naïf. In case you failed to notice, I'm the one with the power to dismantle your foolish hope of remaining here. All I have to do is say one word to Whit, and you'll be gone."

That was the last thing she wanted.

"Don't," she pleaded.

He shook his head, his expression turning curious. "Why

are you so desperate to remain here? It's more than apparent that this is no place for an innocent like you."

Heat crept back up her throat, and she was sure she was flushing redder than a ripe summer cherry. "If you must know, I came here because I am soon to be engaged, and this house party is my last hope for experience before I settle down with a husband."

He stared at her, saying nothing, his gaze so sharp that it may as well have been a knife.

"Well?" she demanded into the uncomfortable silence that had descended. "Have you nothing to say?"

His jaw was clenched taut. He swallowed—she knew because she watched the prominent bulge of his Adam's apple dip in his throat. And still, he said not a word.

"You're soon to be engaged," he said at last. "Who is he?"

"The Earl of Carnis."

He choked. "Carnis? Forgive me, minx, I daresay I heard you wrong. I thought you said that you're soon to be betrothed to the Earl of Carnis, a man who has the personality of a garden bench and the brains of a chicken."

She winced at his description of the man she would one day wed. "His lordship is quite intelligent, if you must know, and he is perfectly kind and sweet to me in all ways. He would never, for instance, lock me in a room."

"If he's so bloody wonderful, then why are you seeking experience with others instead of your future husband?" Richford demanded, ignoring her jibe.

Warmth prickled her cheeks at his familiarity. This discussion was wrong and wicked. But then, so was she, wasn't she? A good, honorable lady wouldn't wish to experience anything romantic or carnal with a man other than the one she was marrying. The kindly, perfectly polite, obsequious man she intended to wed.

"Because I…I admire Reginald," she explained, struggling

to find the words and make sense of her cumbersome emotions herself, "but I don't desire him. Nor, I think, does he desire me. Our union will be built on mutual respect and courtesy. I wish for a husband who will treat me with kindness and give me children. Reginald will do that."

"*Reginald* wouldn't know how to pleasure a woman if he took lessons from the world's finest courtesan," Richford said. "Why would you want to marry such a fool? Does Whit know of this? Please tell me he doesn't countenance a match between you and that idiot."

"Reginald is *not* an idiot," she defended, feeling guilty enough for her plotting. "He is exactly what any lady would want in a husband. And as to whether my brother knows, I'm not certain. He's so oft preoccupied with his own life that I think there is precious little time for him to fret over mine."

"Good God, you're running wild beneath his very nose, and he hasn't an inkling." Richford shook his head. "Little wonder you were able to find your way here. You're cunning enough to rout an army."

She wasn't certain if that was an insult or praise.

Rhiannon chose to consider it the latter.

"I'm hardly running wild," she countered. "Did you not hear any of what I've just told you? I am planning to settle into a comfortable, staid marriage with a gentleman of great honor. One who has professed his deep and abiding love for me."

"Oh, I'm certain he has," Richford said with a bark of snide laughter. "And let me guess, you return his endless and profound love, yet you're still here at a debauched house party."

When he said it thus, it sounded inherently wrong. Because it *was* wrong. But he didn't understand.

"Why should I not experience a bit of life before I wed?" she demanded, planting her hands on her waist. "Have you never stopped to consider how unfair it is that a man can run about doing whatever he likes, bedding whomever he wishes, and all polite society looks the other way? Yet if an unmarried woman should be curious about what she is to endure in the marriage bed, she ought to be scorned?"

"You may be curious all you like, but you cannot wait until you've married the poor bastard?"

She glared at him. "Did *you* wait until you were married?"

"Of course not," he scoffed. "But I'm a man, and I'm not marrying anyone, not now, not ever."

"Then perhaps I shall eschew the marriage altogether and simply take lovers as it pleases me," she declared, frustrated with him.

"You'll be cast from polite society. Your mother and your brother will no longer be able to acknowledge you. Surely that isn't the life you'd want for yourself, Lady Rhiannon."

"So you see? It *is* unfair for a woman. We are judged by a separate set of standards that are far more rigid and unforgiving. That is why I came to this house party. It is my one chance for the freedom that men enjoy. Why should I not seize it?"

Once again, silence fell between them. Richford stared at her. What had he expected? She couldn't humiliate herself by confessing her feelings for him as well.

She raised a brow. "Can you not answer?"

His eyes grew shuttered, unreadable. "You came here to see what pleasure is all about, did you not?"

That same heaviness that filled the air in the hall earlier revisited them. She was furiously aware of him, his proximity, the way his gaze had flicked down her body for just a moment.

"Yes," she answered simply.

"Then come with me, and I'll show you."

CHAPTER 4

He was an absolute lunatic, Aubrey thought as he ushered Rhiannon into the observation room. And if Whit ever found out what was about to happen, his friend would want to bloody well kill him.

As it happened, Aubrey wouldn't blame Whit. It would serve him right. Only a madman fit for the asylum would dream of bringing his friend's innocent sister to an observation room to watch another couple fuck.

"This is certainly an oddly narrow room," Rhiannon observed cheerfully as she looked around. "Whatever is its purpose?"

The chamber had been created by the erection of a wall that had cut off a portion of the original bedroom. Viewing holes, cleverly hidden beneath gilt covers, were strategically placed before comfortable chairs. In this way, lovers who enjoyed being watched could indulge their desires before an audience if they chose to do so. Aubrey knew the erotic whims of each guest. It hadn't taken long to find a couple willing to be watched during their amorous play.

Arranging for Rhiannon's debauchery had taken less than

half an hour. The poor lamb didn't know what was about to unfold before her virginal eyes.

"You shall soon find out, minx," he told her, feeling grim.

He had good intentions, he reminded himself sternly. He wanted to shock her. To show her that she was a naïve babe compared to the jaded souls who came to Wingfield Hall in search of pleasure, regardless of how depraved.

He fully intended to send her running back to London once and for all and of her own volition. The stubborn chit had made it more than apparent that no amount of coercion on his part would make her go.

Yes, that was why he'd brought her here. To horrify her. To disgust her. To pull back the velvet curtain and show her what truly happened at these Wicked Dukes Society fêtes. It was no place for a wayward hoyden who had been cosseted and kept ignorant to the lascivious vices of the world around her. He didn't give a damn how many books she'd read. None of them could possibly compare to what happened within these walls.

A noble cause from the blackhearted, soulless Duke of Richford. He might have laughed were he not preoccupied with making certain she took the seat that would give her the best vantage point after the festivities began.

"This one," he ordered her, pointing at the chair before the viewing portal that was directly in front of the bed.

"I'm to sit?" she asked, looking around. "Why?"

"You'll see. Just do as I tell you."

She didn't like that. Her back stiffened and her shoulders drew back, and damn her, she was glorious when she was angry and spitting fire at him. He had never wanted to bed a woman more than he wanted this one. But he hadn't come here for that. And he could bloody well have his choice of women later when she'd run back to her mama where she belonged.

"You cannot order me about, Richford," she snapped. "What if I don't want to sit?"

"Then stand there," he bit out, willing his thickening cock to wilt like a cut flower too long in the sun.

Her scent wrapped around him, and her lips were beyond deliciously tempting beneath the silk of her half mask. When she pouted like that, he wanted to kiss her breathless.

She sat.

Of course she did.

He seated himself at her side and reached for the gilt covering on his viewing hole, sliding it to the left to determine if the couple within was ready. He hoped to hell they were, because he wasn't certain how much more torture he could withstand. Being so near to Rhiannon was enough to bring a saint to his knees, and Christ knew Aubrey was far from being a saint.

Within, Lord and Lady Elmont were already kissing. One of few married couples who attended club parties together, they were also quite adventurous in their bed sport. They often preferred a third to join them, usually another woman, but he hadn't wanted to give Rhiannon *quite* that much of an education. He had requested they keep their games to the two of them for the lewd bit of theater he had arranged.

"What are you looking at?" Rhiannon demanded, curious.

"Hush, brat," he told her quietly. "You wanted an education in pleasure, an adventure, did you not? This is it, but you must be patient and no bellowing."

Her brows drew together in a frown. "I don't bellow."

"These are observation windows," he said, nodding to the gilt coverings. "There is a glass pane within to keep sound from carrying, but you must be quiet or run the risk of ruining it."

"Ruining what?"

He slid the cover all the way open. Lord and Lady Elmont

were divesting each other's garments, hands moving feverishly.

"Open your window and have a look," he encouraged.

With a questioning glance in his direction, she did as he bade, leaning forward in her chair and sliding the gilt covering to the side. "Oh my," she murmured. "Is that… Are they…"

His lips twitched. "Yes, it is, and yes, they are. Too much already, minx? We can close the viewing holes, and I'll find a maid to help you pack your valises."

"No," she denied loudly.

Too loudly.

The couple on the other side of the small viewing hole appeared to hear her, ending their kiss as Lady Elmont briefly cast a look in their direction.

"Quiet," he reminded Rhiannon. "If you're too loud, this will be over before it's begun, and I promised you an education."

The dim light in the observation room emerging from a single low sconce ensured that the players in the room next door couldn't see who was watching, which was part of the enjoyment for them. Aubrey hadn't told them which members of the party would be in the observation room.

Rhiannon gave him a mutinous glare before turning her attention back to the viewing window. He didn't bother to turn his gaze to what was unfolding within the bedchamber. Viewing her reaction was far more intoxicating at the moment.

Her lips were parted, her creamy neck craned as she leaned forward in her seat. He wondered if her nipples were hard. If her cunny was slick and wet with anticipation. For a wild moment, he thought about lowering himself before her on the Axminster, lifting her skirts, and burying his face between her legs. He could pleasure her while she watched, know the delirious joy of her coming on his tongue.

Fuck.

He had to stop thinking about her this way.

Aubrey shifted in his seat, trying to ease the pressure of his trousers on his rampant cockstand. Rhiannon cast a curious look in his direction.

"Are you not going to watch?" she asked softly.

He clenched his jaw to stave off another agonizing rush of lust. "I *am* watching."

And that was entirely the problem.

~

It was impossible not to be moved by the sight of Richford sprawled with casual elegance in his seat, his long legs before him, his forearms resting on the chair in an indolent pose. Rhiannon was all too aware of his assessing emerald gaze on her. He was watching, like a predator stalking its prey, waiting for a reaction.

He wasn't going to get one.

It was more than apparent that he'd brought her to the viewing room so he could shock her into leaving. But if he thought that merely watching a couple ardently kiss was going to send her meekly back to London, he was wrong.

They stared at each other for a heated moment, and then he averted his gaze to the viewing window before him as dispassionately as if he were regarding his dinner plate. It would seem that nothing could move the Duke of Richford, least of all her.

Disappointment sliced through Rhiannon. Why couldn't he look at her and see that she was a woman, with a woman's desires? Why did he insist upon treating her as if she were a naïve girl who had wandered into the dining room at an inopportune time, interrupting the adult conversation?

In the room next door, the couple had progressed beyond kissing. The gentleman had his coat off and was working at the closures on the woman's bodice, while her fingers flew over the buttons on his waistcoat. They managed all this while their mouths remained pressed together in a series of carnal kisses that was equally revealing. It was almost as if the two intentionally shifted so that the viewing room had a better vantage point as their tongues tangled.

Despite her determination to remain unmoved, Rhiannon slid forward on her seat, holding her breath as she watched the pair slipping out of their clothing. The man was in shirtsleeves now, and the woman's bodice was gone, along with her overskirt. The woman then spun about, presenting her back to the man so that he could untie her corset laces. A coquettish smile played about her lips as she faced the observation windows.

"Do they know we're watching?" Rhiannon asked quietly.

"They know someone is watching," Richford said, his voice a low, pleasant rumble. "But not who."

In the bedchamber beyond, the woman's corset slackened, giving more room to her bountiful breasts. Good heavens, they truly meant to disrobe entirely, didn't they? Rhiannon was beginning to feel faint. They were a handsome couple, the man dark-haired with shots of silver at his temples, the woman red-haired and voluptuous. They kept their masks in place, which Rhiannon found odd.

"Don't they want to know?" she queried, trying to distract herself.

Anticipation had begun to unfurl within her, hot and potent. A new feeling started in the very center of her, a blossoming ache that wasn't entirely unfamiliar.

"Not knowing is part of the thrill," he told her.

She tried not to squirm in her chair as she watched the couple continuing to remove garments, caressing and kissing as they went. Her mind wandered to Richford and thoughts of what it would be like to touch him so freely. To kiss him and take off his coat and shirt. To run her hands over his bare chest.

Her heart quickened.

"Have you done this before?" she asked him, unable to quell her curiosity, slanting a look toward his handsome profile. "Watched a couple like this, I mean?"

"Yes."

His simple answer only left her wanting to know more.

She bit her lower lip, sure she shouldn't ask the next question swirling through her mind and yet needing to know.

"And have you been watched before?"

He finally looked away from the viewing window, his emerald gaze searing her in a place she hadn't realized existed, deep within. "You're terribly interested in me suddenly, minx."

She had *always* been interested in him. There was nothing sudden about it. Just as she had always admired him and longed for him from afar. What had begun as a girl's foolish yearnings had never ended. But her pride wouldn't allow her to admit that.

"I'm meant to have an education," she reminded him instead.

"Yes," he told her at last. "I have."

Rhiannon hadn't been prepared for his response. She had already guessed at the answer, of course, but somehow, hearing it from his lips had a whole new effect on her. The notion of Richford engaging in such debauchery at once thrilled and repelled her. Her body reacted with a mind all its own, a rush of instant desire tearing through her. But she was also painfully jealous of the lovers he'd known, of the mysterious observers who had been privileged to be his audience.

"Do you...do so often?"

He shrugged as if he hadn't a care. "When the mood strikes me."

There was nothing she could think of to say to his frank admission, so she looked away, eyes pinned to the viewing window once more. She was intensely aware of his regard, still on her, of his presence at her side, of everything about him, so potently masculine, so sinful and wicked, so tempting.

"Have I finally shocked you into silence?"

She licked her lips, staring at the couple without truly seeing them. "Not at all. Your reputation precedes you, Richford."

"I can assure you, my dear, that my reputation doesn't even begin to scratch the surface of what I've done," he drawled.

She didn't doubt that either. He was a voluptuary. Although the gossip concerning him was as plentiful as it was scandalous, she had never heard a thing about viewing windows or the observation of others engaged in sexual congress. She was doing her utmost to appear nonchalant and even bored for Richford's sake, but she was secretly anything but.

"I'm sure you go about doing all manner of sinful things," she said lightly.

"As does everyone within these walls, which is why you don't belong here."

She ignored him, watching the scene in the bedchamber continue to unfold. The lady was out of her undergarments now, clad in only a chemise. The gentleman was wearing his drawers, and the lady's hand was cupping the front placket where…

"Oh my heavens," she muttered before she could stop herself.

There, clearly outlined, was his manhood, thinly covered by the cotton of his drawers.

"We can return you to the haven of your room at any time," Richford reminded her.

"I find this far too intriguing," she informed him. "I'm afraid you're stuck with me."

"As you prefer, minx."

He was still watching her; she could see it from her peripheral vision, but she could also feel it, like a touch, sending fire licking through her body. She was flushed and overheated. The narrow room lacked sufficient air. Why hadn't she thought to bring a fan with her?

The man pulled the woman's chemise over her head in one graceful motion, leaving her standing there naked. Rhiannon gaped. She'd never seen a woman nude, except for herself. The redhead's breasts were smaller than hers, but aside from that difference, they were much the same. What shocked her most was the other woman's lack of hesitation or shyness in her nudity, even knowing she was being observed.

The man's head dipped, and he took the woman's nipple into his mouth.

Rhiannon inhaled sharply as the redhead's back arched and she threaded her fingers through the man's dark hair. The expression on the woman's face suggested she was enjoying the gentleman's attentions very much, and Rhiannon's own nipples ached in response. What would it feel like, to have a man's mouth there? She tried to imagine the Earl of Carnis making such a daring overture and couldn't.

Instead, she wondered what it would be like to have Richford's mouth on her. To have those sinful, sensual lips at her breast. The throbbing ache between her thighs said she would like it more than she should.

The man's hands were on the redhead's naked body, traveling over her curves to her hips. They continued their slow caress until one hand came to grip her bare bottom and the other dipped into the cove at the apex of her thighs as he continued to suckle her breasts.

"Are you properly horrified yet?" Richford asked, his voice going husky.

"No," she murmured, keeping her attention upon the window. "Not at all."

Instead, she was intrigued. Interested. She wanted to know what it would be like to be in the other woman's place. To have a man worshiping her with his hands and mouth. Not just any man. Richford.

In the bedchamber, the hand the man had placed between the woman's legs began to move. The redhead's mouth fell open, her head tipping back as her body undulated in time with his ministrations. Rhiannon had never seen such an expression of raw desire on someone's countenance. She watched in rapt fascination as the man suddenly ceased his attentions and guided the woman to the waiting bed.

"Is it over already?" she asked Richford, disappointed.

He chuckled. "Hardly. It's only just begun."

The man helped the woman to drape herself over the bed sideways, then lowered himself to join her. But instead of pressing his form against hers, he remained at her feet, urging her legs to part. Rhiannon could feel her pulse pounding between her own thighs. Her entire body was wound tighter than a watch spring. She was achy and almost feverish. The room might as well have been aflame. Heavens, *she* might as well have been.

Still clad in his drawers, the man splayed his hands on the

woman's inner thighs, pushing them open. The woman cupped her breasts and teased her nipples, casting him a sultry glance down her body.

"What does he intend to do?" Rhiannon asked Richford in a hushed whisper.

Her body was so flushed, her desire so acutely teased to the point of breaking, that the very air around her felt as if it might shatter if she but moved.

"He's going to use his tongue on her."

Richford's words settled over her like a taunting caress.

"His tongue?" Her mind struggled to function properly.

"Watch."

She bit her lip, flushed and achy and needy. She felt things she'd never felt before. It was surely wrong, watching the couple engage in such private congress. It was wicked and sinful, and that was what she liked about it. But having her curiosity satisfied was also a potent lure.

"What if they forgot we are here?" she asked, heart pounding as the man's head lowered.

"They haven't." Richford's voice was deep and low, resonating with certainty.

The man pressed a kiss to the woman's inner thigh. Good heavens, Rhiannon was going to catch on fire.

"How can you be so sure?" she hissed at him.

"Knowing they are watched heightens the enjoyment for them, just as watching is pleasurable to us."

In the bedchamber, the man kissed the woman's other thigh, moving steadily nearer to her mound and yet still not directly touching her there. Did Rhiannon like watching these two strangers tease and seduce each other? She hadn't been prepared to do so, and yet she couldn't deny the effect it was having upon her.

"What is he going to do with his tongue?" she asked, desperately seeking to distract herself.

A thin trickle of perspiration went down her spine, and she shifted restlessly on her chair, seeking an ease to her own agony and finding none.

"Patience, minx."

The gentleman was kissing along the lady's inner thigh now, traveling ever higher. The woman, meanwhile, grew impatient. She rolled her hips and clutched at his dark head, urging him to her center. Rhiannon's heart pounded faster as the man burrowed his face there, in the woman's most intimate place. The man's tongue glided over the woman's flesh, making her writhe and moan.

Good heavens, was he…licking her?

"He's tasting her," Richford elaborated, as if Rhiannon needed to hear the words.

She didn't.

The books she had managed to secret and read had said nothing of *this*.

The man on the bed guided the redhead's legs over his shoulders, and he began feasting upon her in truth.

"Oh my," she whispered. "Is his tongue going into her the way his manhood would?"

"If you want to play wicked games, then you must call it what it is, minx. A cock."

She swallowed hard, still unable to look away from the man pleasuring the woman so thoroughly that she was crying out now, hips pumping against his face. Even with the wall and pane of glass separating them, her lusty moans of rapture could be heard. Rhiannon's face flamed.

She could scarcely believe she was watching two people cavort before her, all while the Duke of Richford sat unaffected at her side.

The man rose onto his knees, reaching for the fastening of his drawers. Rhiannon couldn't deny that she was unbearably curious to see the man's manhood—no, *cock*—spring free. Another button slipped open. Two more to go.

But suddenly, she was being pushed away from the viewing window.

"Enough," Richford growled, his hands clamped on her waist for a moment as he unceremoniously thrust her toward the door before releasing her again. "You've seen all you needed to see."

"But I haven't," she protested, struggling with him without effect.

He was larger than she was, tall and strong and well-muscled, capable of keeping her from returning to the observation window.

"Oh yes, you bloody well have, minx," he said grimly. "Any more, and your brother will have my head on a goddamned pike."

"Not if he doesn't find out." She spun until her back was pressed to the door. "You promised me an education in pleasure, and you can't stop before it's finished."

"Yes, I can," he countered. "And I am. Now, curse you."

His scent teased her. In the shadows, his expression was elusive and unreadable. He seemed furious, but that made no sense. Why would he be angry with Rhiannon if she was only following along with the adventure he had offered?

Unless…

Was Richford not as impervious as he pretended? Could it be that he was every bit as deeply affected by watching the couple as she had been? That he was also currently swimming in an ocean of lust, closer to drowning with every second that passed? And not just because of the couple in the bedchamber, but because the two of them had been alone in this small room together?

"But my education is far from complete," she pointed out boldly, testing her suspicions. "The gentleman was about to disrobe completely when you so rudely interrupted. I didn't even get to see him."

"You aren't going to see him either," the duke snarled.

"Why not?"

"Because I said so." He stalked nearer to her, all but pinning her to the door.

She couldn't leave even if she wanted to.

But she *didn't* want to. She wanted to stay where she was. With him.

"That's hardly a sufficient reason," she protested, a bit breathless now.

"Rhiannon," he ground out, his face lowering toward hers.

Her name. Not *minx*, not *little naïf*, not even *Lady Rhiannon*, not anything else. Just Rhiannon. And oh, how everything within her thrilled at the realization.

Could it be that the Duke of Richford was losing control, and that it was all because of her? Rhiannon's heart leapt.

She smiled up at him, feeling powerful and bold. "Yes?"

"If you don't get out of here in the next five seconds, I'm going to do something we'll both regret," he warned.

But how wrong he was. There was nothing this beautiful man could do to her that she would ever regret.

"I'm not ready to leave yet," she returned, nettled with herself for the unsteadiness in her voice.

The longing.

She had been waiting years for the Duke of Richford to want her, and she wasn't about to move away from the door. Not if her life depended on it.

CHAPTER 5

He wasn't going to kiss her.

He wasn't jealous of Lord bloody Elmont.

But he was going to come out of his damned skin if Rhiannon didn't do as he asked of her and get the hell out of this room. He could admit that much, if only to himself.

And what was Rhiannon doing? The minx was blocking the door with her lush, tempting form, taunting him by suggesting she'd wanted to see another man's cock, when the only cock he wanted her to see or touch or know was his.

That cannot happen, he reminded himself viciously.

You can't have her.

She's forbidden.

Whit's sister.

A fucking virgin.

Yes, she was all those things. But she was also the most potent aphrodisiac he'd ever beheld, flushed and glossy-eyed, all but panting with desire. He might have consigned himself to the fiery pits of hell in that moment just for the chance to lift her skirts and test the slit of her drawers to see if she was wet.

He bit back a groan and struggled to give her his sternest expression. "Be a good chit and go."

"I don't want to be good, and I'm not a chit," she denied stubbornly.

But then she did something else, something that broke him apart like a rock being dashed to bits by a pickaxe. She cupped his face in both her hands, staring up at him with such raw, unfettered desire that he couldn't resist.

He had an excuse for the last time their lips had met. She had been the aggressor then, taking him by surprise. On this occasion, however, he had no such defense. Because he was the one lowering his head toward hers, angling his mouth to claim and plunder. He was the one who pressed her to the door and ravished her lips the way he wanted to with the rest of his body.

And damn her, she tasted every bit as sweet as she had then. Perhaps more so. She opened without hesitation, and he gave her his tongue. Her hands moved from his face to his shoulders, her nails digging into him through the layers he wore as if she wanted to hold him there forever or perhaps make her mark. Some dark and debased part of him hoped she would.

He was on fire for her, and it had precious little to do with the show the couple had enacted for them in the adjacent room. He had scarcely spared them a glance. The only one he'd been watching was Rhiannon. Her swift inhalations, her parted lips, the way her body shifted and moved, as if she were trying to assuage the ever-growing ache deep within. An ache he knew could only be quelled one way.

Realization hit him with a clarity that was so sharp and precise, it may as well have been fashioned from a guillotine. He *had* to touch her. Just once. Had to know if she had been as stirred by watching Lord and Lady Elmont as he thought she'd been. It was wrong, he knew, but he couldn't stop or help himself.

If he never took the opportunity to touch her, he'd regret it to his dying day. This would be his only chance. Aubrey grasped a handful of her skirts, slowly lifting silk and petticoats. Inch by inch. As he did, he deepened the kiss, her tongue slick against his, her breathy moan of encouragement enough to make his cock leak.

It was ridiculous, how much Rhiannon affected him. He was a grown man, an experienced, jaded rake who had known his first lover as a callow youth of eighteen when he had been desperate to lose himself in someone, to escape from the horrors of his own reality. Since then, he'd bedded countless women. There was no earthly reason he should want Lady Rhiannon Northwick more than he'd ever desired another.

Perhaps madness had finally claimed him.

He had been dancing about the devil for years now.

Her lips chased his as she ground her breasts into his chest. Up went her hems, just a scant inch higher. He was closer to what he wanted, but...

Fuck, fuck, fuck. He couldn't touch her cunny. This was his friend's sister.

Unfortunately, regardless of how many reprimands he issued himself, none had an impact on his all-consuming need for the woman who was kissing him as if her life depended upon it. Good. He would make her forget about the couple who were no doubt shagging like mad at this very moment.

Aubrey left her lips, stringing kisses across her jaw and down her throat. He found the place where her pulse pounded frantically and set his mouth over it, sucking at the smooth, soft skin. She tasted sweet here too, like Rhiannon and the faintest hint of her perfume. He sucked harder, some perverse part of him hoping to leave a mark there so that when she looked in the mirror, she would remember this moment. So that she would know who had put his mouth on her there.

"Richford," she murmured.

He dragged more of her skirts upward, running his tongue along her soft skin to her ear, where he gently bit the fleshy lobe with his teeth. "I warned you, damn it."

"I don't heed warnings," she murmured, her voice breathy and thick with desire. "They're dreadfully tedious and boring."

This bloody woman.

What was he going to do with her?

"You're a menace, brat," he told her, nipping at her ear.

Or mayhap he was the menace, because he couldn't seem to stop himself. Nor could he get enough of her. He kissed her temple, leaning into her as he lifted her skirts some more.

"Did you like what you saw?" he asked. "Were you not shocked and horrified?"

"What do you think?" she taunted.

And he surrendered to temptation. Her gown was almost to her waist. He slid his hand underneath the heavy gathering of fabric and skimmed his fingers over the split in her drawers. She was warm, so warm, and inviting and bloody fucking hell, her drawers were damp. He parted the fabric, intent on touching her in truth, finding her bud and teasing her until she spent on his fingers.

"I think you did like it, minx," he managed, his own desire thundering through him like a raging summer storm.

"Of course I did. Was that not the point?"

"Christ no," he admitted, and then Aubrey lost control of his mind and tongue both, because he touched her.

He *touched* her sweet, hot cunny. And bloody, bloody hell.

She was so wet and hot that he could do nothing but groan, running his finger up and down her seam, gathering her wetness. Her pearl was swollen and responsive when he gave her a sleek stroke. Ah, God. She felt so good. Better than good, better than he could have possibly imagined.

His tongue was envious of his fingers, but he knew he wouldn't have a comfortable means of pleasuring her that way. He wanted her in a bed, naked and sitting on his face. He'd eat her cunny and stroke himself to completion. Then he would—

No.

What was he thinking? He couldn't do any of those things. He had to stop this madness.

Except she made a soft, feminine sound of appreciation and rocked her hips, and how could he possibly do anything but give her what she wanted? He swirled his fingertips over her clitoris.

"This is where you long to be touched most, isn't it?" he asked, wickedness overcoming him.

"Yes," she gasped when he increased his pressure and pace.

"You need to come so badly," he whispered, and it was agony and ecstasy, because so did he.

"Richford," she said, her nails digging into his shoulders with greater urgency. "Please."

He could give her this, he decided. What was the harm? She was overwrought, and she was yet a neophyte to desire. Carnal greed took hold of him then, shattering his conscience and his sense of loyalty both. Why should it not be him? Rhiannon wanted to know pleasure. He could show her, give her what she wanted. In return, he could make certain she wouldn't fall into the clutches of one of the jaded rakehells in attendance.

It was almost honorable, when he thought about it.

The door rattled suddenly behind Rhiannon, followed by a loud series of knocks. "Is anyone in there?"

He froze, his hand on Rhiannon's wet, silken quim.

Rhiannon stiffened, eyes going wide as they met his.

Thank God he'd thought enough to lock the door after them when they'd entered. The last thing he would have wanted was for an interloper to appear in a moment like this.

"The room is in use at present," he called out, raising his voice enough so that it would carry as he removed his hand and dropped Rhiannon's skirts as if they had been made of hot coals.

"I beg your pardon, old chap," came the voice on the other side of the door. "I didn't intend to intrude. Carry on."

The fellow sounded foxed, which was just as well. He would likely wander off in search of other amusements, leaving Aubrey to attempt to tidy up the mess he had just made.

He cleared his throat, willing both his racing heart and his hard prick to calm. "Thank you," he called to the man, gratified when he heard footsteps receding down the hall.

Rhiannon was still leaning against the door, looking rumpled and rosy-cheeked.

Damn it all to hell.

What had he just done? Worse, what had he been *about* to do? He had surrendered to his base instincts, casting all thoughts of conscience and loyalty from his mind. How easily he had been overcome. But then, was it any wonder with a temptation like Rhiannon so near to him? For Christ's sake, he had brought her to observe another couple *fucking*.

He was mad.

Madder than mad.

He had been about to make her come on his hand whilst the two of them were standing up and fully clothed. She was Whit's sister, for Chrissakes.

"Forgive me," he managed to say past the agonizing, pent-up lust roiling through his blood and roaring in his veins. "I do believe your education went a bit too far."

"Is it over already?" she asked, sounding disappointed.

He ground his molars. "It must be."

Her blue eyes were on his, searching. "Why?"

"Because I went beyond the pale." His fingers were still wet from her cunny.

It was all he could do to resist bringing them to his mouth and sucking them clean.

"Well." She straightened, moving away from the door and smoothing wrinkles from her silk skirts. "I certainly don't hope you think this was a deterrent. I'm more determined than ever to remain here."

"You can't," he said quickly.

Too quickly.

He had no intention of revealing the effect she had on him to her. The minx would use the knowledge against him like a weapon.

"The longer you remain here, the more likely it is that your brother will discover your presence. And what will you do then?"

"Let that be my worry."

Then the minx moved past him, her skirts brushing his trousers as she went, leaving a cloud of her heavenly jasmine perfume in her wake. Too late, he realized she was going to the observation window. By God, she was likely to see far more than he was willing to allow.

"Rhiannon," he started, "don't."

But she was already looking before he could intercept her, rendered too numb by his own stupid lust to react in time.

"Hmm," she hummed, her voice muffled against the glass

pane, tinged with fresh dismay. "It looks as if our friends have concluded their efforts."

Thank God.

He closed his eyes for a moment, trying to gather his wits before opening them again. "Your education is at an end, I'm afraid. Time to return to your chamber. I'll send the packing maid."

She turned to him, her eyes snapping with fire. "You'll do nothing of the sort, Richford. I'm not leaving."

"Yes, you bloody well are."

She gave him a beatific smile. "If you want me to leave, Your Grace, you're going to have to throw me over your shoulder and carry me out of here whilst I'm kicking, screaming, and cursing you to the heavens. Otherwise, please do keep your distance. Thank you for the afternoon's entertainment. It was most enlightening."

With that, she sailed from the room before he could stop her.

For a long moment, Aubrey remained where he was, her scent still hovering in the air, heart beating furiously in his chest, staring at the door that had closed in her wake. Unable to resist, he brought his glistening fingers to his nose, inhaling deeply of her scent. So damned good. With a groan, he sucked them, savoring the taste of her on his tongue, wishing his head had been firmly between her thighs instead. She tasted perfect, better than the finest desserts, and he wanted more even though he knew he could never have it.

His fingers clean, he stalked back to the door, grimly flicking the lock into place. Returning to his chamber in this state was out of the question. His cock was aching for relief.

He hastily unbuttoned the fall of his trousers with one hand while withdrawing a handkerchief from his pocket with the other. He leaned his forehead against the door, and it was still warm from when Rhiannon had leaned there. Her scent lingered. Fuck. He wasn't going to last long.

Aubrey grasped his cock and worked himself, thinking about how gloriously wet she'd been, how responsive, how plump and swollen her clitoris had felt. He would give anything to suck it until she screamed his name. He still had the taste of her on his lips, in his mouth.

With a strangled shout, he came into his handkerchief, his head knocking off the wooden door, his knees threatening to give out. When it was done, he was sated, though not nearly as spent as he would have preferred. This was all he could have, however. All he could ever have when it came to Rhiannon, and even this was far more than he should have allowed.

Aubrey slipped his soiled handkerchief into his pocket before tucking himself back into his drawers and trousers and buttoning his falls.

He had intended to bring Rhiannon here to teach her a lesson. But he was beginning to fear that the only one who had learned a lesson had been him. And the lesson was that he needed to keep his distance from Lady Rhiannon Northwick.

At all costs.

~

Burying her face in the pillow on her bed, Rhiannon tried not to make any sound as her fingers worked furiously between her legs. In her mind, it was Richford's fingers, not hers. Richford breathing hot and harsh into her ear, telling her how badly she needed to come. Richford stroking her where she ached, playing with her swollen nub until she nearly exploded. A rush of bliss swept over her, her heart hammering, the force of her release taking her by surprise.

But now that she had soothed some of the relentless ache that had been dogging her mercilessly since she had fled the viewing room and Richford both, she felt…incomplete. She still throbbed and longed for more, for *him*. The restlessness hadn't entirely faded.

And that was a disappointment indeed, because she had been nearly out of her mind with the need to bring herself off as she'd raced away. Rhiannon had wrestled herself out of her dress and corset—no easy feat without a lady's maid, but necessary for comfort. In her chemise and drawers, she'd thrown herself onto the bed.

He had touched between her thighs. He'd lifted her skirts, skimmed his hand past the slit in her undergarments, and had found, unerringly, exactly where she needed to be touched. It was the same place she touched, of course, only it was somehow more erotic when the man she had been swooning over for years had been the one doing the touching.

Now, it seemed he had spurred some sort of ache in her that only he could ease. Rolling onto her back with a sigh, Rhiannon stared at the ceiling of her commandeered room. If only Richford had followed her here. Instead, he had reverted to the impassive, aloof duke who regarded her as a vexation and nothing more.

She strummed her fingers over herself lightly, wondering if she might find release a second time. Was it too much? Was it perfectly healthy to do so more than once? The literature Mater had given her—a book on comportment and other topics of importance to honorable young ladies—had sternly warned against touching oneself in a laborious and intentionally vague way. Mater herself had never deigned to speak of anything at all regarding the body, leaving Rhiannon to find her information elsewhere.

Reluctantly, she rolled from the bed and moved to the

pitcher and basin that had been left her by one of the housemaids. Still feeling feverish, her body practically buzzing like a bee, she performed her ablutions. It was soon time to dress for dinner, and Rhiannon had no intention of hiding in her chamber for the duration of the house party.

Richford could go to the devil for all she cared.

She would ignore him. Find her friend Lady Blue and perhaps the two of them could go into dinner together. As her body gradually calmed itself from her agitated state, Rhiannon chose a green evening gown she thought was particularly becoming on her. She donned her undergarments and slipped on the bodice and skirts, fastening and pinning and pulling and draping until she had the desired shape.

Who was she fooling? She didn't want to ignore Richford, and neither did she want him to fail to notice her. He was maddening and irresistible, and her cursed feelings for him had merely blossomed and grown during her time here. If only he would cease worrying about her being Whitby's sister and see her as a woman.

Perhaps she could make him do so.

Tonight.

With a moue of frustration, she stared at her reflection. On second thought, the bodice on this gown was far too modest. The green evening dress would have to go. She required a more daring décolletage. With an aggrieved sigh, Rhiannon worked her way back out of lacing and hooks and layers of silk until she was once more in her underpinnings. The discarded gown fell in a heap at her feet. She stepped from it and riffled through the gowns her lady's maid had dutifully packed. A blue gown and a gold gown sailed through the air. Then a pale-pink and seafoam one as well until finally she found it.

The gown was scarlet and pink, trimmed with silk roses,

and the bodice was incredibly bold. She had yet to wear it in London because Mater, detached and disinterested though she was, had seen Rhiannon in it and disapproved.

"Perfection," she said, smiling to herself as she donned the pink and red silk, draping the lace and skirts before finishing up the fastenings.

When she was done, she regarded herself in the mirror, surprised. She had quite failed to recall just how much of her breasts were on display with this dress. The result was better than she could have predicted. It was just scandalous enough for her to blend in with her fellow revelers without causing too much scrutiny.

After all, the last thing she wanted was to draw too many eyes, lest her brother take note. The house party had so many guests that she had been able to avoid him thus far, and she intended to keep it that way.

Next, she went to work on her hair, coaxing it into a coiled braid and stabbing her head with pins until her scalp was sore and she had a renewed appreciation for the skill of her own lady's maid. Bringing Monford with her, however, had been too great a risk. Although she trusted the woman, she didn't expect her to lie on her behalf, and whilst Mater wasn't cunning enough to suspect anything ill of Rhiannon, her brother certainly was.

Instead, she had invented a visit to their great-aunt, informing Monford that her aunt's maid would attend her and that there was no need for Monford—who detested train rides because they made her ill—to accompany her. The explanation had assuaged her lady's maid's feelings of loyalty and had also ensured that she wouldn't need to fib on Rhiannon's behalf.

A bit of scent at her wrists and throat, the fastening of some earrings and a necklace, and Rhiannon surveyed herself in the looking glass, deciding she was ready.

She turned to leave her room before the dinner gong went but doubled back hastily, realizing she had yet to don her mask again. With the scrap of silk retrieved and tied in place, she ventured back into the mayhem of the house party.

A swarm of guests was filing in and out of the drawing room as they awaited dinner to be announced. Fortunately, all evening meals here, much like breakfast, were informal in nature. With many guests electing to remain anonymous, place settings weren't set, aside from those established at the head of the table for their hosts, including Rhiannon's brother Rhys, the Duke of Whitby. With two of the founding duke members recently married—the Duke of Brandon and the Duke of Camden—that left Richford, Kingham, and Riverdale to round out the four.

And equally fortunate for Rhiannon was that she didn't need to find Lady Blue herself.

"There you are," said her friend from breakfast with a smile beneath her half mask as she approached Rhiannon. "I was beginning to wonder if you would be joining us for dinner."

"I couldn't decide upon a gown," Rhiannon confided quietly, casting a glance around the room in search of Richford and trying not to be too obvious about it.

She didn't see him just yet, and she would recognize his tall, lean form anywhere.

"You have certainly chosen a lovely one," Blue praised.

"Thank you. Your gown is beautiful as well, although I reckon I ought to call you Lady Green now instead."

Lady Blue was wearing an emerald-green gown with a gold underskirt, the bodice ornamented with gilt sequins and jet beads. Her mask matched.

She laughed at Rhiannon's lighthearted joke. "Whilst you are still fully capable of being called Lady Pink. Tell me, are all your gowns this color? It will make it easier to find you in a crush."

Rhiannon smiled back at her friend, thankful she had found at least one amiable person with whom she could converse. "I do admit to a partiality for pink. However, I also own dresses in other colors."

Most of which were presently scattered across her floor and bed. She truly was a dreadful mess without Monford to keep her in order. It had taken Richford's unexpected presence in her bedchamber to make her realize that, however.

The gong sounded then, and their fellow revelers began filing from the drawing room in search of the dining room and their dinners. Rhiannon was in no hurry to be seated anywhere in the vicinity of her brother, so she intentionally stayed where she was on the periphery of the drawing room.

Her friend gave her a questioning look but didn't comment upon her hesitation. They chattered about their afternoons, with Rhiannon intentionally leaving out any mention of the Duke of Richford or the observation room. The less she thought of what had occurred in that narrow viewing chamber earlier, the better off she would be. Rhiannon had no wish to reignite the fires of longing that she had so recently banked. If last night was any indication, dinner would take at least two hours to complete with all the courses and guests in attendance, and she would be forced to sit at the table in pained agony for the duration.

"Are you ready to go in to dinner now, my dear?" Lady Blue queried with a solicitous air.

Richford hadn't come to the drawing room. Rhiannon tamped down the fresh surge of disappointment that rose within her at his absence.

"I suppose we had best do so if we wish to be seated," she said with a sigh.

"You didn't happen to be looking for a certain duke, did you?" her friend asked slyly.

Was she that obvious?

"Merely because I wished to avoid him," she lied airily as they began moving together toward the drawing room door.

"I understand the feeling, believe me." Lady Blue's voice possessed a wry note.

"Has your husband discovered you're here yet?" she asked her friend, keeping her voice low so that it wouldn't travel to any prying ears as they journeyed down the hall.

"He remains blissfully ignorant," Lady Blue said. "And that is just how I wish for it to be until I'm prepared to enact my plan."

Ah, yes. Her plan to incite her terrible husband into divorcing her.

"Have you found anyone of interest?" Rhiannon asked, hoping for her friend's sake that she had.

What kind of a husband would fail to notice his own wife beneath the same roof? And what manner of man would be so terrible that he'd drive his kindhearted wife to adultery just so that she could obtain a divorce?

"I have a few gentlemen in mind," Lady Blue said with a sigh. "Alas, engaging in a wild, passionate *affaire de coeur* isn't nearly as easy as I had previously supposed."

"Surely there are more than a few eligible potential suitors." They were almost at the massive dining room now, and their conversation would necessarily have to revert to a far less personal nature given the proximity of others at the table.

"My dear, I have seen you, and you've only eyes for one of the men here," Lady Blue said slyly. "I daresay you haven't even taken a single look at the rest. But I can assure you, they are all well enough. *Until* they open their mouths and begin speaking."

Her grim pronouncement won a startled laugh from Rhiannon, even if Lady Blue's observation about her having eyes for Richford alone had cut rather close. "That seems to be the problem with most gentlemen, I fear."

Richford included.

She and her friend entered the dining room then, putting an end to their chatter. As if she had conjured him with her thoughts, Rhiannon spied the duke at the far end of the table. Her pulse leapt at the sight of him, a low tingle taking up steadfast residence in her stomach. There he was, drat the man, dressed to perfection in evening black with a white necktie and matching waistcoat, his honey-gold hair glinting beneath the light of the chandelier. He was so handsome it hurt to look at him.

And of course, all Rhiannon could think about was his sinful kisses and his wicked touch. His hand beneath her skirts, his fingers on her pearl, stroking and sending pleasure skating through her. His mouth, his words, his heated stare.

Across the sea of revelers between them, their gazes met and held. Rhiannon was gratified when his eyes dipped to her bodice, taking in the swells of her breasts, pushed scandalously high by her corset and immodest décolletage. His brows snapped together, and his expression turned thunderous.

"It would seem a certain someone has spied you, my dear," Lady Blue said in an aside.

Rhiannon smiled serenely in Richford's direction, as if she hadn't a care.

His glower deepened.

Dinner was going to be an interesting diversion, she thought as she seated herself beside her new friend. Richford was on the opposite side of the table, which meant she could still see him quite well if she tilted her head to the left and shifted in her chair accordingly.

Doing so meant she was unintentionally giving the gentleman at her side an unimpeded view straight down her bodice. Rhiannon only realized it when she caught the masked fellow leering at her with unabashed interest.

She straightened, flicking a glance back in Richford's direction. He looked furious.

"Brava, my dear girl," Lady Blue said at her side. "Make him jealous."

Rhiannon didn't think she had such a hold on him. But there was no denying the irritation she saw flashing in his eyes.

"I'm not certain I am capable of it," she told Lady Blue quietly. "I seem more of an irritation to him than anything."

The company tittered around them, awaiting the first course, oblivious to their conversation, which was just as well to Rhiannon. Lady Blue was her sole acquaintance here at Wingfield Hall aside from Richford and her brother, and she could hardly seek out Rhys. Her brother would scold her and send her directly home in shame. In matters of the heart, she had always found it best to seek the counsel of her female friends.

"You are far more than an irritation if the way he looks at you is any indication," her friend said. "There was a time when I would have given anything for my husband to gaze at me like that."

There was sadness in Lady Blue's voice that tugged at Rhiannon's heart.

"And now?"

"Now, I simply don't care. But enough of my woes, Lady Pink. Let us enjoy the sumptuous dinner, shall we?"

Her friend's words held a grim resignation. Rhiannon wondered if Lady Blue had ever loved her husband. Was he a rake like the Duke of Richford? What had happened between them to make her new friend so jaded, so desperate to escape her marriage?

As the questions rolled through her mind, Rhiannon couldn't resist another glance Richford's way. However, this time, he was distracted, speaking to a brunette near his end of the table. Her stomach curdled. No doubt the other woman was the sort who appealed to him. Someone who was experienced and bold. Someone he didn't think of as a naïve girl.

Perhaps it was for the best.

She had the earl to consider after all. Her feelings for Richford would likely never be returned. Even if she captured his attention momentarily, he was the sort of man who would inevitably stray. She had no wish for a marriage like Lady Blue's. That was why she had agreed to wed Carnis.

Rhiannon turned her attention to the soup course with dour resolve, vowing that she wouldn't spare the duke another glance for the duration of the meal.

CHAPTER 6

"You're scowling again."

Aubrey turned to Kingham—King, as he was better known to friends and foes alike—who was annoyingly observant, particularly when Aubrey didn't want the arsehole to be. "Scowling suits me."

They were seated in the dining room after the ladies had withdrawn, the table a sea of strewn, emptied glasses, the epergne still resplendent with bursts of sweetly scented flowers. He had watched Rhiannon go, annoyed that the minx hadn't even so much as looked in his direction for the whole of dinner.

"Your expression is somewhere between someone-pissed-in-my-brandy and I-just-stepped-in-dog-shit," King continued, unperturbed by his nettled reaction.

"No one has ever pissed in my brandy, nor have I stepped in dog shit," he growled. "So I fail to understand how you would have the slightest inkling of what such expressions would look like upon me."

"An educated guess," King drawled, lighting a cheroot.

"What he's trying to say is that you look like you want to

bloody well throttle someone," Riverdale offered quite unhelpfully.

"I do," he told his friend in a dark tone. "It's you."

Thank Christ Whit had run off after the dessert course had been complete. King had offered something about Whitby wanting to shag the woman who had created the fancy cream ices they'd all enjoyed, which suited him fine. Aubrey hadn't the heart to face his friend, knowing what he'd done earlier that day.

His hand.

On Rhiannon's cunny.

It had been soaked and hot and sleeker than silk. Fucking paradise.

Don't think of that now, you bloody imbecile, he cautioned himself.

"Why should you want to throttle *me?*" Riverdale demanded, sounding hurt. "I'm not the one who said you were wearing an expression that was somewhere between I-just-stepped-in-horse-shit and someone-shat-in-my-port."

"It wasn't I-just-stepped-in-horse-shit," Aubrey corrected. "It was I-just-stepped-in-dog-shit."

"Did you?" Riverdale raised a dark brow at him. "I wasn't aware there were any hounds in residence here at Wingfield Hall."

"You're deliberately misunderstanding me," he growled.

"I'm not misunderstanding a thing. I daresay you've said it all wrong."

"And no one shat in my port," he continued. "That doesn't even make sense. Who would shit in someone's drink?"

"A villain of the worst sort." King shuddered dramatically, then took a puff on his cheroot.

"You said someone pissed in my brandy," he pointed out to King, irritated. "He hasn't even got the right spirit."

"Are we truly quibbling over something so nonsensical?" Riverdale yawned. "How tedious."

"You see? This is precisely why I want to throttle you," Aubrey bit out. "You're terribly fucking vexing."

"I'd rather be fucking vexing than for my fucking to be vexing," Riverdale quipped, raising his glass of wine.

Aubrey stared at him. "Yet again with the proving-my-point bit."

"Where have you been lately, Richford?" King asked. "You've been scarcer than Whitby at this little fête of ours thus far."

"Chasing skirts," Riverdale answered for him.

Something within Aubrey bristled at Rhiannon being referred to in such a dismissive, derogatory fashion. He wanted to smash his fist into his friend's jaw, which was absurd because Riverdale had no notion that it was Rhiannon whom Aubrey had been chasing. And if anyone deserved a fist to the jaw, it was Aubrey himself for daring to debauch Whit's innocent sister.

"I'm not chasing skirts," he snapped, thinking about Rhiannon flirting with the scoundrel at her side during dinner.

Some jaded Lothario, he was sure of it. One who would just as soon lead her into a dark room and lift her skirts for a quick shag than pleasure her. The very notion made him murderous. He told himself it wasn't his responsibility to watch after her. That if she had chosen to spend all of dinner dancing her attention on some roué, he should thank heaven for the mercy that had been shown him.

But he couldn't.

Because he didn't like it.

Rhiannon deserved so much better than some unappreciative rake who wanted to empty his ballocks.

Someone like him.

His lip curled with self-derision.

"Would you care to explain just what you were doing yesterday following the woman in the pink dress about then, if you're not chasing skirts?" Riverdale chortled.

"Don't speak of her," he growled, hating that his friend had noticed Rhiannon.

Good God, Riverdale hadn't lusted over her, had he? If so, he wouldn't have been the only one. Nearly every man on Rhiannon's half of the table this evening had been ogling her creamy, plump breasts in that positively lewd dress she'd been wearing. A beautiful woman clad in a gown that hugged her figure and accentuated her curves in all the right ways like that should be outlawed.

"Seems to me you're smitten," Riverdale said.

"I'm nothing of the sort."

He wasn't smitten with Rhiannon, damn it. He couldn't be. He was bloody well trying to protect her from herself, that was all.

Was that what he had been doing when he had lifted up her skirts and touched her hot, glorious quim?

He scrubbed a hand over his jaw and had to admit to himself that no, it hadn't been.

Fuck. He was everything that was reprehensible. But he wasn't *smitten* with her. The Duke of Richford wasn't capable of something so maudlin. He bedded women. Pleasured them. Walked away and left them with a smile. That was bloody well all.

"If you say so," King said. "Who are we to argue?"

Aubrey could offer nothing to that question. So he sat at the table and stewed, wondering if Rhiannon had returned to the safety of her bedchamber yet. Praying that she hadn't run off with some silver-tongued devil who would take her virginity and break her heart. He tapped his fingers on the table.

"He's horrid company this evening," Riverdale said to King as if Aubrey weren't sitting there between the two of them with fully functioning ears.

He pinned his friend with a pointed glare. "I can hear you, you know."

Riverdale grinned. "Of course you can. How else am I to tell you that your dark mood is quite ruining my good cheer?"

"What you need," King intervened, "is one of my potions. I've a new one that's just the thing."

King's concoctions were notorious. No one knew precisely what was in them, but they were excellent for a diversion when one needed it.

And perhaps Aubrey *did* need it. Rhiannon was driving him to distraction. Why did he have to make her his problem? Why could he not have ignored the fact that he had noticed her yesterday? It was only the second day of looking after her as if he were a governess and she were his rebellious charge, and look at how he'd failed.

He had touched her cunny.

But he hadn't made her come.

His rakehell soul mourned that loss. Some drunken idiot had interrupted before he'd been able to accomplish that glorious feat.

"I'll try your potion," he grumbled. "Give me enough to drown a whale."

"That would kill you, and we can't have that," King told him seriously, finishing his cheroot and extracting a small bottle from within his coat.

"Kill me? What the hell is in this potion of yours?"

King smiled. "The blood of virgins, the bones of saints, that sort of thing."

"You're mad," he said without heat.

"Being sane is so bloody boring," King said with a shrug,

casting an imperious eye over Aubrey. "Are you wearing an embroidered waistcoat?"

"Yes, I am. What of it?"

"The embroidery is a bit much, don't you think?"

Aubrey frowned down at his choice of waistcoat for the evening. "No, I don't. Otherwise, I wouldn't have worn it, now would I?"

"Hmm," was all King said, looking unimpressed.

"Not all of us can be arbiters of fashion," Riverdale said.

"And makers of poison," Aubrey added.

"It's not poison," King countered, looking affronted. "Not in a small dose anyway."

"How reassuring." But Aubrey took the bottle his friend offered just the same.

He needed oblivion.

He needed to forget all about the golden Siren who had been tormenting him the past two days.

"Save some for me, old chap," Riverdale groused.

Aubrey lifted the bottle to his lips.

And in short order, the rest of the night turned into a hazy blur, which was just the way he had wanted it.

He fell asleep dreaming of jasmine-scented breasts on a Gorgon who would make his cock fall off if he met her gaze and an octopus whose tentacles were fashioned from riotous golden waves of hair. The tentacles wrapped around him and told him he was a scoundrel but they loved him anyway.

CHAPTER 7

Rhiannon woke to a low masculine moan.
A moan of agony.
Richford's moan of agony.

She blinked, sunlight streaming through the cracks of the curtains as lucidity returned to her. The pleasant scent of forest, musk, and ambergris teased her nostrils, along with the slight sweetness of day-old spirits. A large, strong body was half atop hers. There was a hand on her hip and a face buried in her breasts.

His face.

He groaned again, mumbling something unintelligible.

Her brows drew together as she gently rolled him to his back on her bed. His eyes were closed, his handsome face screwed up in anguish. He must be having a nightmare, she thought.

"Poor lamb," she crooned, brushing a tendril of hair from his forehead.

His skin was clammy to the touch, with a sheen of perspiration. He was still wearing his shirt and trousers from the night before. Had he taken ill?

He smacked his lips, eyes still tightly shut. "Mmm. Let me touch your cunny."

He reached for her, his arm suddenly flying outward in her direction.

Her sympathy dissipated as she scooted away from his questing hand. Did the rogue even attempt to seduce in his sleep? And had he any notion of whom he was seeking to caress?

He most certainly wouldn't be touching her...her...her *cunny*. Or anything else.

Not whilst he was asleep anyway.

Rhiannon extended her forefinger and poked him in the shoulder, clutching the bedclothes around her like a shield. "Richford."

"Wish I could suck your nipples," he mumbled.

The outrageous rake.

Heat scalded her cheeks. She didn't know if he was even aware of what he was saying or whom he believed he was saying it to. In the early hours of the morning, she had been awakened by a scratching at her door. Half terrified she would find a mouse scurrying around, she had tiptoed about in search of the sound only, heart in her throat, to discover the source had been quite a bit larger than a mouse.

Richford had been in the hall.

When she'd opened her door, he had spilled into her. There was no other way to describe it. For a moment, she'd been horrified until she had recognized him, even in the shadows. She had staggered backward beneath the weight of his muscled body, arms wrapped around him, struggling to keep them both on their feet. He had nuzzled his face into her throat and murmured something she hadn't been able to decipher.

Originally, Rhiannon had thought something had been

dreadfully amiss. Until she'd realized the true cause of his befuddled stupor.

He'd been in his cups.

But he had also been too foxed to return safely to his own room. Why he had sought out hers instead, she couldn't begin to guess. Perhaps, even in his inebriated state, he had been intent upon locking her in her bedroom again. If so, he had failed at his task.

He'd pulled his face out of her neck, told her she was beautiful, and asked her to kiss him. Then he had promptly pitched face forward into her bed and begun snoring. Of all the times she had dreamt of the Duke of Richford coming to her bed in the darkness of the night, not once had she envisioned it unfolding in quite such a manner.

She'd been left to tug off his shoes, coat, and waistcoat, struggling and out of breath beneath his dead weight as he had muttered something about Gorgons and an octopus whilst she had labored over him, her unbound hair falling in his face.

Finally, she had curled up at his side beneath the bedclothes, listening to his snores split the air, oddly pleased that he was with her even under such unusual circumstances. In a moment of utter stupidity, she had told him she loved him.

The memory returned now, making her faintly ill.

She could only hope he had been too soused to notice or remember it if he had.

The reminder made her prod him with more force than necessary, her finger poking sternly into his shoulder until he stirred, eyes fluttering but refusing to open. He snorted out a half snore.

"Richford, you need to wake up," she told him loudly.

At last, he opened his eyes. "What the devil..." He jolted

when he saw her frowning down at him. "Rhiannon? Why are you in my bed?"

His bewilderment was apparent. The foolish part of her that had ascribed some meaning to his appearance at her door withered.

"You're in *my* bed, Richford," she pointed out, pulling the counterpane to her neck, suddenly all too aware that she was clad in nothing other than a prim nightgown.

And they were indeed sharing a bed, as he had pointed out. Not that Richford appeared in any condition to make romantic overtures, of course. His skin was pale, his eyes bloodshot. She would have liked to say he looked dreadful, but Rhiannon was reasonably sure the infernal man was incapable of it.

Even in his ragged state, he was beautiful. Full, sensual lips, eyes the verdant green of spring grass, his lashes unfairly long, his cheekbones sharp slashes, his jaw stubbled with gilt- and cinnamon-tinged whiskers. The top three buttons of his shirt were undone, revealing a mouthwatering vee of his bare chest. His hair was tousled.

She didn't know which she longed to do more, kiss him or box his ears.

"*Your* bed," he grumbled, flattening a palm over his chest and rubbing it. "Oh thank Christ, I'm wearing clothes."

"Of course you are. I had a difficult enough time removing your coat and waistcoat on my own. I wasn't about to attempt further disrobing."

A furrow formed between his golden brows. "You undressed me?"

"Do you truly recall nothing of last night?"

He groaned. "What should I recall? How the hell did I come to be here?"

She pursed her lips. "You walked here, I would imagine. I don't know for certain. Perhaps you ran. I shouldn't like to think you rode a horse down the halls, but given your state, I reckon even that is possible."

"My state?"

"You were foxed," she informed him coolly.

"To have spent the night in your bed, I should hope I was." He scrubbed a hand over his annoyingly handsome face.

Box his ears, she decided. That was the correct first choice of what she wanted to do to the infuriating man.

"Never fear," she said, summoning her pride to keep the hurt from her voice and expression both. "I would have to be deep in my cups myself to allow you into it. As it happens, I hadn't a choice. You knocked at my door, fell upon me, made a lewd request, and then toppled into my bed face first and started snoring like an old cow."

"Do cows snore?"

"I wouldn't know. But *you* most certainly do." She was being rude and unkind, but she didn't particularly care.

He winced. "Forgive me. It wasn't my intention to come to you last night. I can't think of a single reason I would have done so, other than that perhaps I was so soused I got lost on my way to my own chamber."

His bedroom was in an entirely different wing of the manor house from hers, but Rhiannon didn't bother to point that out. He would likely only counter with something else that insulted her vanity in equal measure.

"Regardless of the reasons for your unfortunate visit, you had better be on your way. I need to dress for breakfast."

He nodded and then groaned, eyes going closed. "Give me a moment, and I'll be gone."

"Is something amiss?"

"It feels like a blacksmith from Hades has been hammering inside my skull," he murmured.

"That is generally the sort of thing that happens when one

over imbibes," she pointed out, telling herself she didn't feel bad for him.

"I didn't just over imbibe. I was swilling poison."

She frowned at him. "Someone poisoned you?"

"Yes. Me. I poisoned myself by drinking that goddamned elixir King had."

Rhiannon found herself more confused than ever. "An elixir? Were you ill last night?"

"It was an elixir for distraction, which was precisely what I needed, or so I thought." His eyes fluttered open, his countenance pained. "Ten minutes. That's all I need. And perhaps some water to drink."

Now he expected her to fetch him water?

"This is not the gratitude I anticipated after spending all night listening to you snore," she groused, flinging back the bedclothes.

To her dismay, she realized her nightgown had ridden up over the course of the evening, leaving the hem tangled high about her upper thighs, nearly all her legs bared. It was a most immodest display, and one she hadn't intended. Perhaps he wasn't looking.

Rhiannon slanted a glance in Richford's direction and discovered that he was indeed looking. Quite intently too. Feeling wicked, she flexed her toes and made a show of stretching, raising her arms above her head and arching her back. The action thrust her breasts out and caused the hem of her nightgown to shift, revealing more skin. She took her time, making a low sound of contentment as she did so.

"What do you think you're doing?" he demanded curtly.

She gave him an innocent look. "Stretching before I rise for the day."

"I think you've stretched sufficiently."

Was he affected by the sight of her limbs on display? She certainly hoped he was, the villain. She hoped he was absolutely overwhelmed with lust for her. Mayhap he could drown in it.

"How should *you* know if I've stretched sufficiently?" she countered. "You're not me."

"At least pull down the hem of your bloody nightgown, then," he ordered gruffly. "You're quite indecent."

Rhiannon lingered for another few moments, taking her time.

Then she summoned all her courage as she slid her legs, one by one, from the bed. "I'm not the one who asked to touch my cunny."

The garbled sound he made behind her was either choking, coughing, or perhaps both at once. She couldn't be sure. Her heart pounded at her daring as she walked as calmly as she could manage to the pitcher of water across the room and poured some into a cup.

She could scarcely believe she had just said something so coarse to him. Doing so felt freeing, however. Why must she be the sheltered miss whilst he could indulge in all manner of bawdy sins at his wicked house parties?

"Please tell me you're only trying to shock me," he muttered behind her.

She turned back to him, pleased with herself for her ability to maintain her composure. "My dear Richford, I daresay it would be impossible for me to shock you, given your black reputation. I am merely reporting the facts of what occurred last night."

"I didn't touch you, did I?" he asked, looking even more ill than he had when he had first arisen.

She hoped it wasn't the thought of touching her that did it.

Rhiannon crossed the room and offered the water to him. "You were too busy snoring."

"Thank Christ." He took the cup, their fingers brushing.

Which was fortunate for him, or else she might have been tempted to dump it over his head instead.

"You *did* touch me yesterday," she reminded him. "In the viewing room. Your sins are not entirely absolved."

"My sins will never be absolved." He brought the cup to his lips and drank greedily, as if he had been desperate to quench his thirst.

"I liked it, however," she told him, just to be contrary.

Richford sprayed water all over the bedclothes and then began coughing. She had shocked him. Good. Served him right.

His cough turned into a moan as he clasped his head with his free hand.

"Not the blacksmith of Hades at work again, is he?" she asked sweetly, looming over him.

"I'm never drinking one of King's bloody potions again," he grumbled. "And you're never to repeat such nonsense. What happened yesterday was an aberration. A mistake. It won't happen again."

"Your appearance at my bedroom in the middle of the night, spending the evening in my bed, or your hand under my skirts?" she asked sharply.

"Christ." He glowered into the water cup, avoiding her gaze. "All of them. None of those things will happen again, I vow it. Listen to me carefully, minx. You're to have your belongings packed to return to London today, or I'll be going to your brother. I cannot be following you about this house party any longer. I'm too old for this nonsense."

He still thought he could bully her into leaving? Ha! Poor, deluded Richford.

She clamped her hands on her hips. "I'm not going anywhere. If my presence here disturbs you so much, then perhaps *you* ought to leave."

"Then I'll have no choice but to tell Whit."

The stubborn, infuriating man. If he didn't presently look so pathetic, pale and wincing from his aching head in her bed, she might have boxed his ears after all.

She beamed at him. "Excellent. When you do so, please also tell him about taking me to the viewing room so that I could watch another couple engaging in sexual congress. And then don't forget to tell him about the numerous times you've kissed me. Or the way you pinned my gown to my waist yesterday and slid your hand inside my drawers. Or how you appeared at my bedroom, kissed my neck, spent the night in *dishabille* in my bed, and then wanted to s—"

"Enough," he bit out, interrupting her tirade. "My behavior where you are concerned has been unconscionable, and I own that. But it's also to be expected. Surely you don't think me a saint. I'm an irredeemable rake."

As if she required the reminder. Oh, how she hated to think that she was of no greater import to him than any other liaison he had conducted. And oh, how she loathed to think of the other women before her, who had known his kisses, his caresses. The ones who would inevitably come after her.

Her smile died. "I want to be here, Richford. We have been over this before, and it has grown quite tedious. Now, please do get out of my bedroom because I have every intention of getting dressed in the next minute. I can assure you that the entire process is ridiculously laborious without the aid of a lady's maid, and I need all the time I can manage."

He set the cup down on the table at his bedside, his countenance grim as he sat up fully and swung his legs to the floor. He was vexingly tall, towering over her when he stood. But Rhiannon refused to take a step in retreat. She wouldn't be cowed by him.

"Damn it, minx. What I'm trying to tell you is that you

need to leave this bloody house party for your own sake. If you stay here, no good will come of it."

"I will be the one who decides what is best for me. Despite your assertion otherwise, I am a woman grown, capable of making decisions for myself, and I want to stay here."

"Why are you so determined?"

Because *he* was here. And she wanted him. She had never stopped, not from the first time she had laid eyes on his infuriatingly handsome face. To a rake like him, these last two days likely meant less than nothing. But to Rhiannon, they had meant everything. She had spent years longing for his kisses, for his touches. To be noticed by him.

And now, she had it.

She had *him* within her reach.

She wasn't ready to return to London and accept Reginald's proposal just yet. She had known from the start that the Duke of Richford was not the sort of man who would ever marry or settle. He couldn't be faithful. He didn't fall in love. But for the next few days, perhaps he could be hers.

She had felt it yesterday in his kisses. She felt it now in his heated gaze on her, drinking her in every bit as greedily as he had the water she'd given him. It didn't matter that he was here for the wrong reasons, that he had sought her out of confusion or drunkenness. He desired her. And she had wanted him for what felt like forever.

Something occurred to her suddenly, a realization that lit her up like a flash of lightning across a night sky.

This was her chance.

She held his gaze. "Because I have no intention of leaving this house party a virgin."

"Rhiannon," he protested sharply, his voice hoarse. "Your curiosity will be your downfall."

She had never felt more powerful than she did in that

moment. Never more in control. And what a heady, potent feeling it was. Rhiannon smiled.

"I think otherwise. Now go, if you please. I really do need to dress for breakfast. I find that I'm famished." She reached for her nightgown, which proved all the prodding Richford needed.

"This isn't over," he warned grimly before he stalked from the chamber.

Rhiannon smiled to herself.

He had no idea.

～

AUBREY DIDN'T KNOW which bothered him more as he made his way back to his own bedchamber—his head, Rhiannon's proclamation that she intended to give herself to some undeserving bastard at this house party, or her dismissal of him.

Yes, she had bloody well *dismissed him* as if he were an annoying little dog panting at her heels. And worse? He had allowed it.

Because he had been half asleep, scarcely alive, his head felt as if it had been trampled by a horse, and he had been convinced she was about to take off her nightgown and stand before him, completely naked.

Utterly tempting.

Even in his reduced state, he would have found it impossible not to take what she had been offering. A fierce possessiveness had swept over him at her pronouncement, one that went all the way to his marrow. One that was wrong.

She wasn't his.

She could *never* be his.

He had to keep his distance.

Which would be a bloody lot easier if he hadn't spent the night in her bed.

He had wasted an indeterminate span of time pacing outside her bedroom, inwardly raging at himself for his weakness where she was concerned, torn between pounding at her door and demanding that she accompany him to see her brother so she could begin her preparations to return home and offering to play lady's maid for her and lace her corset and fasten her bodice.

In the end, Aubrey had done nothing. He had simply surrendered to his aching head and queasy stomach and begun making the trip to the opposite end of Wingfield Hall. He was passing through the great hall, temples pounding unmercifully, when a feminine voice stopped him.

"Richford, darling."

Bloody hell.

Turning, he found Perdita, Lady Heathcote, approaching wearing a coquettish grin and a morning gown that clung to her form, leaving little to the imagination. The décolletage would have been more appropriate for evening, but Perdita didn't appear to care.

He bowed. "My lady."

She stopped before him, raising her brow as she surveyed him, from head to toe. "Tell me, where are you going in such haste this morning, and wearing last night's clothes?"

Caught.

Of all the people to have come across him returning to his chamber after he had slept in his trousers and shirtsleeves and drowned himself in King's noxious elixir, the cunning viscountess was the last he would have chosen.

He forced a benign smile for her benefit. "You recall what I was wearing yesterday? I'm flattered."

"You would be surprised how observant I am," she purred, running a finger down his coat sleeve.

He had shrugged into it as he'd been rushing from Rhiannon's bedroom, but it was hopelessly wrinkled from the way she had tossed it onto the floor along with an assortment of scattered underpinnings and gowns. The minx was excellent at making messes, that much he could say for her.

And oddly, he found her chaotic disarray somehow endearing.

He tamped down that feeling as firmly as possible.

"I'm delighted to hear that you are so vigilant," he drawled. "But if you will excuse me, I must carry on."

Her smiled deepened. "Where are you going? I'll accompany you."

Perdita was an enticing woman. On any other day, he would have been more than happy to accept the invitation she was so blatantly giving. But he was too caught up in thoughts of Rhiannon. His cock didn't even stir. And while he told himself that was because he was recovering from his overindulgence in King's poison, his rational mind knew that for the lie it was.

Aubrey had been sporting a morning cockstand from the moment he had awoken in Rhiannon's bed, the alluring scent of jasmine filling him with a different sort of fire entirely. It hadn't helped when she had thrown back the coverlets to reveal her thin nightgown that scarcely shielded her bountiful breasts from view. And when she had made a show of stretching and the hem of her gown had risen perilously near to her pussy, he hadn't been sure which part of him had been throbbing more, his head or his prick.

He shook his head slowly, taking care not to move with too much haste on account of the pain in his skull. "I fear I'm no mood for company at present, Lady Heathcote, though I do thank you for the offer."

She pouted, making no move to leave him in peace, her finger still on his sleeve. "I do wish you would call me Perdita."

"Perdita, then," he repeated, trying to soothe her ruffled feathers.

The last thing he wanted was to rouse her suspicions and have her asking questions about Rhiannon. Besides, he could call the viscountess whatever she requested, and it wouldn't change a bloody thing. She'd never end up in his bed. Not at this house party. He was too damned preoccupied with thoughts of Rhiannon.

Her words were still echoing in his mind, a taunt he couldn't seem to banish, regardless of how hard he tried.

I have no intention of leaving this house party a virgin.

If he had a modicum of honor, he would go straight to Whit before he even changed his damned trousers. He would immediately confess everything he had done, beg his friend's forgiveness, and tell him exactly where to find his minx of a sister, along with informing him of her wildly scandalous, wholly unacceptable plans.

But it would seem he was a completely soulless bastard where she was concerned. A selfish arsehole. Because he couldn't do it, and he didn't even want to begin to contemplate why.

"What do I have to do for a night in your bed?" the viscountess asked coyly.

Her forthright query took him by surprise.

"I'm afraid there is already someone else presently warming it, my dear," he told her smoothly, thinking it the best way to deflect her interest without wounding her pride.

Her blue eyes narrowed. "Pity. I don't like to share. Who is she?"

Rhiannon rose in his mind, her wheat-gold hair cascading down her back and her hard nipples puckered beneath her prim nightgown, the hem pulled nearly to her waist. The woman before him was a beauty in her own right, but she could never compare.

She wasn't Rhiannon.

"A gentleman doesn't reveal such private matters," he countered, growing irritated at her persistence.

"Come now, Richford, we both know all too well that you're no gentleman," the viscountess said, caressing his forearm slowly. "I've heard the rumors about your proclivities in bed, and I can assure you that I wouldn't be hesitant. Indeed, I think you would find me *quite* receptive."

He was familiar with the rumors and scandalous gossip that traveled around society. Not all of them were true, but some of them were.

"I'm gratified to hear it, but again, I fear that I must decline." He withdrew from her caress just as the fall of footsteps and the swishing of silken skirts heralded the arrival of another in the great hall.

The viscountess stiffened, her gaze narrowing upon the newcomer before flicking back to him. "Her?"

Lady Heathcote's voice was sharper than a blade, strident with vexation. His already upended stomach clenched uncomfortably. Aubrey knew in his gut without looking just who had joined them in the great hall.

A glance over his shoulder confirmed it. Rhiannon had stopped midstride, lips parted beneath her half mask. Her gaze slipped from Aubrey to Lady Heathcote as he felt the viscountess's hand return to his arm and her skirts swish against his trousers, as if she were staking her claim.

There was no misconstruing the hurt in Rhiannon's eyes.

He wanted to jerk his arm from the viscountess's grasp and go to Rhiannon instead, but he also knew Perdita was a viper who wouldn't hesitate to ruin Rhiannon if she discovered the truth. The last thing he wanted was for any harm to befall her because of him. This protective surge within him was as new as it was troubling, but he couldn't dwell on it now.

So he covered Lady Heathcote's hand with his and turned away from Rhiannon. "Of course not," he told the viscountess. "I haven't the slightest inkling who she is."

Perdita laughed delightedly. "I ought to have known better. That one has the wide eyes of a neophyte if ever I've seen one. Surely no match for a man of your voracious appetites."

"None at all," he said mildly, tucking her arm into the crook of his elbow. "Come along, my dear."

As he led Perdita from the great hall, he was painfully aware of Rhiannon's gaze burning his back with every step he took.

CHAPTER 8

Following a disastrous breakfast that may as well have been ash on her tongue, Rhiannon had suffered a deadly boring game of blind man's bluff. She had escaped after a blindfolded gentleman had delivered a wet kiss to her ear under the guise of discovering who she was. Now, she was decamping to the haven of her bedroom, vexed with the entire affair.

Vexed with herself.

Vexed with Richford.

With everything, full stop.

Seeing Richford with the woman in the great hall that morning, so soon after he had left her own bedroom, had stung. In truth, it had more than stung. It had torn a great, gaping hole in her fragile heart. She had recognized his female companion from the game of Questions and Commands, when it had proven apparent that the woman had set her cap at Richford. Rhiannon had stopped, shocked at the sight of him standing so near to the woman, who was blatantly caressing his arm as if they were lovers.

His gaze had settled upon Rhiannon before flicking dismissively away, and then he had left with his companion. She hadn't spied him at breakfast, nor had she seen him later. For all she knew, he had withdrawn to his bedroom with the woman in the daringly low-cut dress.

And why should she be surprised if he had? He had made no promises to her. He was an unrepentant rake, a jaded sybarite.

"A bounder," she muttered to herself. "An infuriating, arrogant, overbearing rogue."

But she loved him anyway, the scoundrel. When would her foolish heart ever learn? Just when he had at last shown an interest in her, he had flitted away with someone else. Someone who was worldly and beautiful and everything she was not.

Rhiannon was so lost in her thoughts that she nearly collided with another woman as she neared her bedchamber. Startled, she drew up short, pressing a hand to her rapidly fluttering heart.

"Forgive me," said the striking dark-haired woman who was, quite notably, not wearing a mask.

There was something familiar about her features and voice. Rhiannon studied her intently, trying to dredge up the reason from the murky recesses of her memory. Somehow, she knew this woman, but she couldn't place where their paths had crossed.

Either way, she had no wish to cause the woman to grow suspicious about her presence here in the largely abandoned wing. She had learned from her chambermaid that only a few guests were in residence on this side of the manor house. One of them was her brother, and the other was a lady…

Perhaps this one.

Rhiannon offered her a warm smile. "Oh, I didn't mean to

suggest the fault was yours. I simply meant that I wasn't expecting anyone to be in this wing of the manor house."

"Nor was I," the dark-haired woman offered. "I expect you are one of the houseguests?"

Oh dear. Decidedly not the sort of question she wished to answer.

"I…" Rhiannon faltered, uncertain of how to respond. "Not precisely. And you?"

The woman gave her an inquisitive look. "Not precisely either."

What in heaven's name did that mean? Was this woman her brother's mistress? Rhiannon had heard rumors about Rhys's conquests, for they were quite impossible to avoid. But she didn't think she had ever met one of his women.

Rhiannon felt her smile slipping. "How interesting."

"Indeed."

They stared at each other for a tense moment, Rhiannon still trying to determine what was so dratted familiar about the interloper.

"I do hope you won't mention seeing me here," Rhiannon said hesitantly at last. "It wouldn't do for anyone to know I am present at such a gathering, you see."

The woman offered her a wry smile. "Once again, we find ourselves in similar circumstances. I would appreciate your secrecy as well."

Relief washed over Rhiannon. It would seem that the other woman also required discretion.

"That is easily promised," Rhiannon reassured her. "I haven't any notion of who you are."

"Nor I you."

"Well, then." Rhiannon forced a grin, still feeling awkward. "I shall forget our paths ever crossed, and you may do the same for me."

The other woman inclined her head. "Of course."

She was about to continue on to her own chamber, but inquisitiveness returned, giving her pause. "Are you…staying in this wing of the manor house?"

The other woman's discomfort was etched on her lovely face.

"You need not answer," she rushed to add, feeling guilty. "Curiosity is one of my downfalls, or so I've recently been told by a very overbearing and frustrating arrogant oaf."

It was difficult indeed to keep the sting and bite from her words as she thought of Richford's imperiousness from earlier that morning, followed by his defection with the lovely woman who had been clinging to his arm in the great hall.

"You sound quite provoked by the gentleman in question," the woman observed politely.

Provoked was an understatement. Richford left her infuriated. Hurt. Longing. Desperately yearning.

"Dukes are the most conceited, smug, supercilious beings," Rhiannon said, with feeling. "Particularly when they think they know better than you do, even if the opposite is true."

"I cannot say I would argue with the smugness," the dark-haired beauty commiserated.

And Rhiannon couldn't resist.

"You must know m—" she began, only to cut herself off. Good heavens, she had almost said *my brother*. "The Duke of Whitby," she corrected.

Before the other woman could respond, the muffled footfalls of someone approaching down the hall reached Rhiannon. Misgiving slid down her spine. What if it was Rhys? Or perhaps even Richford? She had no desire to cross paths with either of them at the moment. She was too upset with Richford, and the last thing she wanted was for her brother to recognize her.

She had to escape, but she didn't dare take the time it would require to continue on to her room, risking discovery and questions she couldn't answer. The servants' stairs were conveniently nearby and the perfect means of evasion.

"Oh heavens, what a silly goose I am!" Rhiannon exclaimed. "I've forgotten something that's very important. If you will excuse me?"

Before the other woman could respond, Rhiannon hastened to the staircase, deciding that she was in desperate need of a distraction. Anything to take her mind off Richford. If he didn't want her, then she would find a gentleman who did.

∼

FRUSTRATED, Aubrey stalked along the gravel path in the gardens.

Where the devil was the minx now?

He had searched everywhere until being informed by a sharp-eyed servant that a lady in a pink dress had disappeared into the gardens, accompanied by a gentleman. Pink was Rhiannon's favorite color. She'd been wearing yet another pink gown that morning when their eyes had last met, hers filled with naked hurt.

After escorting Perdita from the great hall, he had delivered her to the breakfast room before seeking his own bedchamber. Still feeling as if he'd been run over by a carriage and in serious danger of tossing up his accounts, Aubrey had fallen into his bed and surrendered to the beckoning abyss of slumber. He hadn't arisen until later that afternoon, feeling marginally human again at last, only to discover he'd slept away half the day and Rhiannon was nowhere to be found.

He had been looking for her ever since, but the moment he'd learned she had gone off unattended with a gentleman, the need to find her had been stronger than ever. Aubrey rounded a curve in the boxwood maze, and possessive fire instantly shot through him.

Rhiannon was seated on a garden bench, the picture of country elegance with her pale-pink silk skirts gracefully draped, the toes of her boots peeping out from her hem. He might have stopped and drunk in the sight of her but for one salient detail.

She wasn't alone.

Rhiannon was in a gentleman's loose embrace, smiling up at the bastard, her head tilted toward him as if to accept a kiss. Aubrey lost his ability to think as he rushed forward, intent upon putting an end to their little tête-à-tête with his fists if he must. He lunged toward the man, grasping his lapels in both hands, ignoring Rhiannon's horrified gasp.

"Richford, what are you doing?" she demanded, her tone aghast.

"What the devil?" Her male companion struggled to remove Aubrey's grip on his coat.

But it was fruitless. Aubrey was far stronger, and he had determination and the element of surprise in his favor.

He didn't bother to answer with words, hauling the protesting man from the garden bench instead. "Keep your damned hands off her," he snarled.

"See here, you haven't any right—" the rogue began.

Aubrey planted a fist in the man's jaw, effectively ending his objection.

The man's head snapped back from the force of the blow.

"I have every right," he countered harshly. "She's mine."

He knew where the assertion had come from. It was a

dark and dangerous place, deep within him. A place he had intentionally kept locked away, for fear of what would emerge should he ever open that door. But he couldn't worry about that now.

"I'm not yours," Rhiannon exclaimed, leaping from the bench and rushing to her beau's side. "Has he hurt you?" she asked her companion.

The other man was rubbing his jaw. "I'll live." He turned furious eyes toward Aubrey. "You're bloody mad, just like your sire."

"Please, the two of you, cease this nonsense," Rhiannon entreated, trying to come between them.

In a blink, the bastard had flung Rhiannon and her concern aside, pushing her away from them with vicious force. She stumbled in the gravel and fell backward with a cry. Aubrey lost his already tenuous grip on control. This man had dared not just to lure her alone into the gardens, but to put his hands on her. To hurt her. Now, he was going to pay for his sins.

Aubrey swung his fist wildly, gratified by the crunch of cartilage as he landed his punch on the bastard's nose. Blood began spurting instantly, raining down the man's face and soaking into his white shirt. He cupped a hand over his battered nose, trying to stem the flow.

"Apologize," Aubrey demanded coldly, staring into the other man's soul and letting him know just how desolate his own was.

He hoped the arsehole saw the madness burning deep inside him.

"I'm sorry," the man was quick to offer, his bravado gone.

"Not to me," Aubrey growled. "To her."

He stalked toward Rhiannon, offering her his hand to help her to her feet. Predictably, she ignored his hand and rose on her own, brushing off her silk skirts and pinning him with a furious glare. "How could you?"

He would deal with her wrath later.

Aubrey glanced back at the sniveling, bleeding beau. "Apologize to the lady."

"Forgive me," the man said hastily, blood leaking through his fingers and dripping in fat droplets onto the gravel at his feet. "It won't happen again."

He began backing away from them, as if he feared Aubrey would follow, traveling in the opposite direction from which Aubrey had just come. Deeper into the maze, as it happened, but he was hardly inclined to offer the man counsel. Indeed, it would serve him right to get lost within the intricate Wingfield Hall labyrinth. Not only had the man dared to be too familiar with Rhiannon, he had also *pushed* her.

He was fortunate Aubrey hadn't ripped off his ballocks and made him eat them for supper. There had been the matter of the insult he'd paid him as well, but Aubrey wouldn't dwell on that now, for Rhiannon was coming for him, blue eyes blazing.

"How dare you attack him?" she demanded as her former beau disappeared into the foliage, retreating like the coward he was. "All he was doing was chatting with me on the garden bench."

Aubrey held her gaze, unaffected by her ire. "He pushed you. I'd break his nose a second time if I could as penance for daring to do you violence."

"I don't think he meant to shove me," she protested, throwing back her shoulders in defiance.

"Don't make excuses for him," Aubrey snarled, feeling particularly vicious. "No man of honor would dare to hurl a woman to the ground as he did."

"How rich." She marched toward him, not stopping until they were breast to chest. "Because no man of honor would viciously attack someone for the supposed crime of merely sitting on a bench with me."

"He intended to do far more. I can assure you of that. You're damned fortunate I found you in time."

Her vivid blue eyes sparkled in the sun as she glared up at him. "Perhaps I wished for him to do more."

Aubrey wanted to touch her, but he didn't trust himself. She was tempting, maddening, bloody glorious. *His.* He felt it to his marrow in that moment, the rightness of it, as if there existed some unspoken innate connection between them. Truth be told, he'd always felt it, but he hadn't been in her orbit long enough to allow himself to truly experience the magnetic pull.

He flexed his fingers at his sides instead, ignoring the ache in his knuckles from punching her companion. "What is his name?"

"I...don't know," she admitted.

"Ah, so you don't know who he is, whether he's married or a bachelor, whether he's kind or cruel, but you wanted him to do what, Rhiannon? Kiss you? Lift your skirts and take your maidenhead on a stone bench?"

"Why should you care what I want?" she asked, raising her voice until it echoed off the maze walls. "Shouldn't you be off with your paramour somewhere?"

"Did you accompany him to the gardens because you were jealous of Perdita?" he demanded, incredulous at the notion.

He had thought her too intelligent to do something so rash. He'd known she had been hurt by seeing him with the viscountess this morning, of course, but he hadn't imagined she would go about the house party, inviting ruin.

"*Perdita*, is it?" Her eyes flashed with renewed fire. "How wonderfully close the two of you are."

He was hardly close with the viscountess, but Rhiannon

didn't need to know that. Perhaps if she believed his interest was firmly elsewhere, he would find it easier to keep her at arm's length.

"It's none of your concern, is it, minx?" he countered.

"Just as what I do, and with whom, is none of yours!" she tossed back, her voice growing louder by the moment.

That was when Aubrey heard the faint sound of footsteps approaching on the gravel from behind him.

"Did you hear that?" he asked, frowning as he concentrated.

"The only thing I heard was an arrogant, haughty, overbearing rake who mistakenly thinks he can dictate my actions."

"Hush," he ordered her. "I think someone is coming."

Her lips parted, but miraculously, she ceased her loud berating. "I have no wish to cause a scene with you. You've done enough damage for one day."

Nor did Aubrey desire to cause any undue attention for either of them, and if they were having a row, they would most assuredly attract attention and curiosity. Perhaps even Whit would take note, despite his recent mysterious absences at the house party.

"This path will direct you back to the main house," he told her, motioning to a place where the trail meandered off in a direction opposite of the one her companion had chosen. "Go now."

"I don't take orders from you, Richford," the minx snapped, defiant to the last. "But I will go because I'm still furious with you."

With that, she turned and flounced down the path. Seeking to give her enough time to escape, Aubrey pivoted and stalked in the direction of the footfalls. If it was Rhiannon's blasted suitor, returning for more of the justice he'd already received, Aubrey would be more than happy to deliver it.

But as he rounded the bend, the man he nearly crashed into wasn't the masked suitor who had been holding Rhiannon in his arms. It was the Duke of Whitby.

Whit looked surprised to see him in the garden maze.

That made two of them.

Aubrey had been able to avoid direct conversation with his friend up until now. Guilt stabbed him like a knife. He hoped his guilty conscience wasn't written on his face like ink scrawled across paper.

His friend's brow furrowed. "Richford?"

"Bloody hell, Whit," he managed, trying with all his might not to think about all the liberties he'd taken with his friend's sister. "You gave me a fright."

He was going to hell. If there had been even the slightest hint of a question as to where he'd be spending eternity, Aubrey knew it without a doubt as he stood in the sunlit gardens, lying to his friend.

"What are you doing skulking about in the gardens?" Whit demanded, his tone tinged with suspicion.

Aubrey gave his friend an unamused look. "I do not skulk."

But he did know it was imperative to distract his friend and give Rhiannon sufficient time to safely retreat from the gardens without discovery.

Whit regarded him solemnly, a raised brow suggesting he disagreed. "As you wish."

"I don't."

Whit shrugged. "I thought I heard you arguing with someone. A female someone."

Damn it. He could only hope Whit hadn't recognized his sister's voice.

Aubrey stiffened. "You must be hearing things. I say, you weren't indulging in another of King's potions, were you?"

Christ knew he'd been as ragged as a centuries-old tapestry after his last bout with Kingham's elixirs.

"Riverdale said something about you and a blonde," Whit countered without answering his question. "Are you dallying with one of the club members?"

Blast it, what was Riverdale doing, wagging his tongue? And since when did Whit give a damn if Aubrey was bedding one of the club members? He wouldn't have been the first to have done so, and neither would he be the last, he was sure. Granted, it had been Rhiannon he'd been dallying with, and if Whit had the slightest inkling of his sins, he'd be drowning him in the garden fountain by now.

"I don't dally either," Aubrey snapped, doing his best to summon outrage and cloak his guilty conscience as he scowled. "Is Riverdale your spy now?"

"Do I have need of one?" Whit asked archly.

"Of course not," he said quickly.

Their conversation couldn't have possibly been going worse.

"Something is afoot," Whit insisted. "Tell me what it is."

"Nothing is afoot," he fibbed, telling himself that he wouldn't think about how Rhiannon had pulled her nightgown hem up over her gorgeous legs that morning and failing utterly.

"You never did have a face for cards. I can tell when you're guilty, old chap."

With great care, he banished the memory from his mind and forced himself to begin counting backward from one hundred in Latin.

"Nothing is afoot," he lied again. "I am merely here in my capacity as one of the leaders of the club, given that two of our members were not able to attend because of women and weddings and other such bloody rot."

He could still scarcely believe that Brandon and Camden had married. Aubrey had disavowed love long ago. He had witnessed what it had done to his father, and he had no wish to have the same hell visited upon himself or anyone he cared about.

"Christ, don't tell me you've fallen in love with someone," Whit said suddenly, a strange expression on his face as he searched Aubrey's gaze.

"In love?" Aubrey sputtered. Again, Rhiannon drifted into his mind, but this time, he was thinking about how he had lifted her skirts, how wet she had been, how much she had enjoyed watching another couple through the viewing windows. His face went hot.

"Of course not," he added, choking out the denial. "Don't be daft."

Whit's expression turned wry. "You don't dally, you've been chasing about a blonde, and you're acting damned odd. But I'm to believe that nothing is amiss?"

Good God. Aubrey could only hope that his friend didn't think too closely about his own words. The only bloody fortunate thing about these ridiculous circumstances was that Whit believed his sister was safely ensconced back in London with their mother where she belonged. But if he began to suspect otherwise, the ruse would be over.

Along with his friendship, should Whit discover the depths of depravity to which Aubrey had sunk.

"Yes," he ground out, "that is what you are to believe, Whit. Because that is what I bloody well told you."

But Whit was no fool, and he knew better; his expression said so. "I know that is what you told me, but I also happen to know it's a lie. What I don't know is why you're so intent upon deceiving me."

There it was again, the guilt, stabbing between his ribs, making his chest go tight. Whit and the rest of the Wicked Dukes Society were like brothers to him. They were the closest thing to a family he'd known since…

No, he wouldn't think of the hellacious past now. He couldn't bear for his mind to return to that dark place, just as he could never see those evils repeated. Unbidden, the images he had witnessed returned to him. The still, lifeless figure. The blood. So much of it, soaking fine silk, pooling on the carpets, seeping away and wasted. Spilled by the hand that should have protected.

Aubrey scowled, summoning the rage he felt for his past to replace the guilt. "You're not my goddamned mother, Whit. Leave well enough alone."

"That rather stings," Whit said, looking hurt. "Fair enough. If you don't want to tell me—"

"I don't," Aubrey interrupted, steeling himself against the urge to confide in his friend.

Because despite his sense of honor and his loyalty to Whit and his threats to Rhiannon, he couldn't bring himself to tell Whit she was here. He didn't want to consider why.

"—then I shall simply have to bide my time and discover what is going on myself," Whit finished with a triumphant air.

Damn it. Aubrey sensed the determination in his friend, and he knew why. Whit couldn't abide by secrets or lies, and it all but killed Aubrey to be the one deceiving him.

"Don't pry where you aren't wanted," Aubrey felt compelled to warn him. "You may not like what you find."

Whit frowned. "What is that supposed to mean?"

"It means that I don't want you interfering in my affairs," he said coolly. "If there was something I wished to tell you, I would have done so by now."

He had to have given Rhiannon sufficient time to

meander out of the gardens and back into the safer crush of guests within the manor house by now. And Aubrey couldn't bear another damned second of deception. He had to flee.

Without waiting for Whit to say anything else, he stepped around his friend, stalking down the path.

The things he was willing to do for Lady Rhiannon Northwick never ceased to astound him. Now, he thought grimly, all he needed to do was keep the cunning minx out of further trouble.

A Sisyphean task if he had ever heard of one.

CHAPTER 9

Rhiannon had found the perfect place to hide from Richford at the ball that evening.

It was in plain sight.

After confiding her plight in her new friend, she and Lady Blue had traded gowns and masks for the evening. She had even donned a red-haired wig that Lady Blue had brought with her for reasons that were still unknown to Rhiannon. Lady Blue's chestnut hair was exceptionally lovely on its own. Rhiannon hadn't dared to ask, however, too pleased with the chance for a disguise. The wig was finely crafted, and it hid her own golden hair perfectly.

As she moved into the transformed ballroom with other guests, she was confident that Richford would have no idea who she was. Her gown and mask were blue, her hair was red, and she was still furious with him for his high-handed behavior. How dare he cavort with another woman before her and then have the audacity to interrupt her in the garden and bloody poor Lord Question Mark's nose?

That was how she had begun to think of her unfortunate would-be suitor—Lord Question Mark—because his name was, indeed, a mystery to her. They had scarcely been alone before Richford had come rampaging down the path, breathing fire quite as if he were a mythical dragon determined to protect the damsel in distress. Never mind that she hadn't been a damsel in distress at all. Rather, she had quite intentionally accompanied Lord Question Mark to the gardens for a stroll.

True, he had shoved her out of his way, and she had landed hard on her bottom—so hard that a bruise had formed, for she'd examined herself in the mirror when dressing—but Rhiannon was persuaded that he hadn't been attempting to push her down. Likely, Lord Question Mark had been trying to keep her safe from Richford's swinging fists.

And my how they had swung. She was reasonably certain Lord Question Mark was presently sporting a broken nose.

"You look lovely, my dear Lady Pink," came a familiar voice at her side then, intruding on her ruminations.

She turned to find Lady Blue approaching, wearing one of Rhiannon's pink gowns and her matching silk mask. "Thank you, as do you. Pink certainly becomes you. I'm indebted to you for trading gowns."

Lady Blue smiled. "I'm happy to help a friend avoid an overbearing curmudgeon for the night. You'll be free to dance and flirt with whomever you like all evening long."

Rhiannon felt her smile slip, because she didn't want to dance or flirt with anyone else. All she wanted was Richford, even if he infuriated her. Also, her head was beginning to itch beneath the wig, and the blazing chandeliers were radiating heat. She felt a trickle of perspiration run down her back.

"He'll never know it's me," she said, trying to hide the note of disappointment in her voice.

What was wrong with her? She should be happy. She

ought to be reveling in the chance to find a gentleman of her choosing without fear that Richford would appear and pummel him.

Lady Blue opened her fan and began waving it. "My, it's hot in here, isn't it?"

"Dreadfully sweltering," Rhiannon agreed, resisting the urge to scratch her head as she began fanning herself as well.

"Is there any gentleman you would like to meet?" her friend asked.

Rhiannon turned her attention to the throng of revelers in the ballroom. All manner of gentlemen were in attendance. Her gaze flitted over a tall, dark-haired man with twin patches of gray at his temples and a strong, angular jaw. He was quite handsome. Then there was a man with golden waves and broad shoulders who was equally attractive. Some wore masks, while others didn't. A few were known to her, easily recognized without a disguise in place.

Oh, how she wished that one of them would incite a spark deep within her.

But inside, she was empty. She felt nothing.

"Not yet," she murmured. "What of you?"

"Me?" Lady Blue laughed. "I'm afraid I've had no success in finding a suitable lover just yet, but there is still time. Perhaps this ball will prove a boon."

Rhiannon continued searching the crush of guests in the ballroom, only belatedly realizing what—or whom—she was looking for.

Him.

"I don't see Richford gracing us with his masculine beauty yet this evening," her friend said at her side, as if she had read Rhiannon's mind.

"I hadn't even noticed," she lied.

Lady Blue said nothing, but Rhiannon was acutely aware

of her friend's pointed stare trained on her from the periphery of her vision.

She turned away from the ballroom and prospective beaus. "Why are you looking at me that way?"

Her friend's expression was contemplative. "Because I suspect you're not being truthful with yourself or me."

"What do you mean? Of course I am." Rhiannon shifted uncomfortably.

"Do you have feelings for Richford?" Lady Blue asked softly, keeping her voice from carrying.

Her stomach tightened, her heart lurching.

"Yes, I do. Feelings of immense frustration, anger, vexation…" She allowed her words to trail off, wondering if she was protesting too much.

"I was referring to a different sort of feelings."

Heavens, was she that obvious?

Rhiannon frowned. "What sort of feelings, then?"

"Are you in love with him?"

Rhiannon had never told anyone about the way she felt for Richford. It had been her shameful secret. He was a beautiful rake, older than she was, beyond her reach. He had never taken notice of her. And yet, over years as she had crossed paths with him at balls and dinners, what had begun as a naïve girl's infatuation had grown and blossomed into something more. Something deep and abiding.

She sighed, hating to admit it, to hear the words aloud. But she also wondered if it would be freeing to unburden herself. She hadn't been able to tell Rhys, of course, because he was her brother and Richford was his friend. Mater was disinterested and scarcely paid note of anything Rhiannon did, aside from urging her to marry the earl. Nor had she ever told her small circle of friends.

"How did you know?" she asked Lady Blue.

"It occurred to me that there could be a different, deeper

reason for your ire with him," her friend explained shrewdly. "He is being an overbearing oaf, to be sure, but I have also seen the way you look at him, and just now, I saw the way your gaze passed over every other gentleman here."

"I am the world's greatest fool," she said bitterly, whipping her fan back and forth.

At least the breeze she stirred was aiding in the itchy discomfort being caused by her blasted wig.

"Loving someone isn't foolish," her friend told her. "Not unless it is someone who doesn't deserve your love."

Rhiannon wondered if Lady Blue was talking about her husband. "Did you fall in love with someone who didn't deserve it?"

"I don't even know if it was love any longer," her friend said sadly. "All I do know is that whatever I felt for him, he most certainly didn't deserve it. Now, all I want is to be free of him. But he ignores all my letters, and I've grown weary of waiting. He's forced my hand."

"I'm sorry." Rhiannon's heart ached for her friend and the misery she had so obviously endured. "If he cannot see how lovely and kindhearted you are, then he is an idiot."

"But enough about me." Lady Blue whipped her fan with greater force. "We were speaking of *you*, my dear."

"I don't want to speak of me either." She sighed heavily for the second time. "He'll never notice me, not the way I want him to."

"See if he notices you tonight," her friend suggested.

"I'm wearing your gown and a wig along with this mask. I should hardly think he would recognize me." She fanned herself aggressively, feeling the wisps curling about her face fluttering. "Besides, I'm determined to enjoy myself without him hovering over me."

"Perhaps he'll surprise you."

"I doubt that."

Because all the Duke of Richford had managed to do thus far had been to disappoint her. Perhaps it was time to finally admit to herself that he simply wasn't for her.

∽

AUBREY SPOTTED Rhiannon at once from across the throng of tittering lords and ladies in their masks and silk and jewels.

It didn't matter that she was wearing what appeared to be a cinnamon-hued wig or that she was dressed in blue instead of her customary pink. He would know her anywhere. She was whirling about the floor in the arms of a dark-haired man, laughing at something the fellow had told her.

He took a glass of champagne from a passing servant and downed it in three gulps, watching her and trying to quell his inner urge to break another nose. Then he took a second glass and quaffed that one as well by the time the dance was done. When she and her partner were finally finished, he didn't waste any time in striding forward.

"I believe the next dance is mine," he said.

Her sky-blue eyes went wide behind her mask. "I'm afraid you must be mistaken, sir."

Was the minx attempting to pretend she didn't know him? Did she truly think he wouldn't recognize her if she donned a disguise?

"I'm rarely mistaken," he told her, sketching an elegant bow before offering her his arm.

Her partner had already wandered off in search of his next dance, leaving Rhiannon standing with Aubrey, clearly uncertain of what to do next.

"That is quite insufferable of you," she said, putting on a haughty air.

He tried not to stare at the way her corset pushed up her breasts like ripe offerings, but it was difficult indeed. The gown was molded to her curves like a glove, and it was little wonder every man in the vicinity was eyeing her like lions who were searching for their prey.

Too bloody bad for the lot of them. This particular luscious lamb was his.

To protect, Aubrey reminded himself sternly. His to protect and keep from throwing herself at scoundrels.

He smiled and placed her hand in the crook of his elbow. "Come along."

"What if I don't wish to dance with you, sir?"

"What is the harm in just one dance?" he countered.

"Very well," she conceded, frowning at him as they linked hands and he pressed a palm to the small of her back. "But only one."

The music began, and he whirled her about, thinking it a damned shame she had hidden her glorious hair beneath the monstrosity she was presently wearing. She was astoundingly lovely despite her attempt to shield her identity. But then, Rhiannon could have donned nothing more than rags and she would have been the most beautiful woman in the room.

Neither of them spoke for a few moments. He liked having her in his arms far more than he should have. They moved together well, seamlessly gliding over the polished floor. The scent of jasmine teased him, and he fought the urge to hold her even closer.

Instead, he lowered his head until his lips were near her ear. "Are you going to tell me why you're pretending to be someone else this evening, or is this another one of your games, minx?"

Her swift inhalation revealed her surprise. "You knew it was me?"

"I would know it was you in the dark without a single lamp lit," he said before he could think better of the statement. "You can hide in wigs and masks and gowns of every color, but you won't fool me."

"You scoundrel." She tipped her head back, her eyes flashing with blue fire. "You didn't say a word."

She must have thought herself immensely clever.

He chuckled, amused by her outrage. "You truly believed I wouldn't recognize you the moment I laid eyes upon you?"

"This wig is dreadfully itchy," she muttered instead of answering him.

Aubrey cast a wry eye over it. "I would wager it is. Why did you try to disguise yourself, minx? Has Whit grown suspicious?"

"I don't think he has. I've scarcely seen him. He seems to leave dinner and disappear each night."

That was because Whit was skirt-chasing, but Aubrey kept that to himself. Riverdale and King gossiped more than a pair of dowagers.

"Hmm," he murmured noncommittally as they spun around the floor.

"Did you know that he's keeping a mistress here?" she asked.

Aubrey nearly tripped over his bloody feet. So much for trying to shield her from the truth.

"I wasn't aware of that," he admitted. But it didn't surprise him to learn it.

"I met her," Rhiannon said. "At least, I *think* she's his mistress. Of course she didn't say she was. One doesn't go about admitting something so scandalous to a stranger. Not even at a house party such as this."

They spun together again, and he couldn't help but notice the lush fullness of her lips. "I reckon not."

"Do *you* have a mistress?"

For the second time, he nearly tripped, this time on her

swaying hems. He narrowly avoided disaster. "Christ, minx. This isn't the sort of question you ought to ask of me."

"Is it the woman I saw you with in the great hall?" she persisted.

"No," he bit out. "Lady Heathcote is an acquaintance and nothing more. Not that it is any of your concern."

"Any more my concern than it is yours when I accompany a gentleman into the garden?" she returned.

She rather had him there. He couldn't deny it.

"Touché, minx," he said grimly.

"Well?" she demanded.

"What was your question?" he deflected, spinning them and beginning to feel dizzied.

Maybe it was the champagne.

Or the dancing.

Or maybe it was just Rhiannon.

"*Do* you have a mistress?"

Aubrey's gaze traveled down the creamy, elegant column of her throat, and it was all he could do not to set his mouth there, to make his mark upon her. "I'll answer your question when you answer mine."

He had never felt this primitive surge for another woman, and it was deuced maddening. He wanted to protect her, to claim her, to throw her over his shoulder and carry her off to his room and spend all night making love to her.

She is your friend's sister, he reminded himself harshly. *She's a bloody virgin.*

"What was your question?" she asked, her voice a touch breathless.

Her gaze had darkened and slid to his mouth.

He searched the ends of his mind and couldn't recall for a few seconds until they nearly collided with another couple and sanity returned to him. "The reason for your disguise."

"Oh, that."

"Yes." He cast a glance over her red wig. "Though you do make a most alluring redhead as well."

"It was you."

"Me?"

She pouted, and he wanted to kiss that pout off her mouth right there in the midst of the ball. He could too. Couples were free with each other here. No one would look twice if he led her to the periphery of the dancers and fucked her against a bloody wall, for Chrissakes. But the last thing he wanted to do was draw any attention to her, so he kept his lips to himself.

"Yes, you," she said. "I wanted to be free to find a lover without you ruining it."

A lover.

His head roared.

She still, after all he had done to persuade her otherwise, was determined to give her innocence away as if it were a frock that was out of fashion.

"Now I'll have your answer," she demanded.

Through the blood rushing in his ears, he almost failed to hear her.

"What answer?" he rasped.

"Do you have a mistress?"

"No," he managed. "I don't."

Because he didn't prefer to have the same bed partner for too long. Lovers were well enough. Mistresses inevitably had expectations of tenderness and affection, and he couldn't give them that. But he kept all this to himself.

"Then perhaps I could offer myself for the position."

He stared at her, lust and a yearning more potent than any he'd ever known intersecting within him. The result was combustible. *He* was combustible.

And tempted.

My God, he was tempted. More than he had even realized possible.

Whit would murder him. She wasn't mistress material. She didn't even know what she offered. And besides, she was marrying the staid Carnis. God, he hated the thought of someone as passionate and lovely and wild as Rhiannon consigning herself to a lifetime of being a proper wife.

The music died around them, signifying that the dance was over. He stood there like an imbecile, doing everything in his power to will away the cockstand that was threatening to rise there in the middle of the ballroom.

"Until the house party is at an end," the minx added. "When we get back to London, it will be as if it never happened. I shall go on my way, and you'll go on yours."

And then she dipped into a curtsy before walking away, leaving him standing there as if she hadn't just set flame to his world and everything in it.

CHAPTER 10

The ball was still well underway as Rhiannon struggled to remove her borrowed gown in her bedchamber, trying not to wallow in humiliation as she did so. Her heavy wig had been the first, and easiest, to go. Now her hair was free of the hairpins holding it in its confining style, if nothing else.

Following her ignominious dance with the duke, she had fled, embarrassed by her immense failure. What had she been thinking, offering to be Richford's mistress? Did her foolishness know no bounds?

And to make matters worse, she had done so right there, in the midst of the ballroom, surrounded by others, where anyone could have overheard her. Meanwhile, what had Richford done? He had stared at her silently, saying nothing.

Not. A. Single. Dratted. *Word.*

"No doubt, he was at a loss," she grumbled to herself. "He has already made his opinion of me known."

It didn't matter that he had kissed her or that he had touched her that day in the viewing room. He was a rake. Were they not ruled by base lust? Had anyone else been in her place, his reaction likely would have been the same. There was nothing special about her. Richford didn't return her feelings. That much was more than apparent.

Rhiannon huffed a frustrated sigh as she continued her efforts. The fastenings on her friend's bodice were small—a neat row of tiny buttons down her back. When she and Lady Blue had convened to make the exchange, they had helped each other dress, giggling and chattering like schoolgirls.

But now, with sore feet, an aching back, and desperately tattered pride, she was struggling to undo the last of them. She couldn't seem to reach, no matter how hard she struggled to stretch her arms.

Likely, Richford had been horrified by her suggestion. That had been the reason for his silence. She hadn't even bothered to find Lady Blue following that wretched dance. It had taken all the confidence she possessed to hold her head high and sail from the ballroom without bursting into tears.

Rhiannon blinked furiously. She wouldn't cry. Not now. Not until she had her gown off. Then she could crawl beneath the bedclothes that still smelled like him and continue feeling sorry for herself in the darkness until she fell asleep. Perhaps in the morning, she would do what Richford had been demanding she do from the first night. She would return to London.

Her friend had forced her to make some realizations this evening. Namely, that she didn't want anyone else. She had come here for one reason only, and it was a golden-haired rake with emerald eyes, a sinner's mouth, and a beard she longed to feel rasping over her throat as he pressed heated kisses to her bare skin.

"Stupid, stupid," she chided herself, snagging a button, only to have her fingers slide off before she was able to remove it from its mooring. "Blast!"

Cursing felt good.

"Damnation," she added, struggling to get her fingers back on the button. "Ballocks. Cock. Son of a swashbuckler!"

There! She had reached the button and pulled it free. Just a few more to go.

Knock, knock, knock.

She gasped and froze as she realized someone was at her bedroom door. Good heavens, it wasn't her brother, was it? Had she been too loud, issuing those oaths? What if he had heard her? What a fool she was.

"Minx?"

The low voice on the other side of the door permeated her wildly whirling thoughts.

Richford.

Her feet started moving, carrying her across the chamber before her mind was even cognizant that she was going to him. Halfway there, her state of *dishabille* occurred to her.

"Oh well," she murmured to herself, thinking she could blame it on the champagne.

There had to be a reason he had come to her.

Didn't there?

She opened the door, and there he was, unfailingly handsome in that way only he had. Rhiannon wondered if he rose every day effortlessly beautiful. Even his tousled hair that morning had seemed artfully intentional, the way it had fallen over his brow in a rakish manner.

"Richford," she said, hoping he could sense none of her thoughts. "What are you doing here?"

His green eyes were blazing, his countenance alight with intensity. "Did you mean it?"

She faltered. "Did I…"

Her words trailed off.

"Let me in before you answer."

She stepped back and opened the door, granting him

entrance. He stalked into the room, and she shut the portal at his back. Richford turned to her.

"Did you mean what you said in the ballroom before our dance ended?" he asked.

There was a studied concentration in his gaze, in his handsome face, that made her tell him the truth, despite all the stern admonishments of her pride.

"Yes, of course I meant it, Richford," she admitted. "Why else would I have said it?"

"What you asked of me is wrong," he said, his voice almost harsh.

He was impossibly beautiful in his evening finery.

She struggled to keep her face impassive, an expressionless mask. "I don't care."

Richford moved toward her. One step. Her breath caught in her lungs.

Then another.

"You want to give yourself to a man before your boring, proper marriage to Carnis," he said, as if the words were hateful to him.

Rhiannon held his burning blue gaze. "Yes."

"Then I'll be that man."

Liquid heat went straight to her core. "You will?"

Another step, and he was standing directly before her. "It can't be anyone else."

Of course it couldn't, the silly man. He was the only one she wanted. The only one she had ever wanted. But she didn't dare say so.

"No," she agreed.

He nodded. "It's decided, then. We have an understanding."

An *understanding*. Was that what gentlemen called it? How polite. Rhiannon wouldn't know, of course. She was a lady. She had been raised to be a man's wife rather than his mistress. Unfortunately for her, the one man she loved and longed for didn't want a wife.

She stared at Richford, wondering if she was dreaming, scarcely aware of the picture she must present, her bodice gaping at the back, her hair half-unbound as she had thrown hairpins in all directions, cursing herself and him and the world.

"We have an understanding," she repeated.

He hauled her into his arms, bringing her body flush against his. "Only until this house party is at an end."

"Yes," she agreed.

Because after this, she would have to return to her life in London. She would have to become someone else's wife. This was all she could have. Richford. *Hers.* For a few days and no more. It seemed an impossible dream, and yet, here he was, his heat searing her body.

"I'm only doing this to protect you," he said fervently, searching her gaze as if he were seeking something of the utmost importance.

If that was what he wanted to tell himself, who was she to disabuse him of the notion?

"Of course," she agreed easily. "And I am only doing this so that I can experience passion before I marry Carnis."

"Don't say his name again," Richford growled, his lips painfully close to hers. "Not while you're in my arms."

"Never." She was the first to move, her mouth seeking his.

"Damn you," he growled in the moment before their lips met.

In a heartbeat, their mouths were sealed.

The kiss was potent and hot and bittersweet. It was everything she had ever wanted a kiss to be, and yet, it was also somehow everything she had never known was possible. His lips crashed over hers, moving softly, demanding yet seeking. She opened for him, her tongue meeting his. He tasted like champagne and temptation, and all she wanted was more.

No, not just more.

All he had to give. That was what she wanted from Richford. What she needed. What she had been longing for all these years spent admiring him from afar. Now, he was here. In her room, his tongue in her mouth, his lips on hers.

Hers.

That was what he was, and even if it was to last for naught more than a few days, she would seize it. Her hands found his shoulders first, her fingers digging into powerful muscle, holding him to her.

"Rhiannon," he murmured into her mouth, half groan, half plea.

One of his hands slipped inside the partially undone halves of her bodice, his fingers skimming over the space between her shoulder blades. Though their skins were separated by a thin layer of cotton chemise, it was as if he had rained fire into her soul, into the very heart of her.

But this wasn't fair. She wanted to touch him too. And she wanted his name. His given name, which she was shocked to realize she didn't know. He had always simply been Richford to her.

"What is your name?" she asked, lips moving against his.

He paused, removing his lips from hers a scant space before answering, "Aubrey."

Aubrey.

Rhiannon needed to form her tongue around that name, to give voice to this sudden alteration in what and who they were to each other. But he was kissing her again, so she decided to save it for later, when his mouth wasn't on hers, stealing her ability to think. She held on to him, leaning into him. Everywhere they touched, she was aflame. Her breasts into his chest, her hips into his, even with her cumbersome skirts twisting between them.

His hands traveled, finding her half-undone buttons.

He broke the kiss, staring down at her with raw, naked hunger. "Turn."

She didn't offer protest, just spun, presenting him with her back.

"You're certain about this, minx?" he asked, voice low and deep.

More certain than she had ever been about anything.

There was no hesitation in her response. "Yes."

His fingers moved over her buttons, pulling them free, the silk of her bodice gaping more with each one. With the gentlest of touches, he peeled her bodice down her arms and tossed it to the floor, where it joined the piles of discarded dresses she had yet to tidy. Her breath caught as his fingertips grazed the bare skin of her upper arms, her elbows. Good heavens, her *wrists*.

She was aching in places that were ordinary and commonplace. Her body was greedy and desperate, wanting his touch on every part of her.

"Your bedchamber is a bloody mess," he observed without any bite to his words.

"My lady's maid would have stood me in great stead, but I didn't dare risk bringing her with me."

His mouth fluttered over her nape, and she nearly jumped from the electric shock of it. "How did you come to be here? You never said."

He wanted to have a conversation whilst he was undressing her? Rhiannon shivered and leaned into him, cursing the annoyance of her bustle getting in the way.

"I didn't tell anyone where I was going. I just left."

He nuzzled behind her ear, and Rhiannon's legs almost gave out.

"Christ. What if a cry has been raised over your disappearance?"

"My mother won't notice," she managed breathlessly. "She scarcely knows I'm alive."

Except in regard to the earl's courtship. But Rhiannon had already promised not to speak Carnis's name again, and she didn't want to think about the future awaiting her now. She wanted to live in this moment, in the impossible hope she had been clinging to for years, finally made real.

As real as the duke's lips on her nape, his fingers finding the hooks on her skirt and setting them free. His hands clamped suddenly on her waist, and he spun her to face him.

"Promise me you won't do something so reckless again."

She opened her mouth to argue, to ask why it should matter, to remind him that this was her last chance before her boring life began as someone else's wife. But he laid a finger over her lips.

"No arguing. Promise." His voice was stern, his expression intent.

"I promise," she said, then gave in to the urge to kiss his finger.

"Good."

His fingertip slid along her lips, over her chin. He skimmed it down her throat, making her tilt her head back. Slowly, slowly, he trailed his touch across the center of her chest, between the swells of her breasts beneath her chemise and corset. Then he hooked his finger in her corset and tugged her into him, his lips claiming hers again, and promises, the future, and all else fell away.

There was nothing but him and her, their mouths melding. Nothing but the night and the two of them. He cupped her cheek with one hand and made love to her mouth, feeding her voracious, deliciously carnal kisses. Her dream lover, hers at last. Perhaps she was asleep, but if so, she would sooner revel in this forbidden fancy than wake.

As if to prove he was real, she coasted her hands over his chest, finding the buttons that kept her from him too. His coat and waistcoat fell to the floor. More buttons. She sucked on his tongue as her fingers flew over additional fastenings. Rhiannon lost patience and clawed at his shirt, her nails raking over his chest.

He grunted, and she tore her lips from his, aghast that she had scratched him like a wildcat.

"Forgive me."

His gaze was as dark as forest moss. "Hush." He caught her hand and brought it to his lips, pressing a feverish kiss to her knuckles. "Never apologize with me."

Aubrey's shirt hung open, revealing a tempting swath of chest and the lean, muscled slabs of his belly, all dotted with a sprinkling of golden hair. Three pink lines rose above his flat nipple, and she leaned into him impulsively, pressing her lips to his heated skin just above his heart. She absorbed the rhythmic beats with her mouth, inhaling deeply of the scent of him, masculine and beloved.

His shirt fluttered to the Axminster. Her petticoats went next. Their lips met again as he walked her toward the bed. She nearly tripped in the particularly voluminous skirts of a discarded day gown and clung to him. He caught her to him, keeping her from falling.

She was drunk on him. Or perhaps on the champagne she had consumed during the ball. Mayhap both? The lights swirled around them, and everything became a blur of color and sensation. He one-handedly plucked open the laces of her corset while kissing her breathless and pulled open the hooks on her busk with the other. Her chemise and drawers were next, and then he backed her onto the bed while she was clad in nothing other than her stockings and garters.

Strong hands on her waist lifted her until her bare bottom settled in the soft nest of the bedclothes. She reached for the counterpane, thinking to shield herself, but he caught her hand in his.

"Let me look at you," he rasped. "Please."

It was the reverence in his voice that shattered her embarrassment. She thrust back her shoulders and raised her chin as his heated stare devoured her.

"As you like," she invited him, her own gaze traveling lovingly over every detail of his bare upper body.

Long, strong arms that flexed as he moved. How was it possible for him to be even more beautiful without his clothes? It seemed an impossibility, and yet, somehow, he was.

"I like." He flattened his hands on either side of her on the bed, his big body bending toward her. Their lips met in a kiss. "Very much." He kissed down her throat. "More than words…" His mouth moved along her collarbone, then dotted across her shoulder. "…can possibly convey."

She swallowed as his lips trailed lower, finding the curve of her breast. Her nipples were already hard, aching to be touched. As if he could sense what she wanted, he took one in his mouth and sucked.

A cry left her as she arched her back, a new pulse beating to life between her legs.

He released the peak of her breast.

"Hush," he reminded her.

Suitably chastened, she bit her lip.

"You're so damned beautiful, Rhiannon." He dipped his head, and his hot, knowing mouth closed over the distended peak. He sucked hard.

Her fingers threaded through his hair, and she arched into him. The feeling between her legs intensified. It was as overwhelming as when they had been alone in the observation room. He moved to her other breast, flicking his tongue around her nipple in maddening circles before suckling until a muffled cry slipped from her lips.

"So responsive," he praised. "I wonder if you could come from my mouth on your breasts alone."

A ragged breath escaped her.

He chuckled, the sound a wicked rasp. "Perhaps we'll test that later. For now, I'm too impatient to taste you."

A forbidden thrill shot through her at his words. For she knew what he meant. What he intended. Aubrey wanted to use his mouth on her just as the man had done to the woman in the viewing room.

And she wanted him to.

He sank to his knees on the carpet, his hands gliding over her bare thighs. "Open for me, minx."

Rhiannon realized she had been holding her legs together tightly, trying to quell the ache. He kissed a path from her hip to her knee like a devoted supplicant. If watching another couple had felt wicked, having him on his knees before her, intent upon kissing her most intimate place, felt deliciously wrong and yet oh-so right. This was Richford, the man she had yearned for all these years. Finally, at last, seeing her.

Touching her.

Desiring her.

She relaxed at once, parting her legs, and he wasted no time in burying his face there. He pressed a kiss to her mound, his soft hair brushing against the insides of her thighs as he caressed her hips. When his tongue flicked over her sensitive nub, she gasped, fingers tightening on his hair. He licked at her, teasing softly at first and then exerting greater pressure as dizzying pleasure overtook her.

She forgot modesty. Forgot to worry about the uncertainties awaiting her beyond this room. Instead, she surrendered to him. He made a low sound of enjoyment that rumbled through her core and radiated outward, his tongue still playing over her, alternating between quick, light licks and long, slow explorations. It was the most divine sensation she had ever known. Little wonder he had all the ladies in London falling at his feet. If he was capable of this…

His lips closed around her, and he sucked.

A noise fled her, half gasp, half moan. The wicked, wicked man. He paused for a moment, his gaze meeting hers as his mouth continued to deliciously torment. And then he found a part of her that was deliriously sensitive, using his teeth to lightly nip. Something inside her came apart. Her crisis took her quickly. She stiffened beneath his tender onslaught as wave after wave of bliss washed over her.

He stayed with her all the while, continuing to lick and lave and suck. His fingers parted her folds, slicking her wetness up and down as his mouth worked at her highly stimulated flesh. There was a new sort of pressure, different from his tongue, and she realized it was his finger, poised at her entrance. Did he intend to…?

Yes, he did.

In the next breath, he sank a finger inside her, all while sucking at her clitoris. The sudden fullness sent a sharp rush of desire through Rhiannon. It was almost painful, the pleasure, as he moved in and out of her, the wet sounds of her own desire echoing in the hush of the night. It was too much. She twisted beneath him, desperate for more, seeking, searching. The crescendo within her built again to a fevered pitch. Her body seized, and she lost control. The pleasure this time was every bit as violent as the last, wringing a moan from her.

"God," he murmured. "You taste so sweet, and you're so wet, so perfect."

He withdrew and rose to his feet, his expression slackened with desire, his lips wet and glistening. What a beautiful sight he made, bare-chested and towering over her. But he was still wearing his trousers, and that hardly seemed fair. She wanted to see him, to touch him.

Rhiannon reached for the fastening on his trousers.

"Minx." He caught her hands and brought them to his lips for a kiss. "You're sure?"

"Yes. I want it to be you."

His lashes lowered for a moment, and he appeared to collect himself. She admired him in the warm glow of the lamplight, loving him like this, all his defenses gone.

"Lie down on the bed."

She shifted and did as he asked, watching as Aubrey undid the fall of his trousers and pushed them down his hips along with his drawers. His cock rose, stiff and ruddy and... *large*. So much larger than the man's in the viewing room. The mechanics of what was about to transpire eluded her. It seemed an impossibility for him to fit inside her.

But then he was lying with her, murmuring tender words, kissing and caressing her everywhere, and her concerns fell away.

∼

Aubrey's cock was harder than it had ever been, and he wanted nothing more than to sink it deep into Rhiannon's pretty pink pussy and fill her with his seed until he was boneless and mindless. He'd never been so overcome by the primitive urge to claim someone, to make her his, the way he was with her.

He was a man possessed.

But as he dappled kisses over her breasts, he forced himself to regain control. She was a virgin. He didn't want to hurt her. Even if it bloody well killed him, he would seduce her slowly. With maddening intent. Because if there was one conquest in his life that truly mattered, it was this one. It was her. He would drown Rhiannon in pleasure, and then, when she could bear no more, he would finally take her.

Yes, he could hold on just a bit longer. This was what he was made for. Desire. Not anything else.

The musky, sweet taste of her yet flooded his mouth as he kissed every part of her he could. A mole high on her stomach entranced him. It was shaped like a heart, and he kissed it twice for good measure. Her curves were perfect for his hands, her skin as sleek as silk. He kissed her belly, then realized she was still in her stockings.

He plucked at a garter and dragged it down her knee, kissing as he went. "I want every part of you bare for me."

No barriers.

Just her.

Soft and sensitive, sensual and tempting. Slowly, slowly, he rolled the stocking past her calf to her ankle, then her foot. He tossed it over his shoulder into the mess she already had left everywhere in her wake, and then he kissed her instep. Somehow, even the chaotic state of her bedroom—increasingly in disarray each time he entered—made him paradoxically harder.

It made no sense. *She* made no sense, and neither did his desire for her. There were a hundred reasons why he shouldn't want her, and yet not one had kept him from her door. He wasn't persuaded that anything or anyone could. He had no control where she was concerned. A few days alone with her and he was lost.

Aubrey moved to her other garter, savoring the slow glide of it and her stockings down her leg. All the while, she watched him, a sensual goddess who knew what she wanted and wasn't afraid to seize it. She was dangerous, Lady Rhiannon Northwick.

He kissed his way back up her body, starting at her toes.

God, she was intoxicating. He couldn't get enough of her. When he reached her hip bone, she writhed impatiently beneath him.

"Aubrey."

Her protest made his cock twitch. He hadn't been prepared for the effect her calling him by his given name would have on him. With a groan, he nuzzled her cunny, inhaling deeply of her scent. And then, because he couldn't resist the urge to make her come again, he used his thumbs to part her, running his tongue along her swollen clitoris. She was so deliciously sensitive everywhere, and awakening her to her passions was a privilege as much as it was a joy.

He sucked hard and then licked down her seam, sinking his tongue into her cunny, fucking her as she writhed and bucked and moaned. Aubrey ground his rigid cock into the mattress, staving off his own release as he tended to her. He replaced his tongue with two fingers this time, stretching her, helping her body to relax and prepare for the invasion that was next.

He had no wish to hurt her. He'd chop off his own arm first. This was Rhiannon, and everything about her first time had to be special. He concentrated on her, listening to her sounds, the way her body moved, learning what she liked and where she was particularly sensitive. He lapped lightly at her pearl as he moved his fingers in and out of the tight, slippery grip of her soaked cunny. His cock was jealous, tunneling into the mattress.

Fuck, she was soaked. Moaning, meeting the motions of his fingers, her hips tipping upward in innocent invitation. Her body stiffened beneath his lips. She was close to reaching her crisis again. Aubrey suckled her pearl and sank his fingers deep, and she came. Came as he lapped up her juices. Came moaning his name.

And he couldn't bear to wait another second to be inside her.

He dragged his lips over her belly, back to her lush, bountiful breasts and the hard pink nipples that begged for his mouth. Obligingly, he sucked each one as he positioned himself over her. Leveraging himself on one forearm, he gripped his aching cock in his other hand, pressing the crown into her soft, slippery folds. She was even wetter than before, her body primed for his.

He notched his cock at her entrance and paused, kissing her throat, her ear. "Are you ready for me, minx?"

Her hands had fluttered to his shoulders, and she was gripping him as if to forever keep him there. Her nails bit into his skin, his wild hellion marking him. And he bloody loved it.

"I've always been ready for you," she said.

There was something enormous in what she had said. Something that his mind couldn't readily compute. All the blood in his body had seemingly rushed to his cock, and he was poised at the gates of heaven itself, ready to conquer and claim. He would revisit those words later, try to make sense of them. For now, he was a man driven by desire.

He sought her mouth, feeding her the taste of herself on his tongue as he thrust forward. The tip of his cock was engulfed in wet heat as he breached her. She inhaled into his kiss, her body tensing.

"Relax," he murmured against her lips, using his forefinger to play with her bud once more.

He stroked lightly, and the stiffness leached from her body. He deepened the kiss and thrust forward again. She clenched on him, gripping him snugly, and it was all he could do not to rampage forward. But for her, he would be gentle. He wanted her to experience pleasure beyond what he had given her with his mouth.

Another thrust, then another, and he was seated fully and she was gloriously tight around him. His conscience tried to tell him how wrong this was. He had just taken Rhiannon's virginity. But all his primitive male brain could think was that she was his.

"How are you?" he asked, kissing the corner of her lips.

"Wonderful. Are we…finished?"

Her naïve curiosity tore a chuckle from him. "No, minx. We've only just begun."

"Oh good, because I was thinking that it would be lovely if you moved again as you did with your fingers and—"

He silenced her further chatter by kissing her again and gave her what she wanted, beginning a rhythm that was slow and steady, still giving her body time to adjust. His sweet minx, even trying to manage him in the bedroom. If he wasn't careful, she'd be leading him about by the ballocks in no time.

But he wouldn't think about that now.

Instead, he quieted his mind and turned all of his attention to the play of their bodies. Beneath him, her lush curves were smooth and supple. Her nipples teased his chest. His control unraveled. He surged into her faster, harder, his own release embarrassingly within reach. He hadn't come this quickly with a woman since…perhaps not ever.

But there was no help for it. Rhiannon was making breathy sounds that were carving away at his very soul, and the snug heat of her cunny was about to make him explode. She moved with him, meeting him thrust for thrust.

"Oh, that's good," she hummed. "So good. Yes. More of that."

He caught her bottom in both hands and shifted them, rising up so that he could penetrate her from a different direction, giving her what she wanted. He fucked her fast and hard, watching as her breasts bounced and her eyes closed, her sultry mouth open.

She was so bloody beautiful. A fucking goddess. He never wanted to stop. Never wanted this moment to be over. Her nails raked his shoulders and her cries lit up the night. He forgot to care about keeping her quiet. Forgot everything. His body was a machine, claiming, taking, giving.

Rhiannon came on him without warning, a sudden clamp of her sheath that made him lose all control. Aubrey's release roared through him, heat singeing up his spine as his ballocks drew tight. He withdrew from her too late, painting her pretty pink pussy with the last lashes of his seed.

CHAPTER 11

Rhiannon woke to the smell of breakfast.

Which was quite odd, considering that she was in her bedroom.

She blinked and yawned, stretching as she looked for the source of the decadent scents. Her stomach rumbled. There was nothing on her bedside table. And besides, who would have brought her breakfast this morning? She hadn't had a tray in her room since arriving, and—

"Good morning."

She emitted a high-pitched squeal at the masculine rumble and turned to find Aubrey moving toward her, bearing a large silver tray laden with an assortment of food. The source of the smell.

Her heart leapt, and her stomach rumbled in unison.

"Good morning," she returned, feeling suddenly shy as she sat up in bed, holding the bedclothes over her bare breasts.

He was the picture of a dashing rake this morning, an easy grin on his sensual lips, his hair a bit damp at the ends, as if he had recently bathed, his whiskers neatly trimmed.

"How are you?" he asked softly, bringing the tray to the table at her bed and placing it there.

How was she? What kind of a question was that? And how to answer?

"I am well," she managed, wondering how an experienced mistress would respond.

Likely, she wouldn't have squeaked like a mouse, she thought grimly.

"Good." He sat on the edge of the bed, studying her. "I thought you might like some breakfast."

The gesture was so unexpectedly sweet and considerate, she couldn't help but to smile. "That was kind, thank you."

His expression shifted, taking on a wariness that had been absent at first. "I'm not a kind man."

"Yes, you are."

He frowned. "No, I'm not. Nor am I a particularly good one." He turned to the tray, picking up a plate. "What would you prefer? I managed to obtain some freshly baked bread and jam, sausages, a rasher of bacon, raspberries, pineapple, and strawberries."

"You needn't feed me. I'm hardly an invalid."

"I am responsible for you now," he said to the tray.

The passionate lover from last night was gone, and in his place was a brooding stranger. After they had made love, he had tended to her, washing her and bringing her to climax yet again before he had slid into the bed with her. They had fallen into a blissful sleep. Rhiannon didn't like this abrupt shift. Not one whit.

"I'm responsible for myself," she countered. "And I'm fully capable of walking to the dining room for breakfast. I've managed to do so every day thus far without you spiriting a tray of food to me."

"Don't argue, minx. Eat." He presented her with a plate laden with food.

All things she liked, of course. And she was hungry. She could dislike the cool demeanor he was presenting her and still accept his offer of food, Rhiannon decided, taking the plate from him.

Their fingers brushed, and a frisson of awareness skipped up her elbow and landed low in her belly.

Those fingers of his had been all over her last night. Inside her. And his tongue.

Heat blossomed on her cheeks at the memory.

"Are you going to eat as well?" she asked, trying to shake her embarrassment by distracting herself.

"I already ate hours ago. It's nearly noon."

"Noon?"

The revelation surprised her. Rhiannon wasn't ordinarily a slugabed.

"The time of day when it is officially afternoon and no longer morning," he drawled. "Also known as midday."

The vexing man. She glanced back up at him, holding her plate with one hand and her blankets with the other. How did he expect her to eat whilst she was naked and he was presiding over her?

She pinned him with a glare. "I am more than aware of what the word noon means."

His lips twitched. "You seemed confused. I was merely attempting to aid you."

"Hmm," she said, deciding to settle the plate on the bed at her side.

The fork clattered and skittered to the sheets, but she retrieved it, determined to have her repast. Her body had certainly worked up an appetite the night before. She was also deliciously sore in places she hadn't previously known existed. And she soon had to make use of the water closet. But none of these were things she had any intention of telling the ridiculously gorgeous man sitting on her bed. She could hold her pee for an eternity if it meant avoiding the mortification of telling him she needed to relieve herself.

So instead, Rhiannon turned her attention to eating the small feast he had brought her. Despite his protestation otherwise, it had been both thoughtful and kind of him. She hoped he didn't regret what had happened between them, for she had every intention of it happening again.

A not-quite-comfortable silence fell between them as she began to eat. But a few bites and she grew weary of his quiet regard.

She glanced up at him, waving a hunk of fresh pineapple that she had skewered on the end of her fork. "Do you do this with all your mistresses? Bring them breakfast and then stare at them in thorny silence?"

"I wasn't aware that silence could be thorny. How delightfully descriptive you are."

She narrowed her eyes at him. "Well?"

"I don't have mistresses."

"Your *mistress*, then. When you had one, that is." Rhiannon popped the pineapple into her mouth.

It was juicy and delicious. But thinking about Richford's other lovers left a sour taste in her mouth all the same. Why had she asked? She swallowed hard, the pineapple going down her throat like a lump.

"I've never had a mistress," he said coolly.

She glanced back up at him, surprised. "But you're a wicked rake."

He gave her a small smile. "One who dislikes arrangements involving commitment of any sort."

Rhiannon had the distinct impression he was trying to build a separation between them. Or perhaps manage her expectations. Was he warning her away from him?

"Then I am your first mistress," she decided.

"You're *not* my mistress, minx."

"Of course I am. You agreed to an understanding last night."

"No, I agreed to relieve you of your virginity so that you wouldn't do something foolish and give yourself to some callous cad who wouldn't give a damn about your pleasure."

She stabbed another pineapple with the tines of her fork and wondered if she should point out that he was behaving like a callous cad at the moment, his offering of breakfast aside.

"Does that mean I am free to find another lover for this evening?" she asked instead.

"Don't even think about it, minx."

"Why not? If you don't want to bed me, then I'm sure I can find someone else who will." Grinning, she chewed her pineapple, quite pleased with herself.

"I'll beat any man here to within an inch of his life who dares to lay so much as a finger on you," he said conversationally.

But the underlying current of menace in his voice told her Aubrey was deadly serious. The frustrating man. He had been so attentive last night, so considerate. His intentional coldness was discomfiting. She was baiting him, it was true, for there was no other man she wanted. Not here at Wingfield Hall or anywhere else.

Only the beautiful emerald-eyed rake currently glaring at her from the edge of her bed.

"I should think that would be quite detrimental to your club's ability to attract new patrons," she pointed out, stabbing a sliced strawberry and bringing it to her lips.

His gaze slid to her mouth. "I could not care less about new patrons at the moment. I'm too busy trying to keep a headstrong hoyden from ruining herself."

She swallowed the sweet berry, then licked the juice from

her lower lip. "What if it isn't your job to keep her from doing so?"

He groaned. "Are you trying to kill me, woman? You are, aren't you?"

"I can assure you that I'm not in the least bit homicidal." She took up a raspberry next.

And that was when her grip on the bedclothes slipped, sending them pooling to her waist and revealing both breasts.

His expression changed, his eyes darkening with lust. "Bloody hell, Rhiannon."

Could it be that she was having an effect on the cool, calculated rake? Emboldened, she left the blankets where they were, the cool air of the room making her nipples go hard.

She placed the plump red raspberry in her mouth and chewed. "Mmm."

"Are you finished with breakfast?" he asked, his voice low and deep.

"Why?"

"Because I find I'm hungry for a second breakfast after all."

"Oh?"

He moved across the bed toward her. "You."

Well. It would seem he *could* be tempted.

Rhiannon bit back a smile. "I'm still a bit hungry."

"Then I'll feed you."

Heat unfurled deep within her. "How gentlemanly of you."

He pulled his lean form alongside her, bracing himself on one hand as he reached for a strawberry with the other. "Eat."

She intentionally nipped his fingers as she took the berry slice from him.

"You bit me."

She chewed, enjoying herself immensely. "Forgive me. I didn't mean to."

His eyes narrowed. "Hmm."

He picked up a hunk of pineapple next, and she licked his thumb.

"You would test the patience of a saint, madam."

She chewed the pineapple and swallowed. "Fortunately, you're not a saint. However, you did say that you didn't want to honor our understanding, so if I nipped you, I can't be blamed."

"I never said I didn't want to honor it. Those were your words, not mine. I said that I don't keep mistresses, and certainly not the innocent younger sister of my friend."

She held his gaze. "Not so innocent now."

"Better me than bloody Carnis," he growled.

The reminder of Reginald was most unwanted. At the moment, she would prefer that she was never leaving this idyll. That Aubrey would somehow fall hopelessly in love with her over the remaining days of the house party and ask her to marry him instead, preposterous as such a dream was.

"I thought you said I wasn't supposed to speak his name," she managed, all too aware that the bedclothes were still at her waist.

"You're not." He reached for a raspberry next, but this time, instead of bringing it to her lips, he placed it on her nipple. "Now hush, because I'm famished."

His head bent toward her breast, and he sucked the raspberry from the tip. She curled her toes beneath the coverlets as pleasure swept over her. A pulse beat to life between her thighs. Suddenly, neither her hunger nor her need for the water-closet mattered nearly as much as another urge.

He chewed the berry, giving her a sinner's grin. "Delicious. I think I'll have another."

Carefully, he placed another raspberry on her other

nipple before claiming that one as well, sucking and licking as he did so. She arched her back, reaching for him, thinking it a terrible shame he was fully clothed.

"I think you're going to have a difficult time managing the strawberries and pineapples," she said breathlessly.

"Nonsense. Watch." He placed a strawberry slice on the curve of her breast, then licked it off.

"Perhaps I was wrong," she admitted.

He settled a pineapple on her other breast and caught it in his teeth, chewing lustily. "Divine."

A hint of juice trickled down her bare skin, and he licked it up, then lingered, sucking and nipping. She gently pushed the plate to the side.

"Aubrey?"

He kissed the hollow between her breasts, then lower. "Yes?"

"I'm not hungry for breakfast any longer."

~

Aubrey was resigned to his fate.

If he hadn't already been going to perdition, that was most assuredly his inevitable destination now. But as Rhiannon so enthusiastically came beneath the play of his fingers and tongue, her thighs clamping on his head, he decided that eternal damnation was utterly worth it.

And he would defy both heaven and hell to be inside her again.

He gave her another slow, soothing lick as the last wave of her pinnacle ebbed. She tasted better than any ripe berry or hothouse fruit ever could. He couldn't get enough. He'd known, of course, that he should stay away. He had done what she asked him to. There was no need to continue debauching her.

But he couldn't resist. He had her for the next few days that remained in the house party. Why should he deny himself? Moreover, why should he deny her? Rhiannon was a naturally passionate woman. It was a sin for her to never taste true desire.

He kissed her clitoris and caressed her thighs as he lifted his head.

"Are you sore, love?"

Her creamy skin was flushed, her hair was a wild tangle over the pillow, and her eyes were a dark, sparkling blue he could easily forget himself in. Her nipples were sweet, erotic points beckoning him, the swells of her breasts equally inviting. More than a handful. Enough to overflow his palms. He wondered what they would look like coated in his spend. His cock, already rigid in his trousers, grew even harder at the thought.

"A bit," she said breathlessly, running her fingers through his hair in an adoring caress he couldn't help but to find erotic. "But not too sore for more sexual congress, if that's what you're asking."

He winced. "Do stop calling it that, if you please."

"What would you have me call it, then?" She ruffled his hair some more.

It was ridiculous, the way she liked playing with his hair, but he didn't complain. He rather liked the way it felt.

"Fucking," he told her and then licked his lips, savoring the taste of her.

She smiled down at him, brushing a lock of hair from his forehead now. He thought he might happily spend the rest of the house party right here, between her legs, with a glorious view of her pink, perfect pussy.

"I'm not too sore for more fucking," said the minx. "Unless you're too tired, that is…"

"Ha! I ought to spank your luscious derriere." He gently

bit her inner thigh. "I've never in my life been too tired to fuck."

Her expression grew serious, though her hand still sifted through his hair. "I suppose you've had very many lovers."

Damn. He dragged his whiskers along her sensitive skin. Poor choice of words. He didn't want his past lovers interfering in the present. Because he couldn't shake the feeling that of all the women he'd bedded and those he may one day seduce, none would compare to her. The acknowledgment settled deep into his marrow, unavoidable as the sun rising every morning. The way he felt for Rhiannon simply *was*.

"I suppose you've only had one," he said teasingly instead of answering.

Him. And dear God, how he wanted to be the only one. But she deserved so much better, and he was not a man who could offer himself to a woman in matrimony. He would never visit such misfortune upon her.

"For now." Her expression turned serious.

Almost sad.

He couldn't bear that. Nor could he bear thinking of any other man in her bed. Or, for that matter, any other woman in his. So Aubrey did what he did best, which was seducing. He brushed aside the breakfast plate, sending it and the remainder of fruit and meat to the floor, and then he rolled to his back, bringing Rhiannon with him so that she straddled him, naked.

Naked and so damned erotic.

"Enough of that for now," he said. "It's time for your lessons to continue."

She flattened her palms on his chest and leaned over him, her hair falling in riotous waves around her face and down over her breasts. "Another lesson? But you're fully clothed."

Disappointment laced her voice, and he might have laughed at his impatient minx if he weren't about to spend in his trousers like a green young man touching his first bare bubby.

"Your bawdy books were woefully lacking in creativity," he told her, reaching for the fall of his trousers and flicking open the first few buttons.

"Oh," she murmured as he reached inside the placket and withdrew his erect cock. "I'm beginning to think they were."

He stroked his length, swirling the moisture seeping from his tip over his crown. "Fortunately, I'm here to rectify that sad state of affairs."

"I can see that." Her eyes were on his cock, watching him run his hand from the base to the head. "May I touch you?"

If she touched him, there was every reason to fear he would come and ruin everything, but he wasn't about to deny either of them the pleasure of her hand on his prick.

"Always."

Hesitantly, she reached out, grasping him as if she feared he might break.

"Harder," he told her.

She increased the pressure incrementally.

"It's a cock, love, not Sèvres porcelain." He wrapped his hand around hers, showing her how much pressure to exert, guiding her hand up and down. "Just like that."

"Oh."

The wonder in her voice...*fuck*. She was the best and the worst thing to have ever happened to him. He wanted to keep her forever. But he couldn't do that to her. Instead, he'd have to settle for this little slice of heaven that could be his for now.

He released her hand, and she continued. "Like this?"

"Perfection," he bit out. "But if you don't put me inside you soon, I'll never last."

Her eyebrows rose. "Don't you need to be atop me? How can we..."

"The other part of your lesson." He guided her until she rose a bit on her knees, and then he helped her to run his cock through her wet folds. "Like this. And now..." He aided her in moving him into place. "You settle down on me."

"Oh my." She shifted forward, the kiss of her wet heat on his crown enough to steal his breath. "Oh, that feels quite lovely."

Better than lovely.

It was sweet torment.

He rolled his hips beneath her as she sank down on him, and he filled her with one thrust. He planted his hands on her waist, helping her to find her rhythm. She moved tentatively at first, and then with greater confidence as she discovered what pleased her most.

"There you are, love," he praised. "Ride me and come all over my cock."

She leaned forward, trying a new angle, her full breasts tantalizingly near to Aubrey's lips. He couldn't resist taking the tip of one in his mouth and sucking as she fucked him.

Like last night, he wasn't going to last long. He was already on the edge, and now that she was astride him, taking her pleasure, it would be impossible to hold on to his control. He sucked harder as she moaned, her cunny clamping deliciously on his cock.

He released her nipple and latched on to the other, sucking hungrily as she rode him faster, harder, taking him deep. She rocked on him, clutching his head to her breast, and then she suddenly clenched down on him as her release swept through her, nearly squeezing him from her body.

He held her to him, thrusting upward a few more times, savoring the slick glide, the incredible sensation of her wrapped around him, until he lifted her away and pulled his cock free. Gripping himself hard, Aubrey shot a stream of spend across her inner thigh. Rhiannon rolled to her back at his side, her breathing ragged, as exhausted as he was.

In the aftermath, he lay there, half panting, heart pounding, body boneless and sated. He had never come so hard fully clothed. Good God, what a depraved beast he was. Later, he would feel guilty for taking her yet again. For so thoroughly debauching her. For now, all he could feel was an eerie, imperative warmth that felt alarmingly like happiness.

CHAPTER 12

Rhiannon found Aubrey where he had told her he would await her that afternoon, beneath the shade of a towering old tree, a fair distance from the manor house and stables. He was handsome as ever in country tweed and a dashing hat, a bicycle on either side of him. Leaning against the tree trunk, he took an idle puff of a cheroot, unaware of her approach as he stared into the distance at the rolling park of Wingfield Hall.

As usual, he quite stole her breath. She took a moment to admire him whilst he was unaware, wondering what occupied his mind and secretly pleased that he had arranged this private time away from the house party for the two of them. She had no wish to participate in further games when she could spend time with him. He was like the sun, and she was a plant that needed to soak up his presence and warmth to thrive.

She didn't even want to contemplate what would happen in three days when she would have to return to London and their time together was naught more than a memory. Her heart went bleak and cold at the mere notion, so she shut it away, a worry for another day.

"Isn't it a bit early in the day for a cheroot?" she asked as she neared him, jolting him from his ruminations as he turned toward her.

"Have I taught you nothing, sweet naïf?" He laid a hand over his heart in dramatic fashion. "It's never too early for a vice."

She smiled, easily charmed. "I stand corrected."

His gaze swept over her. "Good God, are you wearing trousers, minx?"

Rhiannon glanced down at her daring costume, which she had commissioned without Mater's awareness, and at which her brother no doubt would have balked had he been aware of its existence.

It consisted of a jaunty purple coat worn atop a white blouse with a ribbon at the throat. Not so shocking from the waist up. But from the waist down, she wore loose Turkish trousers in a matching shade that ended at her knees, beneath which peeped embroidered stockings and her favorite pair of boots. A handsome straw hat with a purple satin ribbon completed her ensemble. The whole effect was remarkably freeing—and so much lighter than the cumbersome skirts and trains to which she was accustomed.

"It's called a bloomer suit," she informed him. "I have it on good authority that this costume shall be the latest craze for bicycle riding."

"It's criminal, is what it is." He tossed his cheroot to the ground and stomped it with the toe of his boot. "Christ, woman. Your calves in those boots."

"Do you like them?" She pointed her right toe, showing off the flower embroidery on the wholly impractical footwear.

The heels were too high and the leather was stiff and

unforgiving, but she would be pedaling, and she had wanted to look her best for this outing with Aubrey. If she had blisters on her heels later, it would be worth every second of agony just for the look on his face—unabashed admiration.

What a powerful feeling it was to have this man's attention.

At last.

She had only waited years. And now, finally, he was noticing her when it was almost too late. But she wouldn't spoil the moment by thinking of that just now.

"They don't look suited to bicycle riding," Aubrey said, his gaze still clinging to her limbs on bold display, "but they do look suited to making any man who glimpses you in them into a ravening beast."

"Hmm, then maybe I shall have to go back to the drawing room," she mused lightly, tapping her chin with a gloved finger. "I do believe they were about to unleash a new game of naughty charades."

"I think not. You're mine for the afternoon. I've already claimed you." He made an elaborate bow. "Madam, your fine steed awaits."

He gestured toward the bicycles.

"Are you certain no one will see me where we're riding?" she asked, thinking of the silk mask she had stuffed into her coat pocket on her approach.

Having the boundary removed was a relief and a worry in one. She had grown weary of wearing it whenever she left her chamber, but she also had no wish to be discovered. Particularly not when she had finally managed to gain what she wanted in sneaking into this house party in the first place.

"I'm as reasonably certain as I'm able to be," he reassured her. "We have the only two bicycles at the house party, and the path I've chosen isn't suited to horseback riding."

"Where did you manage to find these, and how did you come to have the only two?"

"They're Kingham's. Had them hidden away in the stables. He intended to employ some manner of experimentation with them. He's forever toying with things. I simply availed myself of them before he could begin tearing them apart."

She raised a brow. "Do you mean to say you've stolen them?"

"That's a harsh word. I'm borrowing them."

"Does Kingham know you're borrowing them?"

"He will when I tell him about it later," Aubrey informed her smoothly. "Now come, the skies are growing dreary again, and if we don't soon begin our ride, I'll be tempted to carry you back to your bedchamber and show you the effect that blasted bloomer suit of yours is having on me."

She grinned. "Now you tempt me. Would you truly be able to carry me the whole way, though? It's an awful long way, and I'm no waif."

"On the bicycle, minx," he said, holding it out for her. "I promised you an excursion, and I think you'll like it."

She mounted the bicycle, pleased at the ease of doing so in her new costume. "You see? It's ever so much better to ride when one's limbs are freed from the tyranny of skirts."

"I do believe I've demonstrated that I'm more than happy to keep you free from the tyranny of skirts," he quipped with a wicked grin.

A flush stole over her cheeks. Yes, he most certainly had. And she had fallen a little more in love with him, one kiss, touch, and forbidden pleasure at a time.

"You have indeed," she acknowledged. "I may require another demonstration this evening, however, just to refresh my memory."

He laughed as he swung a leg over his own bicycle, seating himself. "Saucy baggage. Follow me."

Like that, he was off, pedaling away from her. Rhiannon had ridden a bicycle before, but it had been quite a few months ago. She followed in his wake, a bit shaky at first before her confidence swiftly grew.

"Wait for me, you scoundrel," she called after him.

Her poor legs were no match for his much longer, stronger limbs. Fortunately, he slowed his pace and allowed her to catch up with him. They rode in a companionable silence, following the path into the wooded area on the edge of the park.

"Where are you taking me?" she asked at last, curious.

"You'll see. We have almost arrived." His voice was amused.

"Why do you not simply tell me now?"

"Because I want it to be a surprise, minx."

Something wet landed on her nose.

Rain, she realized, glancing up at the sky, which had darkened to a dull gray.

"The skies are opening up," she pointed out. "I do hope we shall arrive at our destination soon."

"Patience. We are nearly there."

The drops began coming down with greater insistence. Rhiannon bit her lip as rain spattered her cheeks but pedaled on without comment. Despite the uncooperative weather, she was ridiculously pleased to be with Aubrey. This excursion had been his idea as well, which delighted her even more. He was so often aloof and cool, detached beneath his rakish façade. But since this morning, a sea change had occurred.

One she wouldn't take for granted, lest it reverse its course.

Which it inevitably would. She knew him too well by now.

From the overgrowth of the forest, a building suddenly emerged amidst the foliage. Not a moment too soon, as the clouds truly began releasing their fury overhead.

"Here we are," he announced cheerfully, as if they weren't being pelted with cold, fat raindrops. "We'll leave the bicycles in the stables."

The meandering path had led them to a charming brick cottage with a small building alongside it. She followed him into the stables and allowed him to assist her off the bicycle.

"What is this place?" she asked as she watched him tuck their bicycles out of the weather.

"An old gamekeeper's cottage. It hasn't been in use for the last decade or so, but we recently refurbished it so that it can be used for house party guests who require additional privacy."

"A place for assignations, you mean."

He shrugged. "A place for whatever one wishes. Dinner, luncheon, perhaps an orgy."

Her eyes widened. "You didn't bring me here for an orgy, did you?"

Aubrey had informed her of the meaning of that word earlier, and it was quite unforgettable.

He extended his hand. "Come and see for yourself."

She placed her gloved palm in his. "But I'm not wearing my mask."

He closed his fingers around hers. "Do you trust me?"

"Yes." Her response was instant, without hesitation.

She trusted him with her body, with her secrets, with her heart.

"Good. Then come."

He tugged her back out into the rain, which was by now a full downpour. They rushed through the deluge and into the cottage, both of them soaked by the time they were inside, giggling like children. Aubrey pulled her into his arms and gave her a thorough kiss, the brims of their hats knocking together.

When it was over, she was breathless as she reached up to remove her wet millinery, glancing around the pleasant interior of the cottage. The entry hall was small but neat, the scent of fresh paint in the air. To her left, a staircase presumably led to bedchambers. To her right, a door was open to a small parlor where a fire crackled in the grate, accompanied by a settee and some chairs.

"It hardly looks like a den of vice," she observed.

"That is upstairs," he commented lightly, taking off his hat and hers and hanging them on a hook by the door.

"I also don't see an orgy."

"Is that disappointment I detect in your honeyed voice, minx?" he teased.

She couldn't stop her smile at his antics. This lightness was a new side of him, and she liked bantering with him far better than sparring with him.

"Of course not, rake," she countered as she tugged off her gloves. "I fear I am yet too much a novice for such depravity."

He shrugged out of his coat and hung it on a hook alongside their hats, then removed his gloves and took hers as well, laying both pairs neatly atop his coat. "What makes you think *I* am not too much of a novice for such depravity as well?"

"Your reputation." Rumors about him were plentiful. She'd heard many.

"Exaggerated, I'm sure. Let me help you with your coat." He stopped before her and began undoing the buttons of her coat. "You'll catch an ague if you stay in this sodden fabric."

She held still for his ministrations, feeling odd to be tended by him so intimately and yet enjoying it all the same. "I am fully capable of undoing buttons myself, you know."

"Yes, but judging from the state of your bedchamber, if I allow you to do so, you'll simply toss it onto the floor." His gaze flicked to hers as he continued his task. "Besides, I like tending to you. You're like a little lost lamb who needs to find her way."

She pursed her lips. "I don't think I prefer to be likened to a lamb."

"You're *my* lamb." He finished and drew the sleeves down her arms, which wasn't the simplest of tasks given their fitted and wet state. "At least until the house party's end."

She didn't want to think about the house party's end.

Didn't want it to end at all.

But she rather did like being his.

At last, he had the coat removed and moved to hang it on the last empty hook. She admired his fine form as he did so, noting the way his tweed trousers lovingly silhouetted his firm derriere. There was something about the moment that felt so wonderfully domestic, as if they were husband and wife taking care of each other. But that was not to be.

Before long, she would be another man's wife.

Aubrey turned back to her, his gaze searching. "Why so Friday-faced suddenly?"

She didn't want to confide her foolish yearnings to him, so she shook her head. "I was only wondering why you have brought me here, aside from sheltering from the rain."

"Come with me, and I'll show you." He offered her his arm.

She accepted it, and he led her down the hall.

HE WAS A BLOODY IDIOT, but Aubrey couldn't recall when he had last been so eager as he led Rhiannon down the hall to the kitchen of the cottage. He had spent the afternoon arranging a surprise for her, telling himself that he was doing so only to bed her again, this time somewhere that he wouldn't need to fret over how loud she was when she came. That he was a heartless, despicable cad who was intent upon ravishing his good chum's sister and he would go to any lengths to get what he wanted—namely her, beneath or atop him.

But in truth, spoiling her pleased him. She had been like a girl with her excitement over his proposed bicycle ride. He could lie to himself no longer, however, as they crossed the threshold of the kitchen to where a sumptuous picnic had been laid out for their delectation. He had plotted this jaunt with her not to seduce, but to win her smile.

She had him wrapped around her damned pinkie finger.

"A picnic dinner for the two of us," he said, leading her to the table.

"You did this?" she asked, taking in the room with an astonished look on her lovely face.

"With the help of some servants," he admitted. "I thought it would be nice to enjoy a meal together, and since we cannot do so in the dining room, I reckoned this cottage would suit the purpose well enough."

"Oh, Aubrey." She turned to him, looking at him as if he were a knight errant who had just returned from grand exploits in her name. "This was so thoughtful of you."

Chrissakes, there she went with prattle about him being thoughtful again. He truly had to disabuse her of the notion that he was anything other than a dark-hearted villain who was bedding her for purely selfish reasons.

"We've been through this, have we not, my dear?" he

reminded her. "There isn't a modicum of thoughtfulness in me."

She arched a golden brow, still looking at him as if he were noble. "I think that is what you would like for me to believe, but this is the second time you are feeding me a meal today alone."

Damn it, perhaps arranging this idyll for them had been a mistake. Except, being alone with her didn't feel like a mistake. It felt like a bloody relief. It was refreshing to have her where he wanted her without having to hide behind masks or steal into her bedroom. He wanted to enjoy her thoroughly before he had to leave Wingfield Hall and pretend as if none of this had ever happened.

Still, she needed to understand who and what he was. He wasn't thoughtful or considerate or caring. He was the son of a madman. He was a selfish sybarite. A dishonorable scoundrel who had betrayed Whitby—his own friend—and had taken his sister's virginity. Not just that, but he intended to bed her as many times as he possibly could to get her out of his system until they parted ways.

"I like to eat. I like to fuck." He waved a hand toward the picnic dinner. "Here we are."

"Why do you do that?" she asked, studying him with her vibrant blue gaze in a way that made him feel as if she saw him.

Saw him far too well.

"Do what, minx?"

"Try so very hard to persuade me that you are irredeemable when we both know the opposite is true?"

"Ah, but I *am* irredeemable." He started moving them toward the table in an attempt to distract her. "If I weren't, what would I be doing here with you?"

"Just because I am Whitby's sister doesn't mean that you cannot desire me," she pointed out.

"It means that I shouldn't. You're my friend's sister. A lady and an innocent. Yet I've treated you like a seasoned mistress, all to slake my own lust. That ought to convince you, if nothing else."

He stopped before her chair, pulling it out for her. She seated herself, and the tempting scents of jasmine and bergamot mingled with rainwater and fresh air reached him.

"Has it never occurred to you that I have lust also?" she asked sharply. "That perhaps I have a mind of my own and that I am not so much an innocent lamb as a lioness who has decided to seize what she wanted?"

He stared at her, awed by her boldness. One part menace, one part goddess, she was intoxicating.

"I can honestly say that no, it has not." He inclined his head. "Perhaps I stand corrected in that regard."

"As every lady at this house party confirms, women can experience lust every bit as strongly as our masculine counterparts," she continued. "Being a lady doesn't make one incapable of feeling desire, and neither does being a virgin. You may feel guilty all you like about what has happened between us, but don't think for a moment that you somehow seduced me into bending to your sinful whims."

Wryly, Aubrey seated himself at the opposite end of the small table. "Believe me, my dear, I am more than aware who seduced whom when it comes to the two of us."

It had been her, of course. He had been no match for a determined Lady Rhiannon Northwick. He hadn't the willpower to deny her. Even today when she had approached for their ride together, she had all but brought him to his knees. Sweet Christ, that bloody bloomer suit of hers had nearly proven his undoing. He'd had half a mind to take her then and there against a tree. Call them whatever she liked, but Rhiannon in trousers was a bloody revelation.

"There. Now, if you would please cease all attempts to

persuade me that you're Beelzebub so that I may enjoy dinner, I would greatly appreciate it," she said.

But he wasn't finished warning her yet. "I'm not a good man, and the sooner you accept it, the better off you shall be. I'm not kind, and I don't do anything if it doesn't benefit me."

She smiled. "If you say so."

"I do, and had you any idea how depraved I truly am, you wouldn't be sitting here at this table with me," he continued sternly. "You'd be on your bicycle pedaling as fast as those delicious legs of yours could possibly manage."

"You think my legs are delicious?"

This bloody hoyden. What was he to do with her? He knew what he *wanted* to do with her—keep her here in this cottage and shag her like mad for the next few weeks at least. Long enough to ease the poison of lust from his veins. But that was impossible.

"Quite," he bit out. "But you are missing the point entirely."

"Which is?"

"That I'm a very bad man, the sort you ought not to know, and absolutely the kind you shouldn't welcome into your bed."

She arched a brow. "I fear you are a bit tardy with that particular warning. Moreover, I hardly think that you are as depraved as you suggest. Why, you've scarcely shown me anything thus far that I haven't already come upon in the bawdy books I have managed to read."

"Your mother and your brother haven't an inkling what you do with your days, do they?" Good God, if Whit knew what Rhiannon had been reading and—worse—doing, he would be bloody apoplectic.

"I should think not, and I prefer it that way."

"But as for depraved, my dear, we have barely scratched the surface."

She held his gaze, challenge sparkling in her eyes. "Show me, then. You are conducting lessons for my edification, are you not?"

The minx. She had trapped him neatly.

"Yes, but there are limits—"

"Nonsense," she interrupted archly. "You are a very bad man. You've just told me so yourself. There should be no limits where you are concerned. You promised to educate me. I demand that you do so."

His cock went positively rigid. "You demand, do you?"

"Yes," she returned, defiant and bloody gorgeous. "But first, let's have dinner. I find that I'm famished."

The death of him, that's what she was.

He was certain of it.

Aubrey reached for the lemonade he'd had the cook bottle for them, opening it to pour Rhiannon a glass. "Then let us begin."

CHAPTER 13

*D*inner was complete. Rain was still lashing the windowpanes in a rhythmic tinkle, and the occasional rumble of thunder split through the skies. It shocked him how comfortable he felt sharing an informal meal with Rhiannon. They had much to converse about, discussing everything from books to art to poetry and wine. He was more content than he had been in as long as he could recall.

Aubrey hadn't anticipated the possibility of a storm trapping Rhiannon and him at the gamekeeper's cottage when he had first settled upon this plan. But now that it appeared to be the inevitable outcome for the evening, he hardly minded.

Having her to himself all night long would be anything but a hardship. He had precious little interest in the naughty games or the players at the manor house. And he didn't lie to himself about the reason for that—she was staring at him from the other end of the table.

She was all he had seen, all he had been able to think about, from the moment he had first spied her at Wingfield Hall.

"Will you now show me the den of depravity upstairs?" Rhiannon asked him.

He nearly spat the mouthful of lemonade he had just taken all over the food they hadn't managed to eat.

Aubrey swallowed hastily. "Yes, but only if you walk up the stairs before me."

She narrowed her eyes at him. "Why?"

"So that I can watch your arse swaying in those trousers of yours."

Her cheeks pinkened. "They're not trousers. They're bloomers."

She was so damned lovely, and despite her bravado, she still was very much an innocent. He was enjoying every second of thoroughly debauching her, however.

"They look like trousers to me," he argued mildly, enjoying himself.

She glared. "They look nothing at all like a gentleman's trousers. Which is precisely why they are called bloomers."

He grinned. "Whatever you wish to call them, they look positively sinful on you. A man cannot help but to think about peeling you out of them when he looks at you."

But then, he also had that same feeling when he looked at Rhiannon, regardless of what she was wearing. So perhaps it wasn't the bloomers after all, but him. He was naught but a randy beast in her presence.

She rose from the table, wincing. "Perhaps you might peel me out of my boots first. My poor feet ache."

He didn't doubt it, though he certainly had been guilty of admiring her in them. The heels were high, the flowery embroidery as flamboyant as her personality, the ankles impossibly narrow.

Aubrey stood as well. "I'll just gather the rest of our meal for the larder before we go."

"You mean you won't leave it for the servants to clean up?" she asked, sounding surprised.

There she went again, looking at him as if he were her knight errant.

"Not because I am noble and considerate, however," he corrected at once. "I am merely selfish. I want you all to myself, without interruptions. I instructed the servants not to come until I request them."

That much was also true.

"Of course," she agreed easily.

Too easily.

But he didn't bother arguing, because he knew what would happen when that obstinate expression appeared on her lovely face. She would continue to fight him. He would simply have to prove it to her another way.

Together, they emptied the remaining food into the larder. He couldn't keep his eyes off the sway of her hips as she made her short trips from the kitchen to the small alcove. Her curves were on full display in her bloomers and shirt-sleeves.

Thunder cracked loudly overhead as they completed their task.

"I do believe we may be stranded here for the night," he told her. "There is no sense trying to ride back to the manor house in the dark and the rain, particularly with it being so wet from the storm."

Rhiannon gave him a searching look. "Is there anyone who will take note of your absence at the main house? It wouldn't do for someone to come looking for the both of us and find us here together."

"Perhaps King, Riverdale, or Whit, but I doubt very much that any of them would search for long. They would assume I'm with a woman and leave it at that."

"Ah, of course," she said lightly. "Silly me. This is hardly your first assignation, is it?"

Aubrey almost told her that this was far more to him than any assignation had ever been. But he stopped himself. He was trying to convince her that he was no bloody good for her, damn it. When they inevitably parted at the house party's end, he had no wish for her to have developed tender feelings for him. Already, he feared they were treading a dangerous path. He had meant every word of warning he had issued to her earlier. She deserved far better than he could ever give her.

He held her gaze now, unflinching. "It is not my first, nor will it be my last."

She nodded, her lips tightening as if she forced a smile. "I am already aware of who and what you are. You needn't fear I shall forget."

Good. That was what he wanted, wasn't it?

Of course it was.

"Then shall we adjourn upstairs?" he asked, offering her his arm.

Her gaze never faltered as she settled her hand in the crook of his elbow. "Of course. I have been promised an orgy, and I am determined to see it."

"I am afraid you may be doomed to disappointment on that count, minx. I have no intention of sharing you this evening."

He guided her back down the hall to the staircase at the front of the cottage. With the darkness of the skies and the shade of the tree foliage, the steps were shadowy and mysterious. He fetched a small, handled oil lamp, lighting it to illuminate the way.

Aubrey gestured for Rhiannon to precede him. "You first, and I'll light our path from behind."

She made her way up the stairs with hesitant care. They were steep and fashioned of worn, slippery old wood, which didn't suit her fashionable heeled boots. He didn't want her falling and injuring herself, and this way, he could be sure to catch her if needed whilst also ogling her bottom.

And what a fine bottom it was, particularly when lovingly outlined by her bloomers.

"I think I'm going to have to burn these bloody things before the house party is at an end," he grumbled, hating the thought of anyone else admiring her in them.

Especially that boring bastard, Carnis. The earl wasn't worthy of Rhiannon's passionate fire. But then, neither was Aubrey.

"Burn what things?" she asked, sounding indignant. "Not my boots. They're my favorite pair."

"Your trousers," he growled.

They made it to the second floor, and she whirled about to face him as he reached the top of the stairs, her countenance adorably indignant. "They're not trousers, you vexing man. They're—"

He slanted his mouth over hers, stealing a kiss because he couldn't possibly exist for another second on this bloody earth without having her lips beneath his. Her arms went around him, and she kissed him back immediately with a hunger that rivaled his own.

"Bloomers," he supplied as he reluctantly tore his lips from hers before he did something idiotic like drop the lamp and set the cottage ablaze.

"You know quite well what they're called. I think you enjoy nettling me."

He enjoyed everything about her.

But he couldn't say that, so he grinned instead. "I do admit to a partiality for when your eyes flash with irritation at me. They turn the color blue the sky gets just after a summer rainstorm has passed."

She would never know how many times he had been tempted to kiss her senseless through their various clashes here at Wingfield Hall. It seemed an impossible dream that he could have her soft, lush mouth beneath his now whenever he wished.

Temporarily, he reminded himself harshly. *You have but a few days to get her out of your blood, and then your time with her must be at an end. Three more, to be precise.*

How the hell would that ever be enough?

Her face softened and she smiled at him, and he tried very hard to believe that it would be possible to grow tired of this sweet, seductive hellion.

"Where is the bedroom?" she asked softly.

His cock, already hardening, went rigid as a fire poker. "Come with me."

～

RHIANNON WOKE in the middle of the night to the music of rain on the cottage roof and Aubrey's ragged sleep breathing.

"No," he groaned. "Please, no."

A possessive arm was wrapped around her waist, and their bodies were nestled together, her back to his chest. His hold on her tightened, his breaths growing more erratic as he made a choked sound.

Something was disturbing him. A nightmare, perhaps?

"Don't go," he muttered.

She rubbed his arm soothingly. "I'm not going anywhere, my love."

He burrowed his face into her throat. "Blood. Oh God. So much blood."

And then he made an odd sound, almost as if he were

weeping. Which was truly unusual, for he was always so self-possessed, so cold and calculated. The Duke of Richford, sobbing in his sleep?

"Aubrey," she murmured in a hushed tone. "You're having a bad dream."

To her relief, her words seemed to pacify him. His breathing gradually settled down and his grip on her eased, the sobbing sounds slowly stopping. For an indeterminate span of time, she lay there, listening to him sleep, stroking his arm, wondering what manner of nightmare had been haunting his slumber.

Her own sleep remained elusive, her mind flitting with far too many thoughts. In the hush of the night, she simply lay there, savoring his proximity. When he slept, all the protective walls he kept around himself were lowered. This, she thought, was the true Aubrey. The lover who tended to her pleasure and her every need with unhesitating care. The man who wrapped her in his arms and held her close.

These were the moments when she allowed herself to hope that perhaps one day, if she worked diligently enough to chip away at the ice he kept around his heart, he might love her as she loved him. That mayhap one day, he would see how perfectly they were matched. Even if she knew those hopes were foolish.

She huffed out a small sigh, staring into the shadows, admiring the way the moonlight dappled his forearm where it rested over her above the bedclothes. They had adjourned to the largest of several bedrooms upstairs, and they had made love until well after midnight, until they had both been sated and exhausted in the very best way.

How she wished that tomorrow would not come, bringing her one day closer to the end of the house party, when they would inevitably part. What would she do when she saw him again in London? Would they meet as strangers,

Aubrey pretending as if they had never been lovers? Would he have his newest conquest on his arm?

Rhiannon shuddered as heavy dread curdled her stomach. She didn't want to think about Aubrey carrying on with his life any more than she wanted to think about returning to hers. Carnis was awaiting her acceptance of his proposal. Like morning, her return to her ordinary life was inevitable.

Aubrey shifted, and she felt the press of a warm mouth to her bare shoulder. "Are you cold, love?"

She had been too caught up in her ruminations to realize he had awakened. "No."

She wondered if she ought to ask him about his nightmare but decided against it. Whatever had brought it upon him, the dream was over.

He dotted another kiss on her shoulder. "Then why did you shiver just now?"

Because I was thinking of my future without you in it, she almost confessed.

But she couldn't. Her pride wouldn't allow it. Aubrey had been painfully honest with her, ad nauseum, even as she already was more than aware of his reputation. He was a rake. This was nothing more than a temporary arrangement between them. It didn't matter how much her heart recklessly yearned for it to blossom into something more.

"Perhaps I *am* cold," she lied, not wanting to broach the subject of what was bothering her. "Do you think you might warm me?"

"Of course." He tightened his arm on her waist, pulling her more snugly against him. "But I can also start a fire in the hearth for you."

"I don't want a fire in the hearth. I just want you."

He gently nipped the skin of her upper arm. "You have me."

But for how long? Each second that passed was one less

that she would have with him. She missed him already, and he was still here, holding her in his arms. Tears pricked her eyes, and she fluttered her lashes frantically, willing them to disperse before they slid down her cheeks. Thank heavens for the darkness surrounding them. He couldn't see her ignominy.

She snuggled her bottom against him and felt the distinctive ridge of him prodding her backside. "It would seem I certainly do have you."

If only desire were sufficient to hold him to her.

She knew now the power she held in that regard. He wanted her every bit as much as she wanted him. Not even his sense of loyalty to her brother had stopped him.

He nuzzled her throat. "Minx. Hold still. I can't make love to you again. Your poor body needs a respite."

The ache deep within her suggested otherwise.

Rhiannon wiggled her rump again. "Are you certain it does?"

He made a low, growling sound, his cock gliding between the cleft of her bottom. "I'm trying to be a gentleman."

"And yet you keep telling me that you aren't one," she pointed out, undulating her hips just a bit so that he settled at her entrance from behind. "You're a bad, conscienceless rake. You're not caring. You're not kind. You're not even honorable."

"That's right," he murmured into her ear. "And don't forget it. Would an honorable man do this?"

He slid his arm under the bedclothes and guided her left leg over his, angling her so that she could feel the full press of his cock against her entrance. Oh, that was nice. Better than nice, but not quite good enough. It didn't matter that they had made love earlier. She already wanted him again.

The more she had of him, the more she needed, or so it seemed. Her appetite where he was concerned was voracious. He dipped his hand between her legs, his fingers parting her folds to find the tender bud that longed for his touch most.

"I don't think an honorable man would," she managed breathlessly. "But fortunately for you, I don't think I like honorable men very much."

He kissed her ear. "Fortune's fickle wheel has finally served me a good turn. Pity it cannot last. But I fully intend to avail myself of it whilst I can."

Aubrey nibbled at her earlobe as his fingers moved with greater purpose, teasing her pearl. She closed her eyes and surrendered to the pleasure he bestowed upon her, banishing all thoughts of their time coming to an end. For these few, stolen hours, it was as if they were the only souls in the world. She could love him with her whole heart. She no longer had to admire him from afar. He was here, in her bed, holding her in his arms. And she was surrounded by his strength and warmth.

What a miraculous gift these days were, theirs alone.

"You're soaked," he said in her ear, his voice laden with frank sensual appreciation. "So wet for me. Your body was made for mine."

"Yes," she whispered, turning her head, her lips seeking his.

They found each other through the darkness, meeting in an open-mouthed kiss that swiftly deepened. And for a few moments, they stayed that way, kissing each other with all the pent-up mutual passion they possessed. The rain overhead sped up, and she swore it was in time to her frantic heart's rhythmic beats.

The world fell away. It was just the two of them in the charmed little gamekeeper's cottage, making love in the night. There was no one to keep them apart. She sucked on his tongue and reached back, threading her hand in his thick golden hair, her fingers tightening on the soft strands as he plundered her mouth.

They had no need for words. All they required was each other, and that was what they had. He fed her slow and steady kisses, thrusting against her without penetrating, each slick glide of his length through her folds making her increasingly breathless. His fingers flew over her with greater speed, finding the spot that was so deliciously sensitive that she couldn't keep herself from...

Oh, dear sweet God, it was there.

Right there.

So close, so close, so close.

She held her breath and gave him her tongue, and he moved against her, prolonging the moment until she was delirious with pleasure. Her release hit her fast and hard. She cried out into his kiss, her body trembling beneath the force as ripple after ripple of bliss tore through her.

He withdrew his touch and gripped himself, shoving his cock inside her with one thrust. His low, satisfied groan when he was seated to the hilt reverberated in the pulses she felt in her clitoris. Her body was so uniquely attuned to his. She could spend from nothing more than thinking about what they had done together as her own fingers moved over her intimate flesh.

Aubrey began making love to her slowly, passionately, exquisitely, as if they forever instead of just one stolen night in an abandoned cottage. He kissed her all the while, his free hand drifting to cup her breast as he moved in and out of her. The unique angle was glorious. He held her hips and buried himself in her again and again until she was climaxing once more, moaning helplessly into his lips.

He was not far behind her, the frenzied bursts of his movement telling her that he was ready as well. She sucked on his tongue, moaning. He withdrew from her body with a helpless groan, and she felt the hot spurt of his seed on her lower back. Their lips moved as one, still seeking, kissing, until they finally slowed, breathless and sated.

Rhiannon had never loved him more.

Nor could she recall a time in her life when she had ever been happier.

CHAPTER 14

Aubrey woke to late-morning sun spilling golden rays into the window, Rhiannon's burnished tresses trailing across his bare chest, and the most acute sense of contentedness he'd ever known. She was slumbering serenely, her head on his chest above his heart, and somehow she had come to be lying on his right arm, which was presently numb.

He didn't give a damn, and neither was he possessed of even the slightest inclination to move it.

Hell, he thought he might saw it off just to give her a softer place to sleep.

It was almost impossible to believe the effect she had on him. He didn't care about anyone or anything else. Not the house party, not the erotic distractions he'd been hoping to find at Wingfield Hall prior to his arrival. Not his friendship with Whit or the Wicked Dukes Society itself. She was all that mattered to him, this wild, wonderful, forbidden hellion who was stubborn and bold and wicked.

Who was everything that called to him in a way no woman before her had.

She shifted against him, emitting a soft, breathy sound that told him she was still soundly asleep. He had a bit more time, then, to admire her uninterrupted, and he was going to take it. After today, the house party would all too soon come to an end, which meant he needed to seize every second he could. This paradise of theirs would soon be empty, the bed linens stripped and replaced by capable servants, the cottage closed up until a future house party and its guests made use of it.

A house party at which she would not be a guest. Because by then, she could well be a married woman. And even if she were a married woman who sought to join the club as a member, she was Whit's sister. They would be forced to deny her.

No, this was his one chance. *Their* one chance.

With his free hand—the one that hadn't been rendered numb beneath her—he gently stroked his fingers over her unbound hair. The attraction they shared was damned rare. They connected, as if they were two halves of the same coin. Some part of him had always suspected that would be the way of it between them.

When she had made her debut in polite society, she had been just eighteen; he had scarcely taken note. Girls had never interested him, even when he'd been a lad of eighteen himself. But in the intervening years, she had become a woman. He had first noticed her about a year ago at a ball Whit had held in her honor.

She had been wearing her favorite color—pink, of course. He had seen her from behind and had begun plotting ways he could seduce her. And then she had turned, and he had seen her face, and to his utter shock, he had realized that Whit's younger sister was two-and-twenty and she was no longer a girl but a woman.

He hadn't spent the last year largely avoiding her for any

other reason, save that magnetic pull he felt for her and the fact that she was Whit's beloved, innocent sister. Instead, he had watched her from afar, admiring her stubborn determination, her easy wit, her graceful beauty, her boldness.

Yes, he had known he wouldn't be able to resist her.

But he had failed to realize just how far his obsession with her would go. He hadn't been exaggerating when he had warned Rhiannon against him. And yet, he still wouldn't have believed himself capable of such disloyalty, ruining his friend's sister.

And for what reason?

Oh, he had told himself his cause was noble. But in truth, he had wanted her for himself from the second he had spied her in the drawing room wearing that pink silk mask, and despite telling himself that he would send her safely home, he had selfishly wanted her to stay. And stay she had, thank God. Because now he had her. She was his.

Whilst he could have her.

"Mmm," she hummed, stretching and beginning to come awake.

Disappointment sliced through him. She would soon move. He would have to leave this bed. And her. He didn't want to go back to the main house, by God. He wanted to stay here with her. Forever.

But that last thought was maudlin and foolish.

Impossible, too.

"Good morning," he told her softly, brushing the hair from her face.

Rhiannon blinked her eyes open, regarding him in silence for a moment, their gazes locked.

"Good morning." She stirred, taking in her surroundings. "Heavens, why did you not wake me? I'm lying on your poor arm."

He retrieved his right limb at last, flexing his fingers with a wince as invisible pins and needles poked unmercifully at his skin from within and the feeling slowly returned. "I didn't mind. You were sleeping soundly, and I hated to disturb you."

Rhiannon gave him a small smile, looking suddenly shy. "I was having a wonderful dream."

He wanted to kiss her. To roll her onto her back and make love to her again, and again, and again until neither of them could move. But he wasn't a complete beast when it came to her, so he tamped down those unworthy yearnings.

"What were you dreaming?" he asked, curious.

Her pink lips parted as if she were about to answer, but then she rolled the bottom lip inward, catching it in her teeth. "I don't remember."

He chuckled. She was bloody adorable.

"Then how did you know it was wonderful, minx?"

"It was a feeling I had." She was at his side now, the bedclothes pulled nearly to her chin.

He tugged at the counterpane lightly. "Nonsense. It had to have been more than a mere feeling."

"Why should you call a feeling *mere*, with the implication being that it is insufficient and ought not to be taken seriously?"

Poor lamb. What must it be like to be so utterly unspoiled by life and all its ugliness? He'd been little more than a child when he had first realized the damage and destruction wreaked by feelings. From then until the bitter end of his parents' miserable union, he had vowed to never allow himself to fall prey to such weaknesses.

"Because a feeling is an illusion," he told her. "Just as emotions are lies we tell ourselves so that we can attribute meaning to our paltry lives."

She cocked her head at him, frowning. "That is a rather cynical view of the world."

He had good reason for it, but he didn't want to discuss the hideous past. Doing so wouldn't change the outcome. In the aftermath of that wretched day, he had learned to live with what was. Death had a finality that superseded all else. He would not repeat the sins of his father.

Unbidden, an image of his hands, red with blood, rose in his mind before he ruthlessly banished it. The blood had been everywhere that day, the metallic scent of it filling his nose, the slipperiness of it on his hands, the red seeping into clothing and carpets. There was a good reason he had ordered the room where it happened dismantled and resurrected as something new.

It was the same reason he avoided supposed love.

He shook himself from his thoughts.

"I am older than you are," he pointed out to Rhiannon. "I've experienced a great deal more of life's inevitable disappointments. That does tend to make one jaded."

Her brow furrowed. "Did someone break your heart?"

"Sweet girl, I'd have to own a heart in order for anyone to break it." He winked at her, trying to lighten the moment, because if there was anything he didn't wish to discuss when he was naked and in bed with a woman, for Chrissakes, it was tender emotions and the bitter horrors of murder and death. "I can assure you that there is nothing more than a desiccated husk where that organ ought to live."

Rhiannon gave him a searching look. "I don't think you are as unfeeling as you would have me believe."

Not with the knight errant nonsense again. What did he have to do to disabuse her of the notion that he was redeemable?

"And I can assure you that I am. Heed my warnings if you know what is best for you."

Her stubborn chin went up. "No. I don't think that I shall."

He wanted to kiss her, to fuck her, to wallow in her innocence and remember what it was like to believe in the goodness of others. Damn her for being so bloody wonderful. It struck him with sudden, awful clarity that if he had been the kind of man who believed in marriage and love and such maudlin twaddle, he would have asked Rhiannon to marry him in a heartbeat.

How horrifying. He banished all such ridiculous thoughts at once.

"Then you'll only have yourself to blame," he warned her.

"You *do* have a heart," the obstinate woman insisted.

There was only one way to make her see reason.

"If I had a heart, I would surely feel guilty for doing this."

To prove his point, he tugged at the bedclothes she was presently using as a shield. They fell away with ease, revealing her gorgeous breasts. He lowered his head and sucked one hard, pink nipple into his mouth.

She made a soft sound of desire, arching her back, her fingers running through his hair, so he sucked harder. "Oh. *My.* That is…" He used his teeth, gently nipping at her. "You are trying to distract me, you wicked man."

He moved to her other breast, running his tongue around the stiff, pouty peak. "Is it working?"

"Perhaps."

"Then I shall have to be more diligent." He whipped the bedclothes away and kissed down her body until he reached the prize he sought.

Gently guiding her legs apart, he parted her folds with his thumbs, revealing the swollen bud at the top of her slit. He sucked her clitoris with lusty appreciation. She tasted so good, her hips undulating beneath him as she surrendered to the pleasure he could give her. She was already deliciously wet and ready. With scarcely any coaxing, he had her legs over his shoulders and her bottom in his hands as he pulled her cunny to his face.

He feasted on her, licking and sucking, fucking her with his tongue, nibbling at her pearl. He lost himself to the velvet heat of her, to the breathy sounds she emitted somewhere above him, to the rolling of her hips as she urged him on. This was what he could give her, lessons in pleasure and naught else. He traded in desire alone, for he had seen firsthand the pain and destruction that love caused.

He had vowed he would never visit that upon another.

When he had Rhiannon at the edge, he stopped, lifting his head. He kissed her inner thigh, mesmerized by how beautiful she was, her hair tangled around her head, creamy skin flushed.

"Why did you stop?" she asked, her breaths ragged, eyes glazed.

"Because I haven't a modicum of compunction, and I want to be inside you when you come." He shifted her and then rolled her to her stomach. "Get on your knees for me, sweet."

"Is this another lesson?" The saucy minx wanted to know.

He bit one soft, fleshy cheek lightly. "Do as I ask."

She turned her head on the pillow, a tendril of golden hair on her cheek. "Or?"

Aubrey traced a lone finger lightly down her slick seam from behind. "Or I won't let you come."

She pouted. "That isn't fair."

He teased her entrance with a light graze, making her writhe. "You see? I'm not a good man. I want you to beg me."

"Aubrey."

"On your knees."

She rose onto her knees, her gorgeous arse in the air, her cunny on full display. He kissed her there, running his tongue through her folds until she was quivering beneath him. And then he stopped again.

"Tell me what you want."

"I want you to admit that you have a heart," she protested, tenacious to the last, even as her body was all but weeping to be claimed.

He licked into her. "Never."

She made a frustrated sound.

"There is only one thing I can give you, minx. I can give it to you so well." He dragged his mouth higher, wanting to shock her, needing to claim every part of her with a ferocity that would frighten him if he took the time to study it. He licked from her entrance then higher, toying with the rosebud of her back entrance, using his tongue on her until she gasped.

"What are you… That is…"

"Wicked." God, the things he could teach her. Show to her. Do to her. If only he had the time. But he was also painfully aware she was still a neophyte and they had a fleeting number of days left. "I'm a very bad man. I did try to warn you. You should have stayed away."

To emphasize his point, he slid his hand under her, his finger unerringly finding her clitoris. She bucked beneath him, closer than ever to coming. He worked her for a few moments before retreating.

"But you didn't listen, did you? I told you that you didn't belong here, and now look at what you've done."

"Please," she said, her voice throaty, steeped in need. "Take me."

He gripped his cock and ran himself through her folds. "I want to hear filthy words from that pretty mouth."

He added just enough pressure to tantalize them both, his cockhead kissed by her silken heat, but he didn't penetrate her. Not yet. Damn. He was so randy that he was about to spend, and he hadn't even been inside her yet.

"Fuck me, Aubrey," she begged, arching into his touch. "I need you."

The words were like a bolt of lightning straight through him. He sank inside her with one hasty thrust. She came almost instantly, her cunny squeezing him so tightly he had to clench his jaw to keep from losing control.

Gripping her hips, he pushed into her again and again, as the liquid heat of her spend rushed down his cock and she surrendered to him completely. He fucked her harder, faster, watching his cock slide in and out of her pretty pink pussy, looking at how well she took him, as if her body had been made for his. God, it was so good. *She* was so good, so right for him. He couldn't look away, even as he tried to stave off his impending orgasm. Her pale back, lush bottom, the elegant column of her neck, her cheeks flushed.

Fuck, this woman was dangerous to his mortal soul.

And as he reached his own climax and spent all over the sheets at her side, he couldn't be sure which of them had emerged from this particular battle the victor. He had intended to prove to her just how heartless he was, but he had managed to prove his utter, abject inability to resist her instead.

Rhiannon was not the only one of them who had surrendered.

∽

Rhiannon was deliriously, ridiculously happy.

Happier than she had ever imagined possible.

It was a guarded happiness, but as she finished breakfast with Aubrey in the small, cozy kitchen of the cottage, she was sure she couldn't keep it from her expression. She was so desperately in love with him. Not even his continued insistence that he was a heartless, conscienceless villain could quell her unabashed bliss. She suspected that nothing could.

"How is your tea?" Aubrey asked as she sipped from her cup.

His dark mood of earlier that morning had improved now that he had broken his fast. Perhaps he believed he had proved his point to her and that she was firmly of the opinion he was irredeemable. If so, he was wrong.

He was a good man. The man she loved. The man she had always longed to marry.

"My tea is excellent," she told him, settling the cup in its saucer. "I must admit that you can pour a proper cup. I wouldn't have expected it of you."

"I am a man of many talents," he quipped with a flourish.

And a man of many facets, she thought quietly, observing him from across the table.

They had fallen asleep again after making love earlier that morning, and then he had treated her to the remaining picnic food from the larder. He had lit the range and toasted bread for her and made tea. Not very ducal and hardly the actions of a heartless scoundrel. He was forever feeding her and tending to her needs.

Rhiannon wisely neglected pointing that out to him.

"Very many talents," she agreed aloud instead, heat rising to her cheeks as she thought of his skilled hands and wicked mouth.

She'd had no idea it was possible to experience so much pleasure.

"I'm gratified you concur." He gave her a rakish wink.

"Oh, I certainly do."

She still couldn't quite believe where his sinful tongue

had been earlier. Rhiannon was reasonably certain she would swoon if she ever mentioned it aloud.

"What has put that expression on your lovely face?" he asked, raising a brow.

He was insufferably handsome this morning, his whiskers a bit more pronounced, his green eyes vibrant and warm on hers.

"The tea, of course," she lied smoothly, bringing her cup to her lips.

"I didn't know you found tea so…moving." He gave her a slow smile that made her bare toes curl on the old stone floor.

She was dressed informally in her shirt and bloomers, her stockings still draped somewhere upstairs in the bedroom. They had been missing and her stomach had been rumbling, so she had eschewed them.

"Quite," she said, giving him a serene smile.

He leaned forward on the table, resting his weight on one forearm as his hair fell across his brow. "Do you know what I think, minx?"

"No, but it looks as if you are about to tell me."

"I think that you're remembering my tongue on you in that forbidden place, how it felt. You liked it, didn't you?"

More heat crept up her throat. Oh, he was wicked. She didn't know if he was trying to fluster her or if this was more of his campaign to prove himself as a cruel, heartless rake. Perhaps both. Either way, she wasn't going to allow him this particular victory.

She forced herself to hold his stare. "I like your tongue on me everywhere."

His gaze darkened and smoldered with sensual promise. "Touché."

He had turned her into a wanton. She scarcely recognized herself. But she liked this newfound freedom to be as bold as she liked with him. He made her feel as if she were capable of anything. Brazen and powerful and so very alive.

How could she have resigned herself to a staid, proper marriage with the Earl of Carnis? Rhiannon couldn't fathom it now. Nor would she return to accept his suit. She couldn't. Not knowing what she would be missing. Not loving Aubrey as she did, and most definitely not with the hope burning to life inside her that he might one day return her feelings.

Despite his protestations to the contrary.

Smiling to herself, she finished the last of her tea.

"What do you think about spending the day here at the cottage again?" Aubrey asked suddenly, surprising her. "I can ride back to the main house and have the servants return and replenish our food supply. You needn't worry that they would see you. You could stay upstairs until they finish their tasks and go back to Wingfield Hall."

The chance to spend another day with him, just the two of them? Rhiannon could scarcely believe her fortune.

"I would enjoy that immensely." She paused. "But I would also dearly love a bath. I suppose having one is quite impossible here, isn't it?"

"What manner of host am I? I've neglected to show you the bath. It was added when we refurbished the cottage. There is a tub which is quite deep and lovely. All I'll need to do is heat the kitchen range again, and you'll have hot water at the ready."

"That sounds divine, but I haven't any soap."

"Tell me where it is, and I'll fetch it from your bedroom when I return."

She thought for a moment, trying to recall where she had left it, but it was no use.

"You've no notion where you put it, have you?" he asked, apparently reading her expression.

Rhiannon winced. "It is somewhere within my room. But where is something of a mystery."

"As I thought. It's likely beneath a mound of dresses you've discarded as not being worthy."

"In my defense, I had no notion you would be spiriting me away to a cottage for days. I thought I was returning."

"You *are* returning. Eventually. Just not today." He gave her a soft smile that was almost boyish. "If you wish it, that is."

Oh, how she liked this charming, softer side of him.

"Of course I wish it," she conceded. "But a bath would still be lovely."

As would a fresh gown, but she couldn't imagine how he might manage to gather such a cumbersome garment and take it through the house without arousing suspicion. She would simply have to settle for her shirt and bloomers until she returned to Wingfield Hall herself.

"Then a bath you shall have," Aubrey told her gallantly. "Unfortunately, I cannot promise what manner of soap I will be able to scavenge. Your bedroom looks as if it has been ransacked by an invading army that has taken anything remotely of value and trampled the rest."

"It looks nothing like that," she defended, slightly insulted. "It looks as if it has been kept by a woman who is accustomed to a clever lady's maid doing most of the work for her and is now rather a bit lost without her aid."

He laughed and shook his head. "When you leave, we shall have to set the room on fire."

"Aubrey," she scolded him. "You are rotten for saying something so appallingly rude to me. You really ought to apologize."

"I will later." He winked as he rose from his chair and rounded the table to her side. "I'll join you in the bath and make certain you're clean *everywhere*."

Heat pulsed to life between her legs. "That sounds acceptable."

"Acceptable, eh?" He bent down and kissed her nose. "Until later, minx."

She watched him stride from the kitchen, admiring him as he went, taking her poor heart with him.

CHAPTER 15

"You see? I told you that it's possible to fuck in a tub."

Rhiannon was still breathless from the staggering climax that had roared through her as Aubrey had made love to her in the bath. She was in his lap, a boneless heap, arms wrapped around his neck for purchase to keep her from sliding limply beneath the water.

She could hear the smug grin in his voice, but she didn't object. Oh, the arrogant, wonderful, beautiful man. He had returned to her with a night rail, his own soap and shampoo, a brush for her hair, and a far more sensible pair of slippers for her feet. A host of servants had arrived with their luncheon and then departed for the manor house, leaving the two of them alone, lost in their own little world yet again.

"Mmm," she murmured, all she could manage for the moment. The water was hot from the range and decadently scented as it sloshed around them.

The floor was a sopping mess they would have to navigate with great care when they emerged. But she wasn't concerned about that just now. In fact, she wasn't certain she cared about anything.

Unless it was the man in her arms.

He kissed her ear, her throat. "I will admit that it was hardly a chore proving you wrong in this particular instance."

Helpless laughter bubbled up in her throat as she turned her head toward him, dazzled by his gorgeous face and the way his smile lit up his emerald eyes. Dazzled by him in every way, full stop.

"I suppose I'll allow you your small victory for now," she teased lightly.

Her heart was so full. Overflowing. The day had been nothing short of wondrous.

"How generous of you, my lady." He cupped her nape and tipped her head, bringing her mouth to his for a long, slow, and thorough kiss.

"I am a remarkably generous woman," she said when his mouth left hers.

"And modest."

"The most modest." She kissed him again before lifting her head to study him, committing every detail of this moment to her memory so that she could recall it later, like a treasured picture in a frame. "Thank you for bringing me here to this cottage."

He gave her a lopsided grin. "You needn't thank me, minx. I can assure you, the decision was a wholly selfish one. I intend to spend as much time on your lessons as possible until the house party is at an end."

"I have been enjoying my lessons immensely." She smiled down at him.

"As have I," he said. "Although I must admit that it rankles to think of you wedding the Earl of bloody Carnis. All your sensual fire will be wasted upon him. The man has the personality of a wet counterpane."

She frowned down at Aubrey, searching his countenance for a hint that he was bamming her.

And finding none.

A hint of misgiving splintered her heart.

"What do you mean?"

He gave a bitter laugh. "Forgive me for insulting your betrothed. But you must know the man is as interesting as a musty old pair of boots. I gather you must have some tender feelings for the fellow in order to agree to marry him, but I dislike him quite intensely."

He thought she was still intending to marry the earl? After all they had shared together? After he had kept her here at this cottage, nothing but the two of them, making love in every manner possible?

She felt her smile slipping. "I wished to marry him to please my mother. I thought that doing so would grant me her favor, or perhaps her attention, two things she has never willingly bestowed upon me. But all that has changed now."

"You are marrying him for other reasons?"

The lingering languor from their lovemaking fled her body. She disentangled herself from Aubrey and moved to the other end of the tub. The movement didn't truly separate her from him, given the size of the tub and Aubrey's impressive height and long legs. But it was all she could manage without rising naked before him like Venus from the sea.

"I do not know if I am marrying him at all," she said, mustering her pride.

Aubrey still believed she would wed the earl.

The shock of this realization was akin to a slap to the face.

She didn't know what to make of it, what to make of *him*. She suddenly felt cold in the water. A shiver passed through her. What if everything they had shared these last few days hadn't changed anything for him?

"You aren't marrying the earl, then?" Aubrey asked, his eyes sharp.

"Perhaps," she said, feeling a bit raw, as if the protective shell she kept around her heart had been suddenly scraped off. "Perhaps not."

"You shouldn't marry him. Carnis is not a good match for you at all."

"Oh? And who would be a good match, then?" she asked him, inwardly pleading for him to realize what his answer should be.

Me.

But Aubrey didn't say that.

Instead, he lifted a shoulder in a shrug, his expression unreadable. "I'm afraid I haven't an inkling, my dear."

He said it with such carelessness, as if her future were passing scenery he watched with disinterest from the window of a railcar. Misgiving settled within her, heavier than a stone. Had she misread him? He had warned her repeatedly, even that very morning, that he was heartless. Before her was surely that part of him now, so callous and cool, as if everything they had shared these last few days—the intimacies, the conversations, the most personal parts of themselves stripped bare—had meant nothing.

She forced a smile, summoning her tattered pride. "Fortunately, I don't have to fret over who to choose as my husband until I return to London."

His jaw tightened, the only indication her words affected him. "Are there others in consideration, aside from Carnis?"

"Of course," she lied, feigning a bright smile. "There is the Marquess of Penleigh as well."

"An arrogant arse," Aubrey declared. "You deserve far better than Penleigh. Why, the man is a widower with two young children. According to common fame, the fellow is responsible for the former Lady Penleigh's untimely demise."

She had heard no such rumor, although she was aware the marquess had two children. He was a pleasant man, and they had conversed on numerous occasions at various balls and suppers. But whilst they possessed a mutual respect for each other, there had been no romantic interest in either direction.

"I must not forget Lord Barclay," she continued.

"Do you mean Viscount Barclay, the mad footballer?" he asked, sounding incredulous.

She gave him a quelling look. "Yes."

He shook his head. "Not clever enough by half for a woman of your immense intellect. The man only gives a damn about football and cricket. You would grow tired of conversing with him after approximately fifteen seconds."

"Then there is the Duke of Weyrich," she carried on, pulling names out of her memory with complete disregard for whether any of the gentlemen in question had even danced with her at a ball, let alone courted her.

"I never liked the bastard," Aubrey muttered.

"You are not required to like His Grace," she pointed out coolly. "You will not be his wife after all. I would, were I to choose to accept his suit."

Aubrey's lip curled in apparent disdain. "Right. Of course not. But I am an excellent judge of character, and Weyrich is not a good man."

"Perhaps I do not need a good man as my husband," Rhiannon dared to tell him. "Perhaps I only need the man who is the right man for me."

They stared at each other, the silence between them so tense that just one more word and it might have shattered like glass. Oh, how she wanted to unburden herself to him. To tell him that the right man for her was *him*. If only he would not be too obtuse to see it. And yet, she was afraid to do so, terribly frightened that if she pushed him too far, he would close himself off to her. She couldn't bear that. Couldn't even contemplate the notion of losing him.

She had clearly inferred far more about Aubrey's intentions than he was willing to admit.

"You are only three-and-twenty," Aubrey said then. "You are yet young. I wouldn't think there ought to be a need for haste in determining your future husband. If you wish for children, there is time aplenty to beget brats."

Was he being deliberately cruel? She couldn't say.

"I am pleased to hear there is time aplenty for me to *beget brats*," she drawled cuttingly, rising from the bath. "I should so hate to think that I am too ancient for my prospective husband. My sole purpose in life is, quite naturally, to provide him with an heir and a spare."

She stood, naked, allowing water to run down her body, and all too aware of his hungry gaze on her, devouring her. But for the first time since they had arrived at the cottage, Rhiannon wasn't thinking lustful thoughts where the Duke of Richford was concerned. Indeed, all she could seem to think about was boxing his supercilious ears.

She stepped over the rim of the tub and onto the towel he had laid on the floor before their bath. Finding a spare, dry towel, she snatched it up and wrapped it around herself. The last thing she felt like at the moment was being on display before him. She already felt vulnerable enough as it was.

"That is not what I was suggesting, minx," he said behind her, punctuated by the sound of him rising from the bath as well. "I was merely cautioning you not to rush with your judgment. Choose wisely. You will be trapped with this chap for the rest of your life. All I want is your happiness."

She wrapped her towel around herself and turned back to him. A mistake, because he was still naked and dripping, looking like some sort of marbled Greek god descended among mortals to torment them with his unearthly beauty. Water ran down his chest, over his muscled abdomen and powerful thighs. His cock was thick and long, rising to attention. She wanted to catch every droplet with her tongue, and then she wanted to splash his insufferably handsome face with water.

But she did neither of those things.

"Why should you care whether I am happy or not?" she asked him instead.

"I want you to be happy, Rhiannon. Surely you know that."

She clutched her towel to her. "Do you?"

He wrapped his own towel low on his hips, securing it. "Of course I do."

She stared up at him, so much emotion inside her. Could he not see what would truly make her happy? That it was he? That she loved him more than words could possibly convey?

Did he feel nothing for her?

"Then who do you suggest I wed?" she asked, daring him to tell her another man.

To tell her himself.

"I hardly think such a tremendous decision must be made tonight," he said, moving toward Rhiannon and sliding an arm around her waist to pull her into his chest. "Must it?"

Her rebellion went liquid inside her. She couldn't resist him when he was looking at her thus, when he was holding her close.

She settled her hands on his shoulders, absorbing his casual strength. "Of course not," she conceded.

"Tonight is just the two of us." He lowered his head and kissed her softly, lingeringly.

All her inner resistance melted. She had no defenses

against this man. Not any longer. She loved him, and that was all.

Rhiannon kissed him back, concentrating on the play of his lips over hers, the strength of his arms wrapped around her. And then she told herself that all would eventually turn out as it was meant to be. She just had to have faith in Aubrey. In herself.

In *love*.

Yes, it was as easy, and as impossible, as that.

~

ONE MORE NIGHT.

That was all he could allow himself with Rhiannon.

This, Aubrey promised himself as he led her from the bathroom to the bedroom they had been sharing in the cottage for the past two days. What she had left unsaid in the bathtub had been in her eyes, easy for him to read.

She didn't want to marry Carnis, which filled him with a relief he had no right to feel. But she did want to marry him, and that could never happen. Because Aubrey had no intention of marrying anyone. Ever.

"Come and sit by the hearth, and I'll brush your hair," he told Rhiannon, taking up the hairbrush she had thrown at him a few days before.

It may as well have been a lifetime ago for how much had changed between them in the intervening time.

"I can brush my own hair," she protested halfheartedly.

He knew by now that she enjoyed the pleasure of someone else running the bristles slowly through her hair, and shockingly, he had found that he liked taking care of her. The revelation had come as a surprise for a man who made a point of looking after only himself and his best interests.

"But you like when I brush it for you," he countered softly, leading her to the armchair.

Obligingly, she sat by the crackling fire, stretching her legs and pointing her bare toes toward its warmth. "You would make an excellent lady's maid."

"I would make a dreadful lady's maid. I'd want to spend all day in bed with you, naked, and you would never leave your chamber. Although I daresay that I would be better at keeping your room from looking as if it had been ransacked by thieves than you are."

She chuckled. "You have a valet to keep your things in excellent order."

"Yes, and he would call for my head on a pike if I were to dream of making such a mess in my dressing area," Aubrey pointed out wryly.

It was better to think of his fastidious valet than to allow his mind to wander to places where it didn't belong. Brown was notoriously particular, and it was true that he never would have stood for Aubrey to fling his garments about the way Rhiannon did. Her poor lady's maid no doubt deserved an increase per annum.

"This house party has been a whirlwind," she defended herself lightly. "In more ways than one."

Aubrey knew what she was speaking of—not just the overwhelming nature of all the entertainments that had been planned. But what had happened between himself and Rhiannon as well. It had been unexpected. Explosive. Addictive.

Utterly fucking ruinous.

He was betraying his friend by being here. Every moment he had spent in her presence, touching her, bedding her, debauching her, had been one more blot against his already black soul. And yet, he had been unable to help himself.

He began passing the brush through Rhiannon's wet hair,

starting at the roots and moving it toward the ends. In the low lamplight, her hair glistened with gold and hints of red. One day soon, another man would have the right to touch her thus. To bathe with her in a tub, to make love with her all night, to kiss her soft lips and lose himself inside her sweet heat.

The mere notion was akin to a blade between his ribs.

But he mustn't think of that now. It was the way of things. He had never kept a lover for long, and Rhiannon was no exception. He couldn't give her what she deserved. A parting of ways was desperately in order before she did something truly foolish like fall in love with him. Their time together had always been finite. He had shown her pleasure, helped her to embrace her innate sensuality.

And now another man would reap the rewards of his diligence.

It would be for the best, he reminded himself harshly. Rhiannon could never truly be his. He was no bloody good for her. Nor was she for him.

"Even whirlwinds must come to an end," he said pragmatically.

"Must they?"

He finished running the brush through her long, beautiful hair. Some perverse part of him hoped she would cut it before she allowed another man to brush through those golden locks as he had. But that was a stupid desire born of a jealousy he didn't deserve to possess.

"Of course they must. Else, we would be trapped here forever, and time would cease to pass."

"That sounds rather like a dream to me. This cottage feels like a place where such magic could happen." She sighed wistfully. "Oh, to be like Eos, the goddess of the dawn, granting her lover Tithonus eternal life so that they could pass each day together, never torn apart."

"A pleasant-enough tale until one learns the end," he quipped, setting the brush aside on a table.

Rhiannon turned to him. "Why should you find the ending of their tale sad? Eos and Tithonus were both granted what they wanted—to be together forever."

"Ah, but do not forget that whilst the poor chap was granted immortality, he didn't retain his youth. So whilst Tithonus and Eos *were* indeed together for eternity, he was doomed to grow old and fade away until she was left with no recourse but to turn him into a grasshopper, of all creatures, just to relieve him of his misery." He offered her his hand. "I cannot speak for Tithonus, but I would sooner lose my immortality than spend the rest of my days as a bloody insect."

Rhiannon settled her hand in his, allowing him to draw her to her feet and into his chest. She wrapped her arms loosely around his neck and stared up at him with that same expression she reserved for him alone—damsel in distress gazing with adoration up at her knight errant.

"You miss the point, I think. Eos's gesture was romantic. She loved Tithonus so much that she couldn't bear to be parted from him."

"But even with immortality, she was still a goddess and he was but a man," Aubrey countered smoothly. "He could never compare to Eos, nor was he ever truly a part of her world. They were too different, a goddess and a mere mortal."

He hoped Rhiannon understood the meaning underscoring his words. In this story of theirs, she was the goddess and he was the mortal, all too flawed and imperfect.

"But Tithonus loved Eos so much that it didn't matter that they were different," Rhiannon argued. "And she also loved him in the same way. Their love brought them together."

"Love is as much a myth as the story of Tithonus and Eos."

"Surely you don't believe that."

"I do. Have you never noticed that in so many of the old legends, it is love that ultimately leads to death and unhappiness? One must fancy the Greeks and Romans were attempting to tell us something."

She wanted to argue with him. Aubrey could read it in the mulish set of her jaw, in the fire sparkling in her eyes. He had been like her once, filled with conviction and fire. But he was thirty years old, and he had buried his mother and father, knowing the damage that supposed love could do. He had neither the time nor the inclination for convictions, and the last of them had been thoroughly dashed into jaded cynicism. He was a man of the moment, chasing whatever pleased him until it no longer did, and then he flitted elsewhere.

Which was what he would do tomorrow.

"I think the Greeks and Romans were telling us that love is always worth the risk and the cost," Rhiannon told him firmly.

"Yet hold me not for ever in thine East," he recited a verse from the Tennyson poem that had always struck him as being particularly meaningful. *"How can my nature longer mix with thine?"*

"If not forever, then perhaps just a few nights more," she said, her gaze plumbing the depths of his, searching.

He wondered what she saw when she looked at him. What she truly saw. He was aware of his looks; they had been all he had to recommend himself, aside from his title and reasonable wealth. But what did she find behind the rakish polish he wore like a shield? She must have fooled herself a great deal when it came to him. He tried to summon a modicum of regret and could not.

More proof of his villainy.

He would not change a single moment of what had come to pass this last week. He would kiss her, know her passion, her body. He would take her, make her his again and again if given the chance. Because Lady Rhiannon Northwick was worth the hell of an eternity as a grasshopper or any fate worse.

But *he* wasn't worthy of her.

Not worthy of so much as the water droplet clinging to the ends of her hair.

"Just a few nights more," he said to her, lowering his head and taking her lips with his.

He kissed her slowly, deliberately.

He kissed her even knowing that he was lying.

Because when dawn painted the sky tomorrow morning, he would be gone, and his goddess would be better off without him.

~

Aubrey carried her to the bed.

They were both naked, for the towels from their bath had fallen away. Her hair was dripping. She didn't care. His lips were on hers as he gently laid her on the bedclothes. She couldn't get enough of him, coasting her hands over every part of his body, committing him to memory. The protrusion of his clavicle, the blades of his shoulders, the sinew of his upper arms, the rigid slab of his abdomen, the sculpted muscles of his chest. She wanted to know him in her fingertips and her heart, to never forget what these charmed nights of passion in the cottage had been like.

Because she couldn't quite shake the fear that these stolen moments would be all they could ever have. His words this evening had been laden with caution. He was warning her away from him.

It hadn't worked, of course.

Like Eos, she would do anything for the man she loved. She would face her brother's wrath. She would battle the demons of Aubrey's past that he kept locked away from her. She would end her understanding with the Earl of Carnis when she returned to London. When she was no longer bound to another, then, surely then, Aubrey would be free to ask her to be his wife.

Nothing could come between them.

Aubrey made love to her with a quiet fervor that was new, raining kisses on her breasts, sucking her nipples until she begged for him to take her. She was awash in sensation, so very alive for the first time, renewed in her lover's lips and tongue and clever hands.

He circled her wrists with a tender grasp, bringing her arms above her and pinning them to the bed as he kissed her deeply, giving her his tongue. She arched into him, feeling utterly at his mercy and loving every second of it. The movement arched her back and forced her breasts into his chest as he fed her wild kisses that went on and on until she was breathless and dazed as he raised his head.

His emerald gaze glittered down at her. "You are more beautiful than any goddess could ever hope to be."

"I am only all too mortal," she said, smiling up at him. "For you, I would gladly be a grasshopper."

He kissed her again. "You are too good for me. Too pure. Too lovely. Too much heart. I want to keep you here forever so that no other man can ever have you."

She knew the feeling. She was intensely jealous of all the women who had known him before her. Who had shared intimacies with him like bathing and sleeping, who had kissed him and listened to him breathe in the night. Not because she feared he had given a part of himself to those women, but because it was less time she'd had with him.

He gazed down at her seriously. "There is something I want to do, and if you don't wish it, you have only to say the word."

"Yes." She lifted her head and kissed him. "I want to do anything with you, everything with you. Show me."

He kissed her deeply, then rolled to the side, releasing her. She admired the ripple of strength in his back as he reached to the floor, retrieving something from the Axminster. It was her embroidered stockings, she realized as he held them up for her inspection.

"I want to tie your wrists to the bed," he said.

And all the wicked rumors she had heard about him descended upon her. But they didn't frighten her. They filled her with desire.

"Would it please you to do so?"

"Immensely, but only if it pleases you. Some find desire can be intensified by restraints, by the knowledge that you are helpless to do anything but receive the pleasure your lover wants to give you."

Her nipples tightened to hard points, and the liquid heat between her thighs was enough to tell Rhiannon that she wanted to try this with him. Not just for Aubrey, but for herself. She wanted to embrace every part of herself with him.

Slowly, Rhiannon extended her arms above her head, just as he had placed them with his grip a few minutes before. "Do it."

His gaze darkened. "You are sure?"

"Tie me to the bed," she told him. "And then make me yours."

He swallowed, his Adam's apple dipping almost violently. "God, minx. You are perfect in every way. Never let anyone tell you otherwise."

She had no intention of doing so.

"I won't."

He moved quickly, his touch gentle as he maneuvered each hand and secured her wrists to the bedposts. The knots held, but the stockings weren't tight. She could freely move.

"Say the word, and I'll untie you," he murmured, returning to brush kisses over her breasts.

She would have answered him, but he cupped her breast in a possessive hold and sucked hard on the peak, making her clitoris throb. "Oh."

Somehow, being at his mercy only heightened the pleasure. She was his to be used, to be pleased, and that knowledge was heady.

He moved to her other breast, sucking and nipping gently with his teeth until she writhed beneath him, seeking more.

"Impatient minx," he chided gently, running his tongue around her nipple.

"Please, Aubrey." Her body bowed from the bed, moving toward his knowing mouth beseechingly.

He gave her everything she wanted, lightly strumming over her pearl as he tormented her sensitive breasts until she was on the verge of spending. But then he removed his touch and kissed a path down her stomach, not stopping until he was between her thighs. He sipped at her sex as if she were fine champagne. Her hips pushed off the mattress, her feet flat on the counterpane, toes curling into the soft nest of bedding.

She was aflame.

His hands coaxed her thighs wider, and then his shoulders wedged into the gap he'd created. He used his mouth and tongue on her until she was slick and desperate, until her breathing was jagged and rushed, until her heart was pounding and perspiration slid down her spine. By the time he worked a finger into her channel, she was all but ready to come, and yet still, he kept her on the edge. He danced light touches over her, sucked hard and then gentled, bit and then licked, penetrated and then withdrew.

It became a game, and Rhiannon was the helpless pawn, spread beneath him for his wicked delectation. And oh, how he feasted. Until she was writhing and moaning, half mindless from the pleasure. Only when she was desperate with the need for release did he give her what she wanted, positioning her legs against his chest before sinking deep inside her with one smooth thrust.

For a moment, she saw stars edging her vision. The intensity of the bliss shooting through her was like fireworks across the canvas of an inky midnight sky, lighting her up. Explosive. She was filled with him, the angle of his cock inside her divine madness as he began a rhythm that took her swiftly over the edge.

She came on a keening cry she couldn't hold back, the force of her climax taking her by surprise. Murmuring sweet endearments, he rode her harder, faster, the intensity of his thrusts telling her he was also close just before he withdrew, coming all over her belly in hot white jets of seed.

In the aftermath, he untied her wrists and aligned his body with hers, nestling alongside her in the rumpled bedding. She was overwhelmed with sensation and emotion, her heart pounding, his spend cooling on her skin. He retrieved a handkerchief and gently mopped up the mess he had made before discarding it.

With the glow of the lamp behind him, he looked golden and beautiful, and she had never been more moved in all her life. She reached for him, cupping his cheek.

"I love you," she said before she even realized it.

The words had slipped from her of their own volition, a confession she'd never intended to make.

Aubrey stiffened at her side but said nothing, and she wished she could retract them. That she could tear them out of the air, expunge them from his mind. That she could unsay them. But she couldn't. It was too late.

Then he leaned over her and kissed her softly on the lips. "Go to sleep, minx."

That was all he said, nothing more. He settled the bedclothes over them both, cocooning them in warmth, and then he pulled her against him.

Disappointment sliced into her heart, but she hastily banished it. What had she expected? That a hardened rake like the Duke of Richford would confess his undying devotion to her?

Aubrey had repeatedly warned her what he was. A rake to the marrow, heartless. She knew it, and she loved him anyway.

Loved him enough for the both of them.

She would just have to keep those forbidden words tucked away inside her heart from this moment forward.

With what remaining time they had.

Telling herself this, she fell asleep wrapped in his arms.

But when she woke in the morning, it was to the sunlight streaming in the windows, the cottage quiet and still, nary a hint left behind to suggest the past few days had been anything more than a figment of her imagination. Not a handkerchief, nor a necktie. Not even a button from his shirt. Nothing but the faint scent of him on his pillow and a bathtub filled with water that was as cold as her heart.

Aubrey was gone.

CHAPTER 16

*A*ubrey had regretted bringing Perdita with him almost the second his carriage had departed Wingfield Hall. She had offered to suck his cock on the short voyage to his country seat, Villiers House, and when he had politely declined, she had pouted for the duration of the ride.

The only pouting woman he could abide was Rhiannon.

And the only woman he wanted in his carriage was her too.

But he couldn't have her.

Which was why he was presently sitting in his study at Villiers House getting roaringly drunk. And which was also why he didn't want Perdita hovering over him like a bloody mosquito, intent upon sucking his blood. Or his cock. Or anything.

He glared at his bottle of gin, his head feeling light and listless and dizzied. As well it might. He had commenced drinking yesterday when he had arrived at Villiers House, and he hadn't stopped since. Getting soused didn't drown out the guilt or the misery that had been his ever-constant companion since he had abandoned Rhiannon in the cottage at dawn the day before.

But it was all he could do to keep himself from going to her.

She loved him. He didn't deserve her. Didn't believe in love. He knew what love led to, and it was naught but death, madness, and destruction. She deserved so much better than that. So much better than him. Aubrey brought the bottle to his lips and downed half of it at once.

The door to his study opened, and the wrong woman swept across the threshold.

Perdita was gorgeous, and her bubbies were hanging out of her bodice in a most indecent fashion, but his cock didn't give a damn and neither did the rest of him. Because she wasn't Rhiannon.

He glared at the viscountess and realized she had two heads and four breasts. "Who let you in here?"

"I let myself in," she said breezily. "I'm growing weary of wandering around alone. You told me you wished for company. Why else did you bring me with you? I could have stayed at the house party for another day."

Damn it, was she pouting again? Aubrey squinted at her. "You're deuced tedious."

"*I'm* tedious?" Her voice vibrated with outrage. "You brought me here and have yet to even so much as touch me."

True. When he had made his decision to leave the house party early, he had known he would need to do so with haste. He'd also known that he would need to do something drastic. Something that would keep Rhiannon from following him with her stubborn determination to see the bloody good in him and to love him.

Christ knew he couldn't resist her.

"As you can see, I'm rather occupied at the moment," he pointed out rudely, lifting his bottle of gin to Perdita.

Gin wasn't his ordinary drink of choice. He saved it for days when he wanted to get so thoroughly soused that he could drown out everything in his mind. He had been on a steady diet of it since his arrival the day before, and he had no intention of stopping any time soon.

"You prefer spirits to me?" Perdita asked, rounding his desk and invading his space.

Her breath smelled of onions. What the devil had she eaten for luncheon? Had it been luncheon yet? Blast, he couldn't recall when he'd last eaten.

Her hands were on his chest, caressing. All four of them.

Why the devil was she here again? Ah, yes.

He had been waiting for his carriage to be readied when Perdita had sailed past him in the great hall. On a whim, he had invited her to accompany him, thinking her the perfect pawn for his plan. If Rhiannon knew he had left with another woman, she would be less likely to come after him. He hated the very idea of hurting her, but he knew without a doubt he was doing what was best for her.

She deserved happiness.

A husband who could give her everything she wanted.

One of Perdita's hands settled on his cock, massaging with firm insistence.

He shoved her hand away. Why had he thought it a good idea to invite a bloody octopus to Villiers House anyway?

"I want to get drunk," he informed her, taking a swig of his bottle for emphasis.

The gin burned down his throat, hardly a soothing elixir. What he ought to have done was drag King from his bed and demand some of his potions. Those would have had him thoroughly and diabolically passed out by now. Perhaps he would have even been so disguised that he might have given shagging Penelope a try.

No, that wasn't her name, Penelope. Was it?

He blinked owlishly, trying to make his blurred vision distinct enough that he could see the woman's face. Mayhap then he could recall her actual name.

She settled in his lap, pouting once more. "But I want to be properly fucked. That's why you brought me here, is it not? I've heard so many delicious stories about you, and I simply must know if they're all true."

Her eyes were brown and gold, her lashes long. Her breasts were ivory mountains, quivering over the edge of her brazen décolletage.

"Persephone," he said.

"Yes," she murmured. "I shall be your Persephone. And you can be my Hades, spiriting me away as you've done."

So that wasn't her name, then. He knew it. Her name was on the edge of his brain, sharper than a needle, poking and prodding.

Phillipa?

No, that wasn't it.

Proserpina? No, that was the Roman equivalent of Persephone.

Priscilla?

"I'll take this," she was saying, plucking his gin from his fingers and settling it on the desk. "You won't be needing that for now."

"Yes, I will be," he argued, reaching for it again.

"No, you won't, naughty Hades," she said, taking his hand and setting it upon her breasts, which were suddenly bare.

No, they had already been bare. Chrissakes, was that her areola peeping from her bodice? What time of day was it?

Aubrey turned toward the windows, where the heavy curtains had been drawn, and found sun streaming through a crack. Surely it was too early to be dressed thus.

"You're indecent," he groused, thinking that perhaps she

was cutting off all the blood to his cock, for he was limp and useless beneath her.

Her breast was cool to the touch and as uninspiring as a pillow. He withdrew his hand.

"I want to be *more* indecent," the woman in his lap was cooing into his ear, and damn him, but he still couldn't recall what her name was.

Pamela?

"That's indecorous. It's got to be...what..." He squinted at the mantel clock and couldn't make out a single goddamn number. "Morning?"

"It's afternoon." She licked his ear, and again the scent of onions washed over him, making his stomach clench. "Why don't you take me upstairs and tie me to your bed? You can birch my naughty bum if you'd like. Punish me until I'm raw."

No, he didn't want this. Didn't want her.

"Perdita," he managed at last.

Yes, that was her name. She was lifting her skirts, placing his other hand on her knee. He closed his eyes as the room began to swirl. He was going to be ill. This wasn't right. It was all wrong. He never should have left the cottage yesterday. Never should have left Rhiannon's side. He could still hear her voice telling him those words he didn't want to hear. The words he couldn't bear.

I love you.

He opened his eyes again, and as if he had conjured her, there she was. Rhiannon standing in the doorway of his study, her blue eyes filled with tears and betrayal. Was she real or a chimera? Was he dreaming or awake?

"Aubrey," she was saying. "What is happening?"

The room was swimming around him. Or he was swimming. Drowning. Drowning in her gaze, in the hurt he saw there, the confusion.

She couldn't be here. He couldn't be with her. He had taken her innocence, and if she let him, he would destroy her.

The woman in his lap was laughing, the sound husky and mocking. She shoved his hand higher so that it skimmed past her garter and he felt soft, smooth, womanly flesh, but it was all wrong, that skin. All wrong, that woman.

Rhiannon was crying, tears streaming down her cheeks. "What have you done?"

He forced himself to speak. "You will thank me later, minx."

"Aubrey," she said again, pleading.

"Can you not see Richford wants a woman and not a mere girl?" snapped the blonde in his lap as she pressed a kiss to his neck. "Go before your reputation is completely ruined."

Rhiannon was shaking her head, backing away. He was losing her. It was what was right. What he wanted. He was no bloody good for her. He was the son of a madman. He was a danger to her, to himself, to everyone.

The door slammed closed, and Pamela was laughing again, only that wasn't her name, and she had wrapped her arms around his neck, forcing his face to hers.

"Kiss me," she said.

He couldn't do it.

The blackness inside him, the awful, ugly, jagged shards he kept buried rose up. He saw blood. So much blood. On his hands, on his shirt, on the floor. Streaking his trousers. He saw the lifeless form draped in fine silk. The eyes staring sightlessly at the ceiling. He heard the report of the pistol firing.

Aubrey pushed the woman from his lap, setting her on his desk. The gin spilled. Glass broke. The walls swirled around him.

He rushed from the study, unsteady on his feet.

But it was too late.

Too late.

Rhiannon was gone.

His butler's frowning face appeared before him. "Is Your Grace ill?"

"Yes, Wickett. I bloody well am." He fell sideways into a wall and cast up his accounts into a potted plant. When he was finished, he wiped his mouth with the back of his hand. "See my lady guest sent on her way, if you please."

Still feeling sick, he dragged his miserable hide to his bedroom and bolted the door before he passed out in his bed just as he deserved to be, alone.

Utterly, damningly alone.

~

THE JOURNEY back to London from Villiers House in a hired carriage was the most miserable one of Rhiannon's life. She had spent it alternately sobbing and in a state of abject shock. Each time she closed her eyes, it was to the picture of Viscountess Heathcote seated in Aubrey's lap as if it were where she belonged, her arms around him, his hand on her breast as it spilled from her bodice.

Her heart was shattered.

Her hopes were shattered.

She was shattered.

Irreparable. That was what she was.

When Aubrey had left the cottage yesterday morning before she had awoken, she had been convinced that he had merely returned to the house party. She had told herself that likely, a pressing matter had arisen he needed to attend to as one of the hosts.

The ride back to Wingfield Hall on her lone bicycle had

been demoralizing. She had been desperately sore in all manner of intimate places, and the seat of the cycle had been wretchedly uncomfortable. Her bloomer suit had no longer seemed quite as dashing as it had when she had set off on her adventure, and neither had the rest of her.

There had been no sign of Aubrey. No missive left for her from him. She'd had to go to the servants and make discreet inquiries to learn he had left earlier that morning, returning to his country seat. The revelation had been like being dealt a physical blow.

It had taken her a night of fitful sleep and misery to realize she needed to go to him at Villiers House. She had allotted herself a full week for the house party, and even that was drawing to an end at Wingfield Hall. The time had come to return to London. But she had told herself she needed to see Aubrey first.

A terrible mistake, as it happened.

A mistake, just like giving herself to him had been. Just like loving him was.

And now, she was almost back where she had started her journey, at her brother's London town house. She had no doubt that Rhys was awaiting her there, along with Mater. She would be required to explain where she had been, and although she had a plan in place and intended to claim she had spent the last week visiting Great-Aunt Bitsy, orchestrating it convincingly seemed far less plausible by the afternoon's grim light.

Her brother wasn't stupid. He would have questions. Questions to which she didn't have suitable answers.

But who could she blame for the straits in which she found herself? Not Aubrey. He had warned her, had he not? He was every bit the villain he had claimed to be, and she was every bit the fool.

If only she could forget the burning memory of his kisses.

His hands on her. His searing eyes that had seemed to see a part of her she hadn't known existed...

No, she chastised herself inwardly. She must be strong. She must not allow her girlish infatuation with a handsome, conscienceless rake to weaken her resolve. He had made his feelings about her more than abundantly clear, dashing her heart to pieces in the process.

She had set off with such hope in her heart, so hopelessly naïve. How horridly wrong her plans had gone.

He had left without warning, without a word. Had disappeared. And then she had found him, much to her everlasting regret. Rhiannon squeezed her eyes tightly shut against a painful rush of heartache and betrayal.

His words still echoed in her mind.

You will thank me later, minx.

Minx, he had called her, daring to use the pet name for her that she had once found so endearing. Now, it felt like a dagger plunging into her flesh, glancing off sinew and bone, making her bleed.

Her hired carriage came to a halt before her brother's town house. Rhiannon didn't know what awaited her within, nor how she would brazen her way through her explanation. If she even could.

But there was one matter of which Rhiannon was deadly certain.

She would never, as long as she lived, forgive the Duke of Richford for what he had done to her.

CHAPTER 17

ONE MONTH LATER

"You're quiet this morning, my dear."

Rhiannon blinked and looked up from the book she had been reading to find Mater smiling brightly at her in the drawing room of her brother's town house. In the month since her return, Mater had been shockingly attentive. Rhiannon could only deduce it was because her unexplained absence had sent the household—particularly her brother Rhys—into turmoil.

Mater was now making amends in the only way she knew how, by hovering.

"I am reading," she pointed out politely, hardly in the mood to converse.

Not with her mother. Not with anyone. The less she said to everyone, the better.

Somehow, she had managed to keep anyone from discovering where she had truly spent her one week of freedom. The excellent thing about using Great-Aunt Bitsy was that she lived a train ride away. She was also fretfully remiss with correspondence. She was forever doting over her ever-growing menagerie of animals and forgetting everything and everyone else. Once, it had taken Great-Aunty Bitsy over a year and a half to respond to a letter Rhiannon had sent her asking her for her cook's recipe for raspberry fool.

"What are you reading?" Mater asked, interrupting her musings.

Rhiannon frowned, hoping her mother had just been passing by the drawing room and didn't have any intention of joining her. "I know you don't care. You needn't pretend as if you are interested for my sake."

Mater's face looked as if it were about to crumple, her eyes welling with unshed tears behind her gold-rimmed spectacles. "But I do care. Must you be so cruel?"

Rhiannon sighed and laid her book in her lap. "It is a volume by Lord Tennyson, if you must know."

She had been searching for answers and solace in poetry. Not just in poetry either. But in ruminations, distractions. In society and alone. In prose too. She had dabbled in drawing and painting, in sewing and playing the piano. She had even taught herself to play the harp.

To no avail.

There were no answers, no explanations for what had happened, save the obvious. The Duke of Richford was everything he had warned her he was, and she had failed to listen. She had paid the price with her heart.

"Since when do you like poetry so?" Mater asked, frowning as she sat on a settee opposite Rhiannon.

Blast.

Since she'd engaged in a discussion about a Greek goddess and the mortal she loved with Aubrey. Since he'd broken her heart. Since she'd been trying desperately to seek reasons and hope.

"Perhaps it is a new interest," she said. "Am I not permitted one?"

"Of course you are permitted, my dear." Mater rearranged

the fall of her skirts. "One is always entitled to new interests. Indeed, have you seen my most recent collection of ferns? I cannot say why, but I find their little Wardian cases so agreeable."

"You have at least twenty of them in the library," Rhiannon pointed out, perhaps a bit unkindly.

The library was also strewn with other bric-a-brac that had held her mother's fancy, however briefly. Mater loved to collect things. Objects, animals, plants, rocks, shells, dead insects. Whatever it was in any given moment, Mater became particularly obsessed with it, governed by the need to obtain more and more the way some were driven to gluttony or others to gambling. Once she started, she couldn't get enough until she eventually wandered off to her next obsession, leaving the scattered remnants of pinned butterflies and taxidermy frogs posed as if they had enjoyed a Bacchanal in her wake.

"It is only eighteen Wardian cases," Mater said defensively. "Though there are yet a few more ferns I should like to collect and preserve. They are so very cheerful, are they not? One can't help but smile to see them."

"It is better, I suppose, than your bout with conchylomania," Rhiannon agreed.

"I still adore my shells. Truly, daughter. Must you make it sound as if I were possessed of a sickness? I am like a curator of a museum or library. If I were not here to preserve such treasures, I shudder to think what would become of them. And I simply like tending to things."

"Things rather than your children," she pointed out before she could think better of it.

Mater's face fell. "You know that I love you and Whitby very much."

"Of course I do." She forced a smile, reminding herself that she didn't want to bring up the unwanted subject of her disappearance a month ago yet again. "And we love you as well, Mater."

It had taken her mother almost the entire week to even take note that Rhiannon had gone. That knowledge still rather stung.

"I suppose you think that Great-Aunt Bitsy would have made a better mother to you than I have done," Mater continued, her tone morose. "I cannot even be jealous of her, for she is as beloved as a mother to me, and I am grateful, in a way, that she has come to be so revered to you as well."

Great-Aunt Bitsy was her mother's treasured aunt, who had all but raised her during her own mother's reign of absences to the Continent and all over the world. The irony of Mater's plight was that she had taken on many of the personality traits of her own mother that she had despised.

"I think Great-Aunt Bitsy has made a fine great-aunt," Rhiannon said mildly, still unable to tell Mater that she had made a good mother.

There were only so many lies she could be expected to tell in the span of one month.

"I do wish you would not have gone to her without warning, however," Mater continued. "You have no notion of how worried I was. And when Lord Carnis came to call, I scarcely knew what to tell him."

Lord Carnis.

Rhiannon wished she could summon even a modicum of tenderness when she heard the name of the man she was meant to marry, but she felt nothing. In the wake of her return, she had been too numb to refuse when Mater had insisted upon the betrothal announcement being made. It had seemed to reassure her mother that she was happy and all was well, and Rhiannon's own emotions had been a disastrous wreckage, like a ship lost to the depths of the sea. She had been content to allow Mater to make the decision for her. What had it mattered anyway? It wasn't as if Aubrey were going to come to his senses and ask her to marry him. He'd had time aplenty.

Now, however, she was beginning to regret her acquiescence.

"You told him that I was ill with a lung infection," she pointed out.

"To preserve your reputation," Mater hastened to say. "Only think of how ruinous it would have been for you if word had begun to spread through London that Lady Rhiannon Northwick was running wild about England on her own. I daresay the earl would not have wanted to wed you after all."

Rhiannon didn't think such an outcome would have been a shame at all. "There is something I wish to discuss with you, Mater."

Her mother frowned. "Does it concern the earl?"

"Yes. I fear that I cannot marry him."

Mater looked aghast at her pronouncement. "Of course you can. My dear, my hopes are high for you, what with Whitby suddenly professing to be in love with that dreadful woman who is divorced from Lord Ammondale and intending to marry her himself."

It was true that Rhys had fallen in love. It had happened for him during the house party. While Rhiannon had been falling deeper under Richford's spell, her brother had been finding love of his own. But unlike Rhiannon, Rhys had found a love that was mutual, true, and ran deep. She had never seen her brother so happy. It was all quite new; he had only just declared himself to Lady Miranda, the former Countess of Ammondale, and she had accepted his proposal, but Rhiannon couldn't be more pleased for her brother. He deserved love and happiness.

"Mater," she warned her mother gently, "you must watch

how you speak about Rhys's future bride. I don't think he would approve."

Her mother made an irritated sound, puffing herself up like a hen who needed to fluff her feathers. "I do wish he would find someone appropriate. Someone suited to him. Someone who would make him a lovely duchess. There are so many debutantes who would make an excellent Duchess of Whitby."

"I don't think any machinations on your part will be well-received. His mind seems firmly made."

Mater sighed. "No, I suppose not. He is a strong-headed, strong-willed man. But you see, dear girl, you are my only hope. Just think of what beautiful children you shall have with Lord Carnis. He is so very handsome."

It was true that the earl was attractive. There had even been a time when Rhiannon had thought about having children with him. But that had been before, when her love for Aubrey had been from afar. There was no denying that everything had changed for her.

The notion of marrying at all left her feeling vaguely ill now. She couldn't do it. She couldn't stand at the altar with the Earl of Carnis and consent to love him and be his wife. Not after what she had shared with Aubrey, and not even if it had all been a lie.

"I don't think I wish for children now," she said.

"You will change your mind."

"No," she said more firmly. "I do not believe I will."

"Think upon it, my dear. There is no need to make up your mind today." Mater rose. "I think I shall return to my ferns."

Rhiannon watched her mother take her leave before turning back to the book in her lap. It was yet open to the poem about Tithonus that Richford had quoted from to her.

Let me go: take back thy gift.

Oh, how those words resonated.

She wished Aubrey could take back the time he had given her. For it had only left her more broken than she had ever imagined possible.

∽

"Sweet Christ, Richford, when was the last time you changed your shirt?"

Seated behind the desk in his study, Aubrey glared at the Duke of Kingham from across an open volume of poetry as he loomed over him.

"Go to the devil, King. No one invited you here."

He was still in the country, rusticating as he had been for the last month. And he had no intention of returning to London any time soon. The farther he stayed away from Rhiannon, the better off he was. Indeed, the farther he stayed away from every bloody living and breathing person, the better off he was.

To that end, the servants followed him about like shadows, too afraid to speak to him directly. And no one was meant to pay calls upon him.

Least of all the smug, arrogant friend who was idly examining the contents of his writing desk now.

King held up a used fork and sniffed the end, making a moue of distaste. "Gads, is that a fish bone down there amongst your correspondence? You're a complete beast, Richford. And if you must know, I invited myself, because you've been acting damned odd ever since the house party. Someone has to watch over you, poor stinking puppy that you are."

He glared at his friend, wishing the study would hold still. It wasn't that he was deeply in his cups. But his bottle of gin was half empty again. Eh, mayhap he was a *trifle* disguised.

He cleared his throat. "I am neither stinking, nor do I resemble a puppy in the slightest. Who appointed you my father?"

"No one, but alas, you haven't many options when it comes to friends who hold you in great esteem and are also free to look after your sorry arse. Riverdale is involved in some manner of contretemps over a woman, Brandon and Camden are happily in love, and Christ knows what Whitby is about these days. Sniffing the skirts of cookery school owners, apparently. I heard something concerning him begging her to marry him or similar rot."

"Good for them. I'm busy, as you can see." He held up the volume for his friend's examination. "You have leave to carry on with whatever it is you were doing before you ventured here. I will just return to my poetry."

"Whatever it is I was doing," King repeated, tsking. "You say this as if I haven't dozens of important tasks to keep me occupied. Tasks that don't involve spending my time calling on a friend who has turned into a stinking drunkard over the past month."

"You have important tasks? What are they? Buying a new waistcoat? Haranguing some poor chap over the cut of his trousers?"

King's eyes narrowed. "You're being an arse, Richford."

"I *am* an arse."

Sweet God, he was worse than an arse. He was the devil incarnate. It didn't matter if what he had done had been for Rhiannon's sake. Her stricken face would haunt him until the day he finally met his grim reward.

"An arse who appears to have been wearing the same shirt for at least the last two days. I'm reasonably certain I spy the remnants of more than one meal marring it, and you smell like an animal suited to the barn rather than a duke to the manor house born."

Nettled, Aubrey glanced down at his shirt, sure he was about to prove his friend wrong. However, there were stains. Several of them, in fact, indeterminate spatters that could have indeed been from more than one meal. He might have known if he could recall precisely what and when he had last eaten, but as it happened, he couldn't. He brushed at the stains, but it wasn't any use. They were quite set in.

"It's only one stain," he lied before performing a discreet sniff of the air. "And I don't smell like an animal better suited to the barn, curse you. That's a scurrilous accusation. How do you know it's not the salmon bones you're smelling instead of my person?"

"Bloody hell. There are *more* bones than just the one?"

Aubrey peered down at the myriad objects scattered over the surface of his writing desk. "There could be a fucking chicken roaming around in here for all I'd know."

King shuddered. "Ye gods, man. I've never seen you like this. First, haven't you any damned chambermaids? Who is meant to be cleaning this filth?"

"Of course I have chambermaids."

"Then they ought to be sacked and replaced," King groused.

"But I don't allow them in here," Aubrey explained.

"Then they ought to enter when you are elsewhere," his friend said as if he were explaining a simple fact to a small child.

Aubrey wanted more gin. Where was the damned bottle? For some bloody reason, he was thinking about the scent of jasmine now and how Rhiannon's hair had glistened, unfurled on his pillow in the lamplight and the way she had spoken with such fervent certainty of Eos and Tithonus and their ill-fated match.

"Did you hear me?" King wanted to know.

"Of course I heard you, but I am ignoring you." He scattered a pile of books in the corner of his desk, sending one tumbling to the floor.

"You need to allow the chambermaids to clean up, or you'll have rats in here soon," King said with great disgust.

"I am thirty years old, King. I am aware of the inner workings of the domestics. But the trouble is that I don't want to leave my study. I am comfortable here, you see. Mrs. Brumley tried, believe me, and on no fewer than four separate occasions, to have one of the maids come in and tidy up my mess, but they annoy me and then I begin to bellow, and it all goes to hell. I've sent three of them away in tears."

"And the fourth?"

"I don't recall. Perhaps I made all four weep. Hmm. It would certainly be fitting if I had." Aubrey shuffled through some correspondence, then tipped over an inkwell. "Fuck. That is going to quite ruin the rosewood unless someone mops it up. Have you seen my gin?"

"Oh, you mean this little thing?" King held up his bottle.

"Yes, that." Aubrey reached for it across the desk, sending a stack of plates to the floor in the process. "Give it to me, curse you."

"It's half past ten in the morning, Richford."

"Then why the Christ are you at my house? Shouldn't you be sleeping off the aftereffects of one of your potions?"

King tossed the gin bottle across the room, where it landed in the hearth with a dramatic crash. "I should be, yes. But presently, I'm concerning myself with a drunken fool who is apparently sleeping and living in his own rubbish."

"I'm not sleeping here," he said, aghast. "I go to bed for slumber."

"Then why have the servants not cleaned the fish bones and dirty plates from your desk?"

"Because I only go to sleep when I'm tired. Half past three or later. When I'm so tired I can scarcely make it up the stairs before I pass out. The maids are all abed. Then I wake before them."

This explanation sounded perfectly reasonable to Aubrey. He was in a hell of his own making. He was miserable. He had broken Rhiannon's sweet, good, innocent heart, and he deserved to be cast into the fiery bowels of Hades for his sins. He would never forgive himself.

"If you continue on this way, it shall be the death of you," King warned grimly.

Yes, and he sure as bloody hell hoped so.

Aubrey didn't answer that, just held his friend's gaze. "Will you go and fetch me another bottle of gin?"

"No."

"Brandy will suffice, if I've gone through all the gin," he said conversationally.

"You don't need any more poison. Good God, Richford." King rummaged through the mess on his desk and produced a pile of fish bones on a plate, coughing as he did so. "I'll just be removing this before we resume speaking."

"No need to resume," he called after his friend.

But King ignored him, returning momentarily without the plate. Even Aubrey had to admit the smell of his study had vastly improved in the absence of the bones.

"I thought I sent you for gin," he grumbled as his friend seated himself at last.

"As I'm not your servant and I need not heed your whims, I ignored you," King returned, grinning brightly.

The bastard. Aubrey pinned him with a glare.

"Are you going to tell me why you've *actually* paid a call on me here? I can count on one hand the number of times you've visited Villiers House."

"Since you've finished rummaging about for your gin like a pig rooting in the mud, I shall tell you."

"I'm beginning to think I don't like you very much, old chum," he said, tapping his fingers on the edge of his desk.

"You will like me even less when I bring you the news."

"I don't give a damn about what is happening in the world."

"I think you will care about this."

Aubrey sighed. "Well, do cease being so bloody mysterious. Impart your news and be done with it."

"Lady Rhiannon Northwick is marrying the Earl of Carnis," King announced, his expression unreadable. "It is being said that the wedding will be held soon. Whitby has announced his intentions to marry the former Countess of Ammondale, and it sounds as if the duchess wishes to see her daughter settled before Whit makes a scandalous match."

Everything within Aubrey seized.

He didn't know why. This was what he expected to happen. What he had known would happen. Granting Rhiannon the marriage she deserved was the reason he had severed ties with her and left her free of him. She would make an excellent countess. She deserved contentedness and a life he could not offer her.

And yet...

And *yet*.

Feeling raw and exposed, he struggled to keep his wildly vacillating reaction from his face.

"Why do you imagine I would care about something so trifling?" he asked King hoarsely.

King's expression gentled, losing some of its customary hauteur and severity. "I know that Lady Rhiannon was at the house party at Wingfield Hall, and I know you were with her."

Shock rendered him silent for a moment. King knew? But that was impossible. No one knew. No one except himself,

Rhiannon, the servants, and Perdita. But he had been certain that Perdita hadn't recognized Rhiannon...

He grappled with what his friend had just revealed, knowing he could deny it or hold his tongue. Or he could concede the truth.

"How?" he asked instead.

King shrugged. "I have my ways. And no, I haven't told Whitby you defiled his sister."

The breath hissed from his lungs. He wanted to deny that he had dishonored Rhiannon, but that wasn't true. He had. He had taken her innocence. And he would do so again if given the chance. Because that was how black his soul was. What a selfish bastard.

"Are you going to tell him?" Aubrey asked at last.

"No," King said simply. "Because *you* are going to tell Whit what you've done."

"It will end our friendship."

"You should have thought of that before you touched her. But you *did* touch her, and what's more, unless I miss my guess, you have feelings for her."

"I don't have feelings for her," he denied harshly, longing to break something.

To send the contents of his desk flying to the floor. He wanted to destroy.

He didn't have feelings for anyone. Love was a fiction. A dangerous delusion.

"She ought to marry Carnis," he said, the words poisonous and bitter.

He didn't mean them. Rhiannon marrying the earl had been indistinct in his mind, some future occurrence he hadn't had to face because he had been in a self-induced gin stupor for the last month. But now King had come with recriminations and the truth, making him face what would happen if he continued to rot away in the country, drinking himself into oblivion and trying his damnedest to forget Rhiannon.

She was going to become another man's wife.

Rhiannon was marrying Carnis.

He ought to be relieved.

That was what he wanted for her, was it not? He couldn't marry her himself.

She would take the earl's name. Lie in his bed. Give him children. Love him.

Aubrey couldn't bear it. He was too bloody selfish.

"Is that what you truly want?" King asked. "You want Lady Rhiannon to wed Carnis?"

"Of course it's not," he admitted, slamming his fist down on the desk and sending papers and cutlery raining to the Axminster. "You already know it isn't, or you wouldn't have come to me with the news."

"If you want to marry her yourself, then why are you hiding in the countryside, swilling gin and living in filth?"

"Because I didn't want to hurt her," he blurted, the deepest, darkest parts of him unleashed. "Because I held my mother in my arms as she lay there covered in blood after my devil of a father stabbed her to death, all in the name of love."

"Your father went mad," King told him quietly.

There it was, the terrible truth. The last Duke of Richford had murdered his duchess. He had been so caught in the maelstrom of his own jealousy that he had believed she had taken a lover. His father had stabbed his mother to death and then shot himself in his study.

All in the name of supposed love.

"I know he went mad," Aubrey allowed hoarsely. "But who is to say that I wouldn't suffer the same fate? That is why I stayed away from her, why I resisted her for so long, until…"

"Until the house party," King finished for him. "Richford,

you're not your father. Indeed, I am persuaded you're nothing like him. What happened was horrific, but you cannot let it keep you from living."

"I was living well enough until her," he pointed out wryly.

"Were you?"

Yes, he was. Everything had been perfectly fine until…

"Were you happy?" King pressed.

He had been happy. With Rhiannon. She was stubborn and maddening and wild. Messy and chaotic and the sunshine to his rain. Beautiful and intelligent and so passionate.

Perfect for him. That was what she was.

And his. That, too. He couldn't let her marry the Earl of Carnis.

She had to marry *him*, damn it.

"Fucking hell," he swore, passing a hand over his face.

"You need to go to London posthaste," King pointed out.

"Yes," he agreed.

"But first, you need a bath, a decent meal, and a change of wardrobe," his friend added with a pointed look of disgust aimed at his shirt. "You can't go to her stinking like a barn, splattered in Salmon a la Chambord, and half soused."

"No need to spare my feelings," Aubrey grumbled.

King grinned. "That's what friends are for."

CHAPTER 18

Rhiannon led the Earl of Carnis into the gardens, gathering her courage for the difficult conversation that was to come.

"It is a lovely day," she said awkwardly as they crunched along the gravel path together.

In truth, it was desperately dreary, but she didn't have an inkling of how to tell this man that she no longer had any intention of marrying him. If only he knew how wretchedly she had betrayed him, he would not look at her with such tender regard as he was now.

"It looks like rain," the earl pointed out.

So it did. She sighed and continued on with him, staring grimly ahead, trying to find the ideal part of the conversation in which she could throw him over.

"You are quiet this afternoon," he observed. "Is something on your mind, my dear?"

She glanced back at him. Reginald was a handsome man. He was tall, if not as tall as Aubrey, and as a skilled horseman, he was in excellent shape. His hair was dark and thick, his eyes were a pale shade of blue, and he was an honorable gentleman.

Yet when she looked at him, she felt nothing.

When he spoke, heat didn't unfurl in her belly, and when she placed her hand in the crook of his elbow, she didn't feel as if she might catch fire. She could scarcely imagine him kissing her on the lips, let alone placing his mouth in places far more scandalous—and pleasurable.

"There is something that has been concerning me, yes," she said at last, wishing she felt something for him.

Wishing she had fallen in love with him. Reginald wouldn't have broken her heart. Reginald wouldn't have walked away from her. He would have loved her in return, this she knew. But perhaps something was inherently wrong with her, because she had ruined everything she had with the earl for a handful of days with a man who was incapable of love. For an illusion that didn't even truly exist.

"Perhaps we should sit," Reginald suggested, gesturing to a nearby bench.

"Yes, perhaps we should," she agreed.

They strolled to the bench and seated themselves upon it, the damp air of the day making her shiver.

"Are you chilled?" he asked solicitously.

She pulled her wrap more tightly about herself, his concern heightening her guilt. "I am well."

"You could take my coat," he offered.

What a wretch she was. Any woman in her place would have been overjoyed to be the future Countess of Carnis. Just not her.

"No," Rhiannon said hastily. "That won't be necessary. Reginald, the thing that I wish to speak about is…" Her words trailed away as she lost her nerve and then regained it, holding his gaze unflinchingly as she spoke again. "I am in love with another man, and I am very sorry, but I don't think I can marry you after all."

"I suspected as much," he said.

She could not have been more shocked if he had sprung up and danced before her.

"You did?"

He gave her a thin smile. "Lady Heathcote paid me a call."

She recognized the name at once, recalling the beauty with the bountiful curves who had been throwing herself at Aubrey every chance she'd managed at Wingfield Hall, the one who had been in his lap that horrid day at Villiers House. But why in heaven's name would the woman pay a call upon Reginald?

"Lady Heathcote?" she repeated, confusion giving way to misgiving as she considered why indeed.

Reginald cleared his throat. "I gather that the viscountess was a…fellow guest at a house party at which you were also a guest."

She inhaled, shocked. "I…I don't know what you're speaking of."

"Don't lie to me, if you please." He took her hand in his, holding it in a firm grip as he gazed into her eyes. "I may be an exceedingly proper man—too proper by the measure of some, perhaps—but I am not a stupid man. Lady Heathcote was adamant that you were in attendance. She said that she saw you unmasked with the Duke of Richford. The two of you were riding bicycles."

Shock swept over her. Instinctively, she drew the hand that he wasn't holding over her mouth. Dear heavens, Lady Heathcote must have been spying on them. It had been plain that she had wanted Aubrey for herself. She could have him now. He had made it equally clear that he no longer wanted Rhiannon.

Lady Heathcote's words returned to her, stinging and

vicious. *Can you not see Richford wants a woman and not a mere girl?*

"Lady Heathcote was concerned that you had perhaps acted with impropriety with the duke, given the nature of the house party and the fact that the two of you were often alone together," Reginald continued, his expression dour.

"Please, you need not say more," she begged. "Now you must see why I cannot marry you."

"Has Richford offered for your hand?" Reginald pressed, unsmiling.

She barked out a bitter laugh. "Of course not."

"I would like you to know that my offer still stands."

"How can it? I have just told you that I love another, and you have admitted to me that you are aware that I have been…improper with him." The words were difficult for her to say.

But she had to say them.

Her brother had often scolded her for being wayward and headstrong, for never considering the consequences of her actions. Well, she was considering them now. She had no other choice but to do so.

"I would be lying if I said that I wish you had not placed yourself in such a position," Reginald told her solemnly. "And I count myself to be many things, but a liar is not among them. The blame for this, I place solely upon your mother. It has been more than apparent to me that she has allowed you to run wild. I can assure you that as your husband, I will be a model for you. I will be more than happy to give you the guidance you require."

She stiffened. "I am not sure that I require guidance. I am a grown woman."

"A grown woman who has made terrible errors in judgment," Reginald pointed out. "Errors which could prove ruinous in the eyes of society."

As he said the last, his grip on her hand tightened incrementally.

A new kind of astonishment took over her. "What are you saying, my lord?"

"I am saying that you need a husband, and I am willing to be that man. To be candid, I sincerely doubt any other will have you, knowing what I do about how you have lowered yourself."

"Lowered myself," she repeated, tugging at her hand. "I do not like the tone this conversation is taking, my lord. Perhaps it is best for you to go. I am sorry, but I cannot marry you."

"Of course you can." His taut smile returned, and for the first time, she saw the hardness and the flinty determination behind it. "Someone needs to take you firmly in hand, and I am pleased to do so. I cannot say I hold you in the same esteem I once did, given your unsavory confirmation of Lady Heathcote's scurrilous gossip. However, I am being more than magnanimous in willing to accept a soiled bride, perhaps one who will even bring another man's bastard to the union."

She gaped at him. Had the earl gone completely and utterly mad?

"I have already given you my answer," she said more firmly, again tugging on her hand to no avail.

"There is only one answer, Lady Rhiannon," he told her, his voice low and seething. "The answer is that you will marry me. If you refuse, I will have no choice but to make my knowledge of your lack of honor fodder for common gossip."

Had she thought Reginald meek and mild-mannered? If so, she had been as wrong about him as she had been about Richford. The Earl of Carnis was furious that she had forsaken him for another man. That much, she could see.

She reeled. "Are you saying that if I don't marry you, you will ruin me?"

"My dear, you have ruined yourself. I am the one who will save you. But only with you as my wife. If you disagree, my sole recourse is to make certain that you are no longer welcome in polite society. Before I am finished, not even your brother will be allowed to know you."

"Whitby would never disavow me," she protested, horrified by the very notion.

"Wouldn't he? I beg to differ. He is marrying a divorced woman. The scandal is already tremendous. Only think of how terrible it shall be for him and his new bride when word spreads that his sister has whored herself for his friend." Reginald paused. "Whitby has no inkling any of this has occurred, has he? You were beneath his nose for the entirety of that filthy house party, and he never knew it. How guilty he will feel. But naturally, he shall have to put his wife first. Perhaps he might send you to the Continent. Or banish you to the country. Certainly, he can never know you again."

Her mind could scarcely grapple with the reality before her. Boring, kind, handsome Reginald was blackmailing her into marrying him. Using the threat of her own ruin and banishment to force her into becoming his wife. Her urgent, instant reaction was to slap him and tell him no.

But the reality of everything his warning entailed terrified her. She knew that her brother would do everything in his power to keep her from being banished from polite society. In the end, however, the choice wouldn't be his. And he was newly content, having won Lady Miranda's hand and love. Rhiannon had no wish to jeopardize their future or their happiness. To say nothing of what would happen if Rhys were to discover that Richford had taken her virginity.

No, she couldn't do that to Rhys. Learning that she had given herself to Richford would destroy him.

She swallowed hard against the bile rising in her throat.

"Very well, Lord Carnis. I will marry you if that is what you require."

He gave her a cunning smile as he lifted her hand to his lips. "That is indeed what I require. It is, at the very least, what is owed to me. We will marry as soon as possible, given that I don't wish for there to be any question should there be issue from our union. I will inform your brother of the happy news about our imminent wedding."

"Please do," she bit out. "I think I shall remain here for a few minutes more and take in the air if you don't mind."

"Of course." He rose and bowed before her.

Rhiannon had scarcely waited until his footfalls faded into the distance before she sank to her knees and retched into a rosebush.

~

As the carriage swayed through the crush of vehicles outside the Duke of Riverdale's town house, Rhiannon pressed a hand over her churning stomach. The starting, then stopping, and then beginning again was making the threat of casting up the meager toast and tea she had consumed earlier that afternoon more acute by the moment.

"You're rather pale this evening," Mater observed shrewdly, peering at her through the low light of the carriage lamps.

"I wish we would arrive at the ball," she said. "I grow weary of being trapped within the confines of this carriage."

"As do I," Rhys ventured, tugging at his necktie and scowling. "I loathe balls. I wouldn't even be attending if it weren't Riverdale hosting."

"It is most unexpected, His Grace's sudden announcement concerning his duchess," Mater added, a note of disapproval in her voice. "What do you make of such an unusual development, Whitby?"

"I was equally surprised to learn Riverdale was secretly married," Rhys said mildly.

Rhiannon squirmed on the Moroccan leather squabs, not liking the subject veering dangerously close to her brother's circle of friends. It was painful enough that she must attend Riverdale's ball. At least she didn't need to fear that Aubrey would be in attendance. When she had made indirect inquiries of her brother related to the ball, she had learned that Aubrey was apparently ensconced in the countryside at Villiers House.

Her relief at knowing she wouldn't have to face him had been palpable. And not just because she wasn't certain how her broken heart and eviscerated pride would weather such a storm. But for another reason as well.

For the last few days, she had begun feeling unwell at unusual times, sometimes even retching. At first, she had told herself the reason was her upset over Carnis forcing her into an unwanted marriage. But now, she wasn't so certain.

It added to her ever-growing suspicion.

Every day, she waited for her courses to arrive.

And each day came and went without them.

Rhiannon was unfailingly punctual in such matters, and she was late. With each new day, a pressing fear crept over her. Richford had been careful. He had not spent his seed inside her. At least, not entirely. Or so she had thought.

What if he hadn't been careful enough? What if she was carrying his child? How could she tell her brother? And even worse, how could she marry Carnis if she was indeed carrying Aubrey's babe?

To her shame, each time the thought arose, along with the fear came the tiniest surge of hope. To have a part of him, to bear his daughter or son, would fill the cracks and voids he had left in her shattered heart.

"I suppose I must count my small mercies," Mater was saying. "If you must wed Lady Miranda, at least you haven't kept it a secret from me. Imagine Riverdale's poor mother. I can only think she is dreadfully ashamed of her son."

"We have been over this, Mater," Rhys said, a note of steel entering his voice. "I must wed Lady Miranda because I am in love with her, and I am hopelessly lost without her. It's a miracle she will have me, sinner that I am."

Mater said nothing, her lips pinched tightly together. She disapproved of Rhys marrying a divorced woman. But where she argued against scandal, Rhys courted it. His love for the woman he intended to marry was admirable. Rhiannon couldn't help but to envy her future sister-in-law, whom she had yet to meet.

Oh, to be loved as deeply as Rhys loved Lady Miranda.

Or to be cared for at all.

Tears pricked her eyes and she blinked furiously, determined not to allow them to fall. She had wept far too many times over the Duke of Richford.

"I will be happy to welcome Lady Miranda as my sister," Rhiannon told Rhys firmly, trying to distract herself.

She meant the sentiment, of course, even if she had begun to worry that the woman she had encountered at the house party—the mysterious black-haired beauty she had presumed to be her brother's mistress—and Lady Miranda were the same. If so, it was entirely likely that Lady Miranda would recognize her. Rhiannon could only hope that her future new sister-in-law would keep her secret.

Just as she hoped Lady Heathcote would, despite her vindictive call upon Lord Carnis. Fortunately, Lady Heathcote was not invited to Riverdale's ball either. Rhiannon had made discreet inquiries and had been relieved to learn her nemesis would not be in attendance.

The evening promised to be a smooth one. Just as long as Rhiannon could maintain her composure and keep from either weeping or casting up her accounts, she thought miserably.

"Thank you, sister," Rhys said. "You've been a boon to me."

She had been there to urge her brother to follow his heart with Lady Miranda. Because her brother was beloved to her, and because she wanted him to find the contentment in life that he deserved.

She had to look away from the earnest gratitude in his eyes now, however, for she was keeping a secret from him, and upholding the falsehood was more difficult by the day. Particularly with Carnis forcing her hand and the realization that she was likely carrying Richford's child.

She swallowed hard against a rush of emotion. "You need not thank me, brother. I only want what is best for you."

"As do I," Mater added, sounding a bit indignant.

"Of course, Mater," Rhys added, not just a bit of sarcasm edging his voice.

Their relationship with their mother was a complicated one. With Rhys's impending marriage and Rhiannon's as well, time would tell if they would be able to build on the tentative progress they had made in the last few weeks. Rhiannon could only hope that her own union to Carnis didn't prove a misery, but she supposed that at least she had her mother's approval.

It was grim comfort.

The carriage at last swayed to a final halt.

"We have arrived," Rhys announced.

Rhiannon took a deep breath. This was her first foray

back into polite society since the house party. She prayed that no one would recognize her.

～

"Cease looking at me like that," Aubrey grumbled at King.

"Looking at you like what?" his friend asked, raising a brow. "Looking at you as if I am both thrilled and relieved that you have bathed and no longer carry the scent of last week's fish course? Or as if I am disappointed in the cut of your coat?"

Aubrey resisted the urge to tug at his sleeves. "What is wrong with this coat?"

"The cut is wrong when paired with that waistcoat," King decreed, ever the arbiter of fashion.

"The cut is perfectly fine," he argued. "Did you know Riverdale had a bloody duchess he was keeping a secret from us all?"

"Do keep your voice from traveling," King drawled, brushing a speck of lint from his own immaculate sleeve. "Of course I did."

"How do you know everything?" Aubrey couldn't help asking, equal parts amazed and nettled.

King gave him a serene smile. "As I've said, I have my ways."

"I hope you and your bloody *ways* are correct and that Lady Rhiannon will indeed be in attendance this evening," he grumbled, feeling as if his white necktie were choking him and just narrowly resisting the urge to tug at it.

Before King could respond, Whit, Rhiannon, and their mother were announced.

His friend was no doubt giving him a smug look, but Aubrey didn't bother sending so much as a glance in King's direction. He was looking at Rhiannon. She was pale, he thought, though elegant and beautiful as ever. Her fair hair was plaited in a Grecian braid and secured at her crown, a few curls spilling free. Her gown was fashioned of gold silk with a leaf pattern, and she resembled nothing so much as the goddess of dawn, bold and glorious.

She was so bloody beautiful, and seeing her again was like taking a fist to the gut. He thought he'd been prepared, but he wasn't. He didn't deserve this woman, but he intended to make her his anyway. Because King hadn't been wrong.

Aubrey was in love with Lady Rhiannon Northwick.

He loved her, and that knowledge was terrifying. Without the haze of the gin clouding his mind, he had been granted the clarity he'd done his utmost to avoid. He should have damned well realized it that morning at the cottage before he'd left her like a coward, but he'd been too foolish to realize. He had believed she would be better off without him in her life.

He still didn't know what he could offer her aside from his hand in marriage. The past remained as it was. He couldn't change what had come to pass. He was the son of a madman. His father had murdered his mother and left Aubrey to find her body. He'd been sixteen, and he had done everything in his power to protect his mother's memory and to keep the salacious whispers of what had happened out of the gossip's mouths.

Fourteen years later, he was no better equipped to handle the wretched violence of that day than he had been then. But King had been right. Aubrey wasn't like his father. He would never harm Rhiannon.

No, all he had done was break her heart.

And now, he had to do everything in his power to mend it.

"Godspeed, old chum," King told him quietly.

Aubrey nodded, eyes on Rhiannon. "Thank you."

CHAPTER 19

He was here.

Rhiannon had felt his presence before she had even looked across the crowded ballroom and found him watching her. The clash of his emerald gaze with hers was electric. Her heart stumbled. Her stomach upended.

Shock washed over her like a cold rain.

She almost tripped on her gown, but somehow, she managed to hold her head high and paste a serene smile to her lips as if she hadn't a care in the world more pressing than who would fill her dance card. As if the man she loved, the man who had left her without a word and betrayed her with another woman, was not staring at her through the sea of guests.

Aubrey.

She had thought he was in the country where she had left him. She had hoped she would never have to set eyes on him again. But that hope, like the belief that he would return her love, was dashed.

How was she to see him and not run to him? How was

she to pretend as if he were a mere acquaintance, when she had been in his bed, in his arms, when she knew his body as intimately as she knew her own? When she could be carrying his babe?

Her breathing was coming fast, and a slick sheen of perspiration trickled down her spine. The heat of the blazing chandeliers and the bevy of revelers was too much. *He* was too much.

Mumbling something to her mother and brother, Rhiannon hastened away, slipping along the edges of the crowd in search of a place where she might take some air. Hide from prying eyes. Where she could spend the rest of the night until enough time had passed so that she could politely take her leave.

Somehow, she found her way to a terrace and slipped onto it, walking to the walled edge and taking in gasps of cooler night air. She didn't have long for her respite, however.

"Rhiannon."

His voice was a low caress.

She stiffened, eyes closing as she summoned her strength before spinning to face him. He moved toward her, faultlessly elegant in a dark suit and crisp white tie, his burnished hair falling in rakish waves and his beard longer than before, though still neatly trimmed.

"Your Grace," she forced out, dipping into a formal curtsy.

He was before her, his gaze searching hers. "It is good to see you."

Her smile felt brittle. "I wish that I could say the same for you."

His jaw tightened. "You're angry with me."

She laughed bitterly. "I feel nothing concerning you, sir."

"Is that so?" His hands settled on her waist, drawing her

into him. "I find that difficult to believe, minx, because I feel everything where you are concerned."

"Don't call me that," she snapped, thinking about the last time she'd heard him refer to her thus.

Lady Heathcote had been in his lap.

You will thank me later, minx.

She tried to remove herself from his hold, but he remained firm and determined, keeping her there, the heat of his muscled form burning into her like a taunt.

"Rhiannon, please," he rasped. "I know you're furious with me, and you have every right to be so, but I need to speak with you."

She stared up at him, thinking he sounded sincere. But he was too late. She was being forced into a marriage she didn't want with Carnis. She had spent the last weeks in utter misery. Aubrey had destroyed her.

"Indeed," she forced out stiffly. "I cannot fathom what you would have need to speak with me about. If you will excuse me, I really must be returning to the ball."

At last, she extricated herself, but as she made to move past him on the terrace, he took her arm in a gentle hold, staying her.

"Please, Rhiannon. Don't go just yet."

She hated herself for the reaction her body had to his touch. Everything within her wanted to throw herself into his arms and forget what had happened. But she couldn't do that.

"Why would you not call on me if you wish for an audience?" she demanded.

"Would you have received me?"

"No," she admitted.

"There is your answer." He stared down at her, his countenance determined. "Nor *should* you receive me. I don't deserve your time or your attention."

"Then why are you demanding both now?" she asked, her voice trembling with the force of her emotions.

"Because I cannot lose you."

She shook off his hold. "You've already lost me, Richford."

Without risking a backward glance, she fled from the terrace, biting her lip to keep from bursting into tears.

~

THREE DAYS after the ball Riverdale had held in honor of the wife no one knew he'd had, Aubrey found himself being led to the Duke of Whitby's study. For each of those days, he had attempted an audience with Rhiannon, and on every occasion, he had failed miserably. She had run from him at the ball, and before he'd managed to find her again, she had pled illness and left early. Each time he had called upon her since, he had been told that Lady Rhiannon was not at home.

The time had come for a change of tactics, much as he dreaded it.

Aubrey took a deep breath as he crossed the threshold of his friend's study. This was going to be one of the most difficult interviews he'd ever had in his bloody life.

"Richford," Whit greeted him with a congenial smile. "Come in and have a seat. Would you care for a brandy and soda water? Perhaps something else? Coffee or tea?"

His heart was thudding hard. So hard that he swore his ears were ringing with the sound.

"Nothing," he managed. "Thank you."

"It isn't like you to turn your nose up at a drink." Whit considered him with a curious regard, frowning. "But then, it isn't like you to pay calls upon me in my study at this time of day either. Is it something serious? You've pissed in your bed, have you? No? Perhaps you've been thrown over by your lady of the moment."

Ordinarily, Aubrey would have grinned at his friend's good-natured mockery, but the news he had come to divulge was burning a hole through his conscience. "Unfortunately, the reason for my call is none that you have just mentioned."

Whitby's teasing air faded along with his smile, his expression clouding and growing perplexed. "Sit then, won't you? Do cease hovering."

Aubrey didn't want to sit. He would inevitably have to stand anyway when Whit learned his true reason for visiting him. And he would also have to accept the punch he deserved.

But he sat, obliging his friend, who would no longer be his friend five minutes from now after he learned the sordid truth about what manner of man Aubrey truly was.

He was the sort of man who fucked his friend's innocent sister.

Who took her virginity.

Who pushed her into the waiting arms of another man.

Who deserved a sound pummeling.

"Christ, old chum," Whit said, his frown deepening. "You look like death."

"How bloody apropos," he said. "I feel like it."

Perhaps he should have accepted Whit's offer of brandy. He could have tossed the drink down his throat and numbed at least a hint of the pain.

Whit straightened in his chair, regarding him solemnly. "Why do I have the feeling I'm not going to like what it is that you have to say?"

He held his friend's stare, unflinching. "Because you won't."

"Go on."

Aubrey took a deep breath, then exhaled. "The reason I paid this call on you was to discuss something of great import."

He was about to continue, but a sudden disturbance in the hall distracted him. He would recognize that voice anywhere, even if he was a corpse six feet in the damned ground.

Rhiannon burst through the door, wild and breathless and so beautiful that his chest ached just from drinking her in. Aubrey shot to his feet, longing to go to her, unprepared for the emotions that charged through him. For a moment, her eyes swept to him before she instantly averted her gaze.

He felt her reaction as keenly as if it had been a slap, and he could hardly blame her. He deserved her scorn and her violence both.

"Rhys, I wish to speak to you," she announced, keeping her gaze trained solely on her brother.

Whitby stood, his countenance growing even more confused as his eyes flicked between Aubrey and Rhiannon, until comprehension slowly began to dawn, taking the place of the befuddlement.

"Can it not wait, Rhiannon?" he asked, a new sharpness entering his tone. "As you can see, I'm speaking with Richford."

Still, she refused to so much as spare Aubrey a glance as she held her head high. "I'm afraid that it cannot."

"My lady," Aubrey began, taking care to keep his tone polite, "I was having a conversation with your brother that is private and personal in nature. One that I don't imagine you would like to bear witness to."

Nor to the drubbing which would inevitably follow, he thought grimly.

"Your Grace," she said coldly, granting him a disdainful glance, "you must forgive me, but I do believe a family matter takes precedence over that of an acquaintance."

"What is going on between the two of you?" Whit demanded, suspicion clouding his voice.

Aubrey stared at Rhiannon, waiting to see what her reaction would be.

"Nothing," she said.

He turned back to Whit. "In truth, that is the reason for my call. I humbly beg Lady Rhiannon's hand in marriage."

Rhiannon's gasp could be heard over his pounding heart.

"You humbly beg what?" Whit demanded, sounding furious now. "To marry my sister? *You*? Is this some manner of puerile joke? Surely you must know she's already betrothed to the Earl of Carnis."

"It's not a joke," Aubrey said grimly.

"I beg your pardon?" Rhiannon asked, eyes wide, stare fixed upon him.

"You're not marrying Carnis," he told Rhiannon. "Marry me instead."

"Why should I marry you? You've made yourself quite clear on the matter of marriage."

Their gazes were locked.

"Which one of you would care to tell me just what the bloody hell is going on?" Whit demanded, his voice bearing the lash of a whip.

Aubrey didn't look away from Rhiannon. "Perhaps you ought to ask your sister."

There was hurt in her eyes; he read it there. And he was the cause of it. She shook her head slightly, as if to deny the truth of what had burned hot and bright between them—the passion, the desire, the yearning.

But he wasn't having it.

She wasn't marrying the Earl of Carnis.

She was going to marry him. And damn the consequences.

But she was staring at him, silent accusation in her sky-blue gaze. Saying nothing. As aloof and removed from him as she'd been these last few days.

So Aubrey did what he had to do.

He turned back to Whit. "You should know that I ruined her."

Whit's brows snapped together. "You did what?"

"I ruined her. I took her innocence. And now, I'll marry her. It's the least I can do to answer for my many sins."

His congenial friend was suddenly emanating with rage. "How the devil… Explain, now, curse you."

"Aubrey, no," Rhiannon said faintly.

He glanced in her direction, thinking her pale again. She was clutching her stomach. Good God, was she going to be ill?

"*Aubrey?*" Whit repeated in a snarl. "Rhiannon, you owe me an explanation. Why are you being so damned familiar with Richford?"

She swayed. Aubrey saw the moment they lost her before her eyes rolled back in her head. He started forward and caught her in his arms as she swooned.

∼

Rhiannon regained consciousness to the sound of two grown men bickering like children.

"Get away from her, you despicable swine."

"She's ill, you arse. I'm tending to her."

"Get your beastly paws off her."

"Would you have preferred I allow her to fall to the floor and injure herself, Whit?"

"I'm going to beat you to within an inch of your miserable life."

Her eyes fluttered open at the last, particularly damning threat. She was reclined on a settee, Aubrey hovering over her in a protective pose, as if to keep Rhys from causing her harm, her hand clasped tightly in his as if he feared she would leave him if he released her. Just beyond him, looking angry enough to tear apart the room with his bare hands, stood her brother.

"I deserve a drubbing and worse," Aubrey agreed. "But let's make certain Rhiannon is well first."

"Do not speak of her with such familiarity," Rhys snapped.

"Stop fighting at once," she managed.

Two pairs of eyes swung to her, both concerned, one also filled with fury.

"How are you?" Aubrey asked, brushing a lock of hair from her forehead with his free hand. "What happened? Have you taken ill?"

She wasn't entirely sure herself what had happened. Only that she had been feeling sick to her stomach, and then the room had seemed to tip sideways, and her vision had gone black around the edges.

"I am well enough, I think," she managed.

"Stop touching my sister," Rhys growled, his voice taking on a lethal edge.

"I'm fine," she reassured Aubrey, tugging her hand free of his grasp. "You should go."

He shook his head. "I'm not going until this is over."

"Until what is over?" she asked, frowning up at him. "I cannot marry you. I'm promised to Carnis."

"To the devil with Carnis. You don't love him."

"Aubrey," she protested, not certain of what to say.

She *didn't* love the earl, but he had entrapped her. Then there was the matter of her brother hovering over them. Rhys knew something of what had happened between the two of them, but hardly all of it.

But before she could say more, Rhys tackled Aubrey from behind. The two of them landed in an inglorious heap on the

Axminster, her brother's fists flying as they tussled. With a cry, she rose to a seated position.

"Stop it, Rhys!"

Aubrey wasn't even bothering to defend himself. He was simply allowing her brother to pummel him. Rhys landed a punch to Aubrey's jaw, the thud echoing sickly in the chamber.

"Rhys!" she cried out again.

But her brother was a man possessed, his fists flying.

"Aubrey, do something," she tried.

"I—umph—deserve it," he managed, wincing when Rhys landed a blow to his ribs. "Let him hit me."

Men! What was wrong with them? She rose from her settee, looking frantically about the room for something she could use as a weapon. Her gaze lit on the fire poker, and she rushed for it, deciding it would have to do.

Rhiannon snatched it up, still feeling dizzied but too frantic to care. Someone had to put an end to this nonsense. She wasn't going to primly sit there whilst Rhys thrashed Aubrey to death and Aubrey did nothing to stop him.

Grimly, she raised the fire poker and landed a blow on her brother's right shoulder. He howled with pain and rolled off Aubrey, pinning her with an accusatory look.

"Rhiannon, why the devil would you hit me with the damned fire poker?"

"Because you were going to kill him if I didn't do something to stop you," she explained.

Aubrey sat up, bruises mottling his face, blood dripping down his nose. "I wouldn't have allowed him to kill me, minx."

Rhys snarled. "What did you call her?"

Aubrey calmly extracted a handkerchief from his coat and pressed it to his nose, absorbing the blood. "A term of endearment. The sort of thing one calls a lover."

"How have you been bedding her, you faithless rogue?" Rhys demanded, moving toward Aubrey once more. "How did you get to her?"

Rhiannon held up her poker in warning. "No more attacking him, Rhys," she warned. "I mean it."

Rhys's eyes narrowed on her. "I'm your brother. It is my duty to protect you from scoundrels like him."

"He is your friend," she reminded him.

"He *was* my friend," Rhys grumbled. "Until he ruined my innocent sister."

"I wanted to be ruined!" she shouted, losing her patience. "I didn't travel to Great-Aunt Bitsy as I said I did. I went to Wingfield Hall instead."

She was practically panting, aware of her brother's eyes on her, staring with shock as she waved the fire poker to punctuate her wild declarations. This wasn't how she had envisioned telling Rhys the truth. Heavens, she had been convinced that she would *never* tell him. But he needed to know. Aubrey wasn't solely to blame for what had happened.

"What do you mean, you went to Wingfield Hall?" Rhys asked, his voice hoarse.

"I know about your club. I know about the wicked house parties." Her cheeks went hot, and for a moment, she had to look away to gather her bravado before continuing. "I was curious. I decided to attend. I knew that Mater wouldn't notice me gone until it was too late, if at all. I also knew that Aubrey was going to be there."

"Richford," Rhys snarled.

Rhiannon nodded. "I have had a *tendre* for him for a long time. Mater insisted I accept the earl's suit, and well, I suppose I considered stealing away to the house party my last opportunity to see if I could make Richford fall in love with me."

She could feel Aubrey's questioning gaze on her. So she

continued, keeping her eyes on her brother as she unburdened herself. "But when I arrived, Richford instantly recognized me, despite my mask. He tried repeatedly to persuade me to leave, and I was convinced I had wasted my time until…"

"Dear God." Rhys shook his head. "You needn't say more."

"You see?" she asked her brother. "I seduced him, not the other way 'round. Everything that happened was only what I wanted. Until it wasn't."

"If you hurt her, I'll bloody well end you," Rhys threatened Aubrey.

"I knew he was a rake who didn't believe in love," she continued firmly. "But I naively hoped he might make an exception for me. I was wrong. He broke my heart. That is all. You mustn't be angry with him."

"I will be angry with him if I wish to be. He was my trusted friend, like a brother to me, and he dishonored you beneath my very nose," Rhys spat.

"I am every bit the villain you paint me to be," Aubrey told Rhys solemnly. "But I am also the man who loves your sister."

She swayed on her feet, inhaling sharply, sure she had misheard.

"What?" At last, she allowed herself to look at Aubrey to find him staring at her, his emerald gaze unwavering even as his left eye began swelling shut.

"I love you, Rhiannon," he said softly.

The fire poker fell from her suddenly numb fingers, hitting the Axminster with a dull thump.

"You…you love me?" she repeated. "But you don't believe in love. You told me so."

He shook his head, lowering his handkerchief so she could see his handsome, battered face without obstruction. "I was wrong. I do believe in love. You taught me that. And you taught me something else too, minx."

She pressed a hand over her mouth, unable to speak past the tears welling up inside, clogging her throat.

"You taught me that I would gladly be your grasshopper for eternity, if it meant I could have a glimpse of you every dawn."

"Grasshopper?" Rhys interjected with disgust. "What twaddle is this?"

"You *do* love me," she said with wonder, ignoring her brother.

"I do." He tried to smile, but it turned into more of a wince. "This isn't how I envisioned asking you to be my wife, but, Lady Rhiannon Northwick, will you marry me?"

Aubrey loved her.

He believed in love.

He had come for her.

Joy mingled with disbelief, emerging as a choked sob. "I want nothing more than to be your wife. B-but I told Carnis I would marry him."

"Throw him over," Aubrey said without hesitation.

She swallowed hard. "I'm afraid it won't be as easy as that. Lady Heathcote paid him a call. She recognized me at the house party. She told him about the time you and I spent together. When I told him I couldn't marry him because I was in love with someone else, he demanded that I wed him anyway or he would let my secret be known. I was afraid of the scandal it would make for Rhys and his betrothed, so I agreed."

"Did everyone know you were at bloody Wingfield Hall except for me?" Rhys demanded.

"That bastard," Aubrey swore, his face darkening with anger. "How dare he threaten and manipulate you into marrying him? And Lady Heathcote, too. I will fix this, Rhiannon. I vow to you that I will protect you and right the mistakes I've made. Do you trust me?"

She stared at him, searching his gaze, and found the answers she was looking for. "I do."

"Grant me a few hours, and it will be done," he said, rising to his feet.

Rhys rose as well. "You aren't going alone, Richford. You've made enough of a mess of things."

"No more fighting, the two of you," Rhiannon scolded them, not sure she trusted Rhys and Aubrey together without her just now. "I'll have your promises."

Aubrey nodded. "You have mine. No more fighting. At least, not with Whit."

She turned to her brother, who looked as if he were in great pain. "Very well. I won't hit Richford again." He paused. "Unless he deserves it."

"*Rhys.*"

"Fine," her brother muttered. "I won't hit Richford. But I'm going to fetch Mater to sit with you until we return."

"I'm perfectly well," she protested, realizing she hadn't had a chance to tell Aubrey her suspicion that she was carrying his child yet.

Which was probably wise. She would do so without an irate brother as an audience.

"Your mother will sit with you," Aubrey added sternly, frowning at her. "Perhaps we should call for a physician, Whit. She looks pale."

Her brother nodded. "She rather does."

"*She* can hear you talking about her as if she isn't standing here," Rhiannon pointed out, nettled. "I will sit with Mater if it pleases you until you both return."

"It does," Rhys and Aubrey said in unison.

Her brother glared at Richford. "She's my sister, damn your hide."

"And she'll be my wife," Aubrey pointed out.

"*If* I give you permission to wed her," Rhys countered.

"You'll give it," Aubrey said, sure of himself.

Rhys grumbled something unpleasant beneath his breath. And then the two of them left the study. Rhiannon watched them go, her hopes for the future dependent upon them both.

CHAPTER 20

They found the Earl of Carnis at the Black Souls Club, which proved a godsend because Aubrey was good friends with the club's owner, Elijah Decker. Decker was more than happy to provide a private room for an audience between Carnis, Whitby, and Aubrey.

The three of them closeted themselves behind the privacy of a closed door, Carnis going pale as he took in the state of Aubrey's face.

"Do you see this, Carnis?" Aubrey asked, grinning even though it hurt like the devil to do so. "This is what your face shall look like if you continue trying to force an unwilling woman to wed you."

"See here," Carnis sputtered. "No one is unwilling. Lady Rhiannon and I have had an understanding for months now."

"As I comprehend it, the lady told you she didn't want to marry you any longer," he said softly, allowing menace to lace his voice.

"And you threatened her with scandal and ruin if she failed to do what you wanted," Whit added, cracking his already bruised knuckles.

Carnis swallowed hard. "There was no threat, and neither was there force, I can assure you."

"Again, that's not what Lady Rhiannon said," Aubrey stated calmly. "And do you know who I believe, Carnis?"

"Y-yes. N-no," the earl stammered, clearly understanding that there was no good way for him to answer the question.

"I believe Lady Rhiannon," he said. "I believe that you flew into a jealous rage when you learned Lady Rhiannon was in love with someone else, so you decided to blackmail her into doing your bidding."

"I was doing nothing of the sort," Carnis blustered, drawing himself up.

Whit cracked his knuckles again. "Do you know who did that to Richford's face, Carnis?"

The earl stared.

"It was me," Whit said conversationally. "And Richford here is one of my closest chums. What do you think I intend to do to you?"

"Please. I...I don't want any difficulties," the earl said, eyes wide. "I didn't mean to blackmail her. I...I wouldn't have hurt her. I'm in love with Lady Rhiannon. I just... I wanted her to be my wife."

"That makes two of us, Carnis," Aubrey told the bastard. "But you aren't the one who is going to win this particular battle. I am."

"You can have her," Carnis said, eyes darting wildly about the room as Aubrey and Whit drew nearer. "I won't tell a soul what I know. I swear it."

"Good," Whit said. "Because if you do, I'll thrash you. And then I'll see that you're ruined everywhere. You'll be turned out of this club and every other. I'll haunt you even when you're dead. Do you understand me?"

"And if you do anything to harm Lady Rhiannon's reputation or cause her distress in any way, I'll gut you like a bloody fish," Aubrey concluded. "Understood?"

"Y-yes." Carnis nodded wildly. "Understood."

"Good." Aubrey shot a look toward Whit through the eye that wasn't swelling closed. "I believe we have another call to pay."

◦

PERDITA'S SMILE vanished when she saw both Aubrey's face and that he had brought a companion with him for his impromptu visit.

"Your Graces," she greeted them with forced cheer. "You honor me with your call."

Despite her words, she appeared anything but pleased to see them.

As if remembering herself belatedly, she dipped into a curtsy in her small drawing room, which was laden with *objets d'art* and other bric-a-brac.

Aubrey didn't bother returning a polite bow, and neither did Whit.

He moved toward her with a calm he didn't feel. "It has come to our attention that you have been spreading false tales about Lady Rhiannon," he said, keeping his voice carefully polite and low.

She wetted her lips. "I would never—"

"Enough," he interrupted before she could offer a lie he wouldn't believe and hadn't the patience to hear uttered. "I know that you did so, as does Whitby. In fact, it was your tales that led to Carnis attempting to blackmail Lady Rhiannon into marrying him."

Her eyebrows rose. "I had nothing to do with the earl's decision concerning Lady Rhiannon. I merely thought it fair for him to be apprised of the manner of woman he wanted to make his wife."

"And what manner of woman is that, Lady Heathcote?" Whit asked sharply.

"I...I..." Her gaze went from Whit to Aubrey and then back as a flush crept over her cheeks. "Forgive me. I didn't mean to say something untoward."

"But you did," Aubrey pointed out coldly. "Apologize."

"I'm sorry," she said hastily.

"You will also apologize to Lady Rhiannon, in writing," he added, knowing Rhiannon wouldn't wish to face Perdita again and sparing her the discomfort.

She was owed an apology, however.

"Richford, you cannot come into my home making demands of me," she began.

"Yes, I can," he countered. "Because if you don't do exactly as I say, I'll go to Lord Heathcote with everything I know about you, my lady. Every vice, each lover. I have detailed notes concerning the particular...activities of the members of our club, you see."

"As do I, my lady," Whit added smoothly. "And I won't be afraid to use those details to protect my sister as I must. I'm sure you understand."

"Please, Your Grace," she entreated. "I meant no harm. You cannot go to my husband with what you know. It would be disastrous for me."

"I don't suppose Heathcote is a very forgiving man, is he?" Aubrey asked idly.

"I don't reckon he is," Whit agreed. "It would be a pity to have to sow marital discord, but if I were to learn that tongues were wagging about Lady Rhiannon again, I would have no other choice, I'm afraid."

"Nor would I," Aubrey added. "Especially not since Lady

Rhiannon has done me the great honor of agreeing to become the next Duchess of Richford."

Perdita gasped. "You're marrying her?"

"Yes." Aubrey grinned, his split lip hurting like hell. "I am."

Perdita shook her head. "I promise never to speak another word against Lady Rhiannon."

"See that you don't," Aubrey told her.

~

THE CARRIAGE PROCEEDED ON, the next destination Whit's town house, where Rhiannon awaited their return.

"Do you think Carnis and Lady Heathcote will heed our warnings?" he asked Whit into the awkward silence that had fallen.

"I think they had better, or they will face our wrath," Whit said. "And the outcome will be even uglier than your face."

He winced and then winced again as the action shot pain through him. "Careful. You may wound my poor feelings."

"You're fortunate I didn't kill you." Whit raised a dark brow. "You have a great deal of explaining to do, Richford."

"I am sorry for the way everything happened," he told his friend at last. "But I cannot say I'm sorry that it happened. I love your sister."

"Like a grasshopper or some such rot," Whit muttered.

"It was a conversation we had about Eos and Tithonus," he began.

Whit held up a staying hand. "I don't want to hear about your romance with my sister, if you please. All I want to know is why you didn't bloody well tell me that the hoyden had found her way into Wingfield Hall the moment you realized it."

Why, indeed?

"I was being selfish," he admitted. "I wanted her to stay. If

I'm perfectly honest with myself, I can admit that I have harbored…tender feelings for Rhiannon for some time."

"Christ." Whit wiped a hand over his face as if he'd just been splattered with something dirty.

"Not always," he defended himself. "In the last year or so, I've found her increasingly difficult not to notice. She's wild and bold and…" He allowed his words to trail off, feeling embarrassed heat creep up his throat and make his ears go hot. "Well, I'm sure you see what I mean, given that you've newly fallen in love yourself."

"What happened between the two of you after the house party?" Whit asked, his brow furrowed. "What took so long for you to come to your senses?"

"You know my past," he said quietly. "I was fearful because of what happened. I thought that she would be better off without me, that I couldn't love her as she deserved. Truth be told, I'm still not certain I can love her as she deserves. She's far too bloody good for me. All I can do is promise that I'll love her and protect her with everything in me, as long as I've breath left in my lungs."

Whit stared at him in a tense silence for a few moments, seeming to look straight into the depths of Aubrey's soul. He didn't care. He had nothing left to hide. He stared back, unrelenting.

Finally, his friend gave a jerky nod. "If Rhiannon wishes to have your sorry hide, then I wish both of you happy."

Whit's approval. Relief hit Aubrey in the chest. He could breathe again.

"Thank you, Whit. You won't regret this, I vow it."

His friend gave him a pointed look. "If I do, then I'll be decorating that ugly face of yours again. Only next time, I won't be so gentle."

Aubrey chuckled. "Touché, old chum."

~

Several hours had passed by the time Aubrey returned to Rhiannon in the drawing room of Whit's town house, where she was seated with her mother. The dowager Duchess of Whitby gazed at him with obvious alarm from behind her gold-rimmed spectacles as he and Whit crossed the threshold.

"Your Grace, what has happened?"

"The settling of a score," he said wryly, casting a glance in his friend's direction.

The blows he had received had been earned, and Aubrey knew it. Moreover, Whit's reaction was no less than what his own would have been had he a sister and Whit had seduced her. What Aubrey had done was wrong. He ought to have asked for Rhiannon's hand from the moment he had pulled her from naughty charades. He should have carried her away to Villiers House, and they could have eloped and avoided all this blasted strife.

But he hadn't carried her away, and neither had they eloped. Instead, their path to love had been long and winding and fraught with miscommunication and his own obstinacy and idiocy.

"What manner of score?" the dowager wanted to know, sounding scandalized as she glanced from Rhiannon to her son. "I had no notion Richford was such a ruffian."

Aubrey chuckled and then grimaced when pain radiated from his split lip. It amused him that having a thoroughly beaten face would render *him* the ruffian, but he was in no condition to argue. He was about to have the most important conversation of his life.

Preferably without an audience.

"Your son is the ruffian," Rhiannon said, pinning Whit

with a scolding glare. "He attacked Richford and is the source of all his injuries."

"Not without provocation," Whit pointed out. "It's hardly my fault he refused to defend himself."

"My actions were indefensible," Aubrey said grimly, hoping not to have to repeat his transgressions before the dowager.

Once had been quite enough.

Now, all he wanted was some time alone with Rhiannon. Supposing he could persuade Whit and the dowager to grant him that.

"I shan't argue with you on that count," Whit said.

The dowager was still frowning at Aubrey. "I do hope your face will clear up before the wedding. It wouldn't do for my Rhiannon to have a groom who looked better suited to prizefighting than being an honorable gentleman."

He glanced at Rhiannon, warmth stealing into his heart, and this time, he allowed it. He didn't force it away or try to tamp it down. He didn't tell himself that feeling was mere lust. He knew what it was.

Love.

"You've spoken with your mother, then?" he asked her quietly.

She had risen from the settee and came to his side now, the symbolism of her action not lost upon him. "I have. Mater knows that Lord Carnis was trying to force me into marrying him against my will."

"Poorly done of him," the dowager said, shaking her head in disgust. "I never thought the earl to be so ill-mannered. To think that I once had the most enlivening discussion with him concerning taxidermy sparrows."

That certainly explained rather a lot about the fellow, Aubrey thought.

But he kept that to himself, instead turning to Whit. "May I be granted an audience with your sister?"

Whit's eyes narrowed. "I don't know if that is wise, given the circumstances."

"I think it's rather too late to fret over me being ruined," Rhiannon told her brother softly.

Which was hardly pleading the case for them.

"Yes, Richford has already managed that, has he not?" Whit asked pointedly.

He deserved his friend's ire, and he knew it would take time to fully regain Whit's trust. Rhiannon's, too. But he was committed to making amends. To doing better. He would prove himself to them both.

"I intend to rectify the matter at once," he said. "I promise to observe propriety. You have my word as a gentleman that nothing improper will occur."

Rhys was silent for longer than Aubrey liked before looking to the dowager. "Mater, what say you? Shall we allow Richford to propose in privacy?"

"Well, *someone* had better propose to her," the dowager said primly. "I do believe she's increasing."

Stunned, Aubrey looked back at Rhiannon, whose sky-blue eyes met his. She was carrying his child? He had been so careful...

Not the first time, his conscience reminded him.

He had been so carried away that he hadn't completely withdrawn from her with enough haste.

"Rhiannon?" Whit demanded, his voice sharp. "Is this true?"

Still staring at Aubrey, she nodded. "Yes."

A grin of sheer elation broke over Aubrey's face, and he didn't give a damn that it felt as if someone were planting him a facer all over again. Rhiannon was with child. His child. Their child. Perhaps a girl with flaxen hair who ran wild or a boy with dancing blue eyes and a penchant for mischief.

"By God," Whit grumbled. "If the two of you don't set a date for the wedding at once, I'll have no choice but to thrash Richford a second time."

"As soon as possible," Aubrey blurted. "I hope."

"Come, Whitby," the dowager interrupted, rising from her seat and sliding a basket of embroidery onto her arm. "I've been meaning to show you my fern collection."

"Christ," Whit muttered beneath his breath. "Not the bloody ferns."

But he obligingly offered the dowager his arm just the same. She accepted it, and the two began leaving the drawing room.

"I've just acquired the most delightful fern that's native to the Mediterranean, the *asplenium billotii*..."

Whit turned back. "You have one quarter hour."

Aubrey wanted to argue that it wasn't enough, but his friend's warning glare kept him silent as he watched Whit escort the dowager from the drawing room. When they were gone and the door discreetly closed, he turned to Rhiannon at last, opening his arms to her.

She flew into them, and no embrace had ever felt more right.

"You're going to have a babe?" he asked, holding her close, his hands on the small of her back.

"Yes. I think so. I've missed my courses." She paused, biting her lip. "I know it is unexpected. I didn't know what to do."

Realization hit him.

"My God, Rhiannon. You were going to marry Carnis while you carried my child?"

Her brows furrowed. "Everything was happening so quickly. I didn't know what to do, and I had the babe to consider. I didn't want our child to be born in shame, without a name. Can you forgive me?"

"There is nothing to forgive, my love." He shook his head, furious with himself. "It's my fault, everything that happened. I should have asked you to marry me the minute I recognized you at Wingfield Hall. If I had, you never would have found yourself in such desperate circumstances, at the mercy of a vile gossip like Lady Heathcote and being blackmailed into a marriage you didn't want."

At his mentioning of the viscountess, Rhiannon stiffened. He knew why.

"There's something I must tell you," he began, his voice hoarse with emotion. "A few things, actually. Perhaps we should sit. Are you still feeling ill? Did your mother send for the physician?" Belated panic swept over him. "What about the babe?"

This was all new, and it was bloody terrifying.

Rhiannon laid a gentle finger over his lips. "Hush. I'm perfectly healthy, so you can stop worrying. Dizziness and an uneasy stomach are to be expected, according to Mater. She suffered the same when she had Rhys and me."

Relief swept over him, and he kissed her finger. "Good. Excellent. Not that you're feeling ill, and not that you told your mother that you're with child out of wedlock... Christ, little wonder she was glaring at me... But the rest, that it's an ordinary occurrence and no cause for concern..."

He was babbling and he knew it. Rhiannon gazed up at him with sympathy.

"This is all new for me as well," she said.

Bloody hell, this woman. She was stronger than he was. So much braver. She had given herself to him, had loved him, and had expected nothing in return. And all he had given her was heartache and fears over how she would provide for their unborn babe.

"You are far too generous where I'm concerned," he said, taking a deep breath. "What I'm about to tell you may change your opinion of me. If it does, I won't blame you. But I must tell you, just the same."

"Is it about Lady Heathcote? Whatever happened at Villiers House, I don't want to know," she began. "It has no bearing on our future, and—"

"Nothing happened," he interrupted. "That was part of what I wanted to tell you. When I left Wingfield Hall, I was desperate to keep you from me. I knew I had to do something reckless or you would stubbornly forgive me and try to make amends. When you told me you loved me, I was terrified. I didn't believe I was capable of loving you or being the husband you deserved, so I left like a coward. And I took Lady Heathcote with me because I thought that if you believed I had betrayed you with her, you would be too hurt to continue pursuing me. I thought you would be better off."

"Do you mean that the two of you didn't… But I saw you together. She was in your lap." Tears welled in Rhiannon's eyes, and she blinked them away. "I don't want to know, Aubrey."

"I didn't bed her, Rhiannon. I've done a lot of wretched things and made far too many mistakes where you're concerned, but that isn't one of them. She was in my lap, trying to persuade me to join her when you arrived. But I never did, and after you had gone, I sent her on her way. If I had thought, even for a moment, that she would have tried to hurt you, I never would have taken her with me."

"I believe you," she said, shocking him.

Heaven knew he'd done nothing to earn her trust. But he was relieved he had it just the same.

"Thank you."

She nodded. "But why were you so desperate to keep me

from you? Why did you push me away? Help me to understand."

Aubrey swallowed hard and forced himself to relive that horrible day. "When I was sixteen years old, my father went mad and killed my mother in a jealous rage. He thought she had taken a lover. They quarreled, and somehow, he took a knife and, well… As she lay dying, he went to his study, took out a pistol, and shot himself. I was the one who found my mother in her sitting room. She was already gone. I… I heard the report of the pistol."

He could still see his mother, lying there in her silk gown soaked with blood. Could smell the coppery tang in the air, feel his throat closing with horror as he tried helplessly to wake her. But just as swiftly as the past rose up before him, the present was there to anchor him. He forced himself to inhale deeply of Rhiannon's jasmine scent, to absorb her vital warmth and softness, to hold her tightly to him and just be.

The past could not harm him.

Not any longer.

"My God, Aubrey." Tears were running down Rhiannon's cheeks now as she gazed up at him. "I had no idea."

"The servants were paid well to keep what had happened a secret. My grandmother did her best to prevent the truth of my father's sins from becoming fodder for wagging tongues, but there were whispers. And you see, I… I vowed that day that I would never be like my father. I suppose a part of me has been afraid that if I fell in love, I would also go mad and hurt the one closest to me. I couldn't bear that. I thought I was protecting you, keeping you safe from me."

"I am so sorry for what happened to your mother and for the horrors you endured. If I could travel back in time and change it, I would."

His sweet minx, always putting him before herself.

"You were naught but a girl then."

"And you were a boy." Rhiannon dashed at her tears with the back of her hand. "A boy who deserved so much better."

"The past is where it belongs." He cupped her cheek, catching another stray tear on the pad of his thumb. "Neither of us can change it, but we can choose the future. I choose love. I choose you and our child. And I hope you'll choose me as well."

"Of course I choose you," she said. "I'll always choose you. I love you, Aubrey."

He lowered his head, pressing his forehead to hers. "And I love you. I'm so sorry for leaving you that morning. I promise I'll never leave you again."

She rubbed her nose against his. "I won't let you."

His poor beak hurt thanks to Whit's fist, but he didn't say a thing. He would suffer the pain a thousandfold if it meant she was his forever.

"Will you marry me, Lady Rhiannon Northwick, and do me the greatest honor of my life by becoming my wife?" he asked.

She didn't hesitate. "I will."

His lips found hers, and he kissed her tenderly, showing her without words what he felt for her.

When he lifted his head again, his minx was back, tears no longer glistening in her eyes. "What took you so long to come to your senses?"

He thought of the wretched state King had found him in and grimaced anew. "I was in a bad way. Kingham came to me and helped me to see reason. He pulled me back from the edge. It took me a few days to collect myself and come to London."

Rhiannon cradled his swollen cheek. "Oh my love, you're in a bad way now."

His face would heal, just as his heart had.

He turned, pressing a reverent kiss to her soft palm. "On

the contrary. I'm in the best way. Because I have you and our babe."

Rhiannon sniffed, looking misty-eyed again. "I want to kiss you, but I'm afraid I'll hurt your lip."

"Kiss me anyway, my love," he said, framing her beautiful, beloved face in his hands.

She rose on her toes and settled her mouth softly against his.

He kissed her back with all the love that was burning for her deep within his shadowed heart.

EPILOGUE

ONE MONTH LATER

Rhiannon awaited her husband in her new bedroom at Richford House, wearing nothing more than a sinfully revealing night rail she had chosen with Aubrey in mind, her hair unbound and flowing freely down her back. It was the night she had been awaiting for the last arduous month whilst Mater had plotted and planned her wedding with the same devoted joy she showed her ferns, shells, and taxidermy.

The latter had proven rather disconcerting. Rhiannon was still bemused by her mother's attempts to show both herself and her brother at least as much attention as Mater paid her collections. It was heartening, however, as was Mater's effort to get to know Aubrey despite her initial concern over the unusual circumstances that had brought Rhiannon and Aubrey together.

Smiling to herself, Rhiannon cradled the slight swell of her belly. She and Aubrey planned to retire to Villiers House well before her lying-in so that they wouldn't cause any undue gossip when the babe arrived. Mater had offered to accompany them, wishing to dote over her grandbaby. Just as long as she could bring her fern collection with her.

A light tap at the door adjoining her chamber to Aubrey's interrupted Rhiannon's musings then.

"Come," she called, eager to have him all to herself after the bustle of the day. First, there had been the wedding, followed by a wedding breakfast that had gone on for hours until she and Aubrey had finally escaped.

Now, their obligations were at last at an end. There was no one but the two of them.

The door opened, and Aubrey came to her, wearing a dark silk banyan and looking so handsome it was all she could do not to throw herself directly into his arms. His emerald stare traveled over her hungrily, and her nipples went instantly stiff beneath the cool silk of her gown.

"My God, minx," he murmured, his voice awed. "The goddess of dawn cannot hold a candle to you. You are the most beautiful bride I've ever seen."

"Thank you." She smiled at him, love for him bursting in her heart. "You are the most handsome groom as well, to be certain."

He stopped before her, taking her hands in his and bringing them to his lips to press reverent kisses on her knuckles. "If I'm dreaming, please don't wake me."

"It feels a bit like a dream, doesn't it? The last month has been an eternity."

"Three lifetimes," he said easily. "I couldn't wait to have you here with me, where you belong." He released her hands and gently caressed her stomach. "Where you both belong."

Warmth spread through her at his touch.

"I felt the same."

"How is our little bean?" he asked.

"Quite well, I'm sure." It was yet too soon for her to detect any movement of the babe.

"And how are you, my love? You're not feeling ill, are you? If you would prefer it, I can leave you to rest."

She grasped his lapel, holding him to her. "You are not going anywhere, husband."

"As my duchess wishes." He grinned down at her. "Besides, I've seen the damage she can do with a fire poker. I have no wish to be bludgeoned on my wedding night."

His beautiful face had thankfully healed from the day Rhys had pummeled him for ruining her, and in time for their nuptials. She didn't regret hitting her brother with the fire poker either. She would do it again in a moment.

"I'm not nearly as bloodthirsty as my brother," she teased.

"No more talk of Whit just now, if you please," Aubrey returned lightly. "I'd hate to have my cock wilt before I can even make use of it."

Rhiannon laughed. "Fair enough. I have rather a lot of plans for your cock this evening."

He groaned and kissed her. "Wicked darling. This is but one of many reasons why I love you so."

She wrapped her arms around his neck. "What are the other reasons?"

Aubrey grinned down at her. "Your intelligence, your bravado, that stubborn streak of yours, your determination, your kind heart, the way you love me even when I don't deserve it…"

"But you do deserve it," she protested. "You make me so very happy, my love."

"Ah, but I could make you happier, I think," he teased, his lips dancing lightly over hers.

"Mmm," she hummed as his hand found her breast, his thumb rubbing unerringly over the peak. "Perhaps you should show me how."

"With great pleasure. But you're going to have to get naked first, darling."

Feeling wicked, Rhiannon stepped back and grabbed handfuls of silk before pulling her nightgown over her head and tossing it to the floor.

"Already making a mess of your new bedroom, duchess?" he asked with mock severity even as he drew her near, his hands traveling over her bared skin. "I'm afraid I'm going to have to punish you."

Rhiannon found the buttons on his banyan and began working them free of their moorings. She quickly grew impatient and began tearing at them. A few rolled to the Axminster.

"More mess," she said breathlessly. "Perhaps you ought to tie me to the bed."

"Fuck," he growled. "You make me wild for you, woman."

And then he clawed off his banyan the rest of the way before taking her up in his arms and carrying her across the room. He laid her gently on the mattress, his rigid cock a temptation she couldn't resist stroking. He was hot and thick in her hand, a bead of moisture seeping from the slit.

He made a low sound of approval, allowing her to explore him.

But that wasn't sufficient for Rhiannon. They had spent the last month apart, and she was ravenous for him. Her delicate condition had left her in a state of perpetual yearning.

"Lie down on the bed," she urged him, changing her mind about what she wanted.

"Minx," he protested.

She gave him a meaningful look. "Do it."

He growled and did as she commanded, arranging himself on the center of her bed. She moved to him on hands and knees, between his legs.

"You don't need to," he murmured.

"Oh yes," she returned, kissing the tip of his cock. "I do."

Tentatively, she took him into her mouth, the salty taste of him on her tongue.

"Just like that, love," he praised. "Suck me."

His low words spurred an answering ache between her thighs. She was already wet for him, desperate. Tending to him like this only served to heighten her need. She took him deeper, hollowing out her cheeks as she did as he directed, sucking and licking as he moaned beneath her, his hips pumping. She was lost in him, loving everything about this new intimacy, from the sounds he made to the way his body moved restlessly beneath her.

"Harder," he urged, his voice thick with desire. "Take me down your throat if you can."

She did what he asked, taking him deep, as far as she could until tears stung her eyes and she feared she would gag.

"Fuck yes," he groaned. "You look so beautiful, your gorgeous mouth full of my cock."

She moaned and continued, her saliva making her lips and chin wet, his cock glistening in the lamplight as she thoroughly licked and sucked him. It was the most potent aphrodisiac, this powerful man in her mouth. She was giving him pleasure as he had done for her, and she loved it.

But just when she thought she had him at the edge of losing his control, he gently moved her away.

"Enough. I want to spend in your pretty pussy first, and if you carry on, I'll never make it."

"But I wanted you to spend in my mouth," she protested, wondering if such a thing were possible.

He groaned again. "Next time, my darling."

So it was, then. Rhiannon smiled, thinking she would like that very much indeed. How good it was to be married at last. To be free to be with him in every way.

Aubrey helped to arrange her so that she was astride him,

and together, they guided his cock to her soaked entrance. She sank down on him as he thrust upward, and they met each other in the middle, finding a rhythm that had them both hurtling toward bliss in no time. Aubrey took her nipple into his mouth as he fucked her, and she came helplessly all over his cock, a rush of wetness bursting from her as stars exploded before her eyes. He cried out her name and filled her with his seed.

In the aftermath of their mutual release, she collapsed atop his chest, listening to his heart hammering fast, matching her own. He sifted a hand tenderly through her hair and kissed her crown.

"I love you, Aubrey," she said, thinking of the miracle they shared.

The miracle of love, of the new life within her. The miracle of how they had found each other, two souls who made each other whole. The miracle of how, even though they had been torn apart and all had seemingly been lost, they had found their way back again.

And here they were, husband and wife.

Her heart was so happy.

"I love you too, minx," he said, his cock already beginning to stir within her again. "I'll always be your grasshopper."

She smiled and kissed his chest, teasing them both by moving up and down on him ever so slightly, testing the waters. "And I'll be your goddess of the dawn."

"Again?" he asked with great interest as he thickened within her.

She sat up and met his gaze, smiling, feeling thoroughly wicked and utterly wonderful. "Again, darling."

And they made love slowly and thoroughly a second time before they fell into a deep and sated sleep, tangled in each other's arms.

Thank you so very much for reading *Duke with a Lie*! I hope you adored Rhiannon and Aubrey's rather scorching path to happily ever after as much as I loved writing it. Brother's best friend is one of my favorite tropes.

More Wicked Dukes are preparing to fall. For a sneak peek at the Duke of Riverdale and his mysterious duchess (Lady Blue, is that you?) do read on for an excerpt of *Duke with a Duchess*.

Plus, I'm thrilled to share with you that I've collaborated with my close friend and phenomenally talented *NYT* and *USA Today* Bestselling author Melanie Moreland on a new Regency romance, *Maid for the Marquess*. Be sure to look for an exclusive sneak peek of Maddie and Alexander's swoon-worthy age gap HEA after *Duke with a Duchess*.

And if you also happen to enjoy dark mafia romance, I'd love for you to check out my book *Brutal Devil*, written as Lora Whitney, featuring an arranged marriage with a possessive, morally gray hero, forced proximity, and loads of spice!

Please stay in touch! The only way to be sure you'll know what's next from me is to sign up for my newsletter here: http://eepurl.com/dyJSar. Please join my reader group for early excerpts, cover reveals, and more here: https://www.facebook.com/groups/scarlettscottreaders. And if you're in the mood to chat all things steamy historical romance and read a different book together each month, join my book club, Dukes Do It Hotter right here: https://www.facebook.com/groups/hotdukes because we're having a whole lot of fun!

Duke with a Duchess
Wicked Dukes Society Book 5

WHEN EVERETT SAUNDERS, Duke of Riverdale, needed to marry in haste, he found the perfect duchess. One who would grant him an heir and a spare and rusticate quietly at his estate, allowing him to carry on with his life of debauchery. At least, that was the woman he *thought* he'd married. Instead, he unwittingly leg-shackled himself to a cunning, fortune-seeking liar. The only solution to his woes is abandoning the conniving baggage and simply carrying on as if he doesn't have a wife at all.

Nothing in her life has ever gone according to plan, and her hasty marriage is no different. But Sybil, Duchess of Riverdale, isn't about to meekly allow her rakehell husband to abandon her and go on with his life. When her letters to him remain unanswered, she takes matters into her own hands, determined to obtain a divorce by any means, fair or foul.

Riverdale, however, is unwilling to let her go unless she gives him an heir. Sybil has no choice but to accept the sinful arrangement proposed by her husband. She'll submit to his desires in the bedchamber, but he'll never again have the power to break her heart. All she has to do is keep herself from falling back in love with the merciless rogue she married.

Chapter One

SYBIL TIPPED the pitcher toward her sleeping husband's head. A stream of cold, clear water poured forth, landing directly on the thick mahogany locks that were a great source of pride and vanity for him, splashing over his unfairly handsome face.

He sputtered and jolted awake, sitting up as water streamed down, his bedclothes falling in his lap.

His chest was bare.

Sybil intentionally averted her gaze. Because whilst the Duke of Riverdale was a terrible, faithless husband, his body, like his face, was as perfectly proportioned as any marble from antiquity. At least he was the only one presently occupying his bed. Otherwise, she might have broken the pitcher on his head instead of merely pouring water to wake him.

"What the devil?" he sputtered, shaking like a dog to dash the water from his eyes.

Sybil had imagined a reunion with her husband on many occasions. Never quite like this, however.

"Good morning, Riverdale," she said coldly.

"Sybil?" He glared at her, his lip curling. "What are you doing in my bedroom? And why the hell did you pour water on me?"

She settled the pitcher in its basin. "Is that any way to greet your wife?"

"Is dumping a pitcher of water on my bloody head any way to greet your husband?" he snarled.

Water was streaking down his throat and rolling south in droplets over his chest now. Sybil told herself not to look, and yet her foolish eyes had a will of their own.

"Perhaps you ought to tell me the proper means of greeting a husband one hasn't seen in more than three months," she suggested. "A husband who abandoned one in the country and refuses to reply to any correspondence."

He gathered up the counterpane and began using it to dry himself, continuing to glower as he did so. "I have nothing to say to you, madam."

His words, like his ire, shouldn't matter. Shouldn't have

the power to wound her. And yet, they did. He had made his disregard for her feelings known, just as he had made his dislike of her more than clear.

"Indeed, but *I* have something to say to *you*." She kept her eyes pinned to his, intentionally not glancing down at his damp chest.

Or his muscled arms, flexing as he moved.

Curse the man. She was looking again.

"How nice for you." His voice was cold, just like his wintry blue eyes. "I don't give a damn."

She hadn't expected a pleasant reunion. Riverdale had made his opinion of her painfully obvious before he had left that awful day. He hadn't waited for her explanation, hadn't bothered to listen to even a word she had to offer. She hadn't been able to defend herself. No matter now. The worst was done. But his seething fury still somehow stung.

"Perhaps you ought to care," she suggested.

"Too late for that." He dropped the bedclothes and ran a hand through his hair, pushing it back from his high forehead. "Get out of my bedroom."

She didn't budge, her feet rooted to the Axminster. "Not until you hear what I've come to say."

"More lies," he snapped. "I have neither the time, nor the inclination to listen to a word you say."

"Yes, I suppose you are eager to return to your carousing. No doubt you have some skirts to chase this morning. Do forgive me for keeping you from them."

Sybil couldn't conceal the bitterness in her voice, though she had tried her utmost. She was still every bit as furious with him as he was with her. But of the two of them, she was the only one with good reason.

"Is that why you've come?" he asked, smirking. "Are you jealous, darling?"

Yes, but she would leap out the nearest window before admitting it to him.

She tipped her chin up, scoffing. "Hardly. I have no claim on you."

He had also made that more than apparent. The Duke of Riverdale had no intention of being a faithful husband.

"You are correct in that, madam. You don't. Now get out, if you please. I need to take a piss, and I'd rather do it without you listening."

He was being coarse and vulgar, trying to shock her. It wasn't going to work.

"No. Not until you hear what I've come to say."

He shrugged. "Suit yourself."

Before she could protest or avert her gaze, he flipped back the bedclothes and rose, naked. Her eyes dropped of their own volition to his long, thick shaft standing proudly erect.

He was hard.

Heat flew over her. He stalked across the room, his buttocks flexing as he went.

"I want you to divorce me," she blurted.

Want more? Get *Duke with a Duchess* now!

∽

Maid for the Marquess

Miss Maddie Smythe
My callous father wagered me to a brooding stranger during a hand of cards, leaving me terrified.
But Lord Wheaton was nothing like the baron who'd forced me into servitude and gave me away.
The handsome marquess was compassionate, honorable, and my only hope for a future.

I married him to save myself, not intending to lose my heart. Never thinking of the danger that loomed, threatening to tear us apart forever.

Alexander, Marquess of Wheaton

The last thing I needed was an innocent to protect, but I couldn't leave the frightened maid to her vile father's mercy.

It didn't take me long to realize Maddie was everything I never knew I needed, sweet and caring and lovely.

She made me whole.

When her villainous father tried to take her from me, I vowed to do everything in my power to save my wife.

Even if it meant sacrificing myself…

EXCERPT

"I will add one more thing," the baron said abruptly.

I frowned at the unexpected offer.

"Which is?"

"A servant for you." Something in his voice set my teeth on edge. He looked delighted, as if he had suddenly thought of a plan.

"I have no need of any servants."

He waved his hand. "This one is special. Been in my house her whole life." He paused. "Untouched. She will be yours to do with what you want. In fact, I hope you use her then cast her aside when done."

I was shocked at his callous tone. Horrified at his suggestion. I met Edward's eyes, who also looked dismayed.

"I beg your pardon," I snapped.

He held up his hand. "I mean no disrespect. I know you are a man who prefers experience. Consider this a gift. Whether you win or not."

I realized he fully expected to win. That in his twisted

mind, I would accept a servant in lieu of funds, never suspecting his fraud.

"Bring her in," he ordered his butler.

Once again, I met Edward's gaze, a silent conversation flowing between us. Whoever this servant was, it was obvious Barnett despised her. Wanted her gone and wished for her to suffer.

Nothing prepared me for the young woman who was dragged into the room and pushed in front of me. I automatically rose to my feet as any gentleman would do when a lady entered. I had to grab the edge of the table to remain standing. It was the chit I had seen scurrying away—the one who had captured my interest for some reason. Seeing her fully was a shock.

Draped in a gown that was threadbare and far too large on her small frame, she shrank into herself, as if used to hiding. Her head was bowed, her shaking arms wrapped around her torso. Small feet peeked out from under the useless garment. It did nothing to hide her form or protect her.

I wondered what the greatest motivation behind her trembling was.

Cold or fear?

I noticed how tiny her hands were that clutched her gown. Surprisingly long fingers gripped the material—digits so slender they were noticeable even through the gloves she wore. That oddity caught me off guard, making me wonder why she would have gloves on at this time of night. Her arms were rail thin—in fact her entire body seemed more childlike than that of a maiden.

With her head lowered, her unbound, wild, dark hair hid her face. I crossed my arms, feigning disinterest.

"I have no need of a child," I growled, furious.

Lord Barnett leaned forward, his voice dripping in anger.

"Show yourself, girl. Push that horrid mane behind you and look up. Or bear the taste of my displeasure." When she didn't move, he stood. "Your father is speaking," he roared.

Another jolt of shock hit me.

This was his *daughter*? Why was she being treated as a servant?

Slowly she straightened her shoulders, using one hand to push away the heavy tresses. She lifted her head, and our gazes locked. I stepped back in disbelief, barely able to hide my horror and shock.

The face she revealed was that of a beautiful skeleton. White skin, beyond pale, stretched taut over high cheekbones. A perfectly formed nose. Small ears. A swan's neck. In contrast with her paleness, her lips were full and red, akin to a slash of crimson on snow. Hers was one of the loveliest faces I had ever beheld with my eyes.

Her hair tumbled past her slender shoulders, and my eyes were drawn to her bosom.

Her breasts were large, heavy. Far too large for her tiny frame. Even standing straight, she tried to hide them, obviously ill at ease.

Her trembling increased as I drew closer. Our eyes met, and I felt the stirrings within my chest as I took in her weary, ancient gaze.

Her eyes were blue—but not the simple blue of the sky or water. They were a shade I could not even describe, that of the ocean on a stormy day, blues and grays mixing and crashing together. Framed by long lashes, they were filled with pain and trepidation.

And pure, abject terror.

I had seen that terror in one other set of eyes. It was a memory I carried close to my heart—that after all these years still had the power to bring me to my knees.

I hadn't been able to comprehend what I was seeing then,

but I recognized it now. And I refused to turn my back on that fear.

"She'll do."

Want more? Get Maid for the Marquess now!

DON'T MISS SCARLETT'S OTHER ROMANCES!

Complete Book List
HISTORICAL ROMANCE

Heart's Temptation
A Mad Passion (Book One)
Rebel Love (Book Two)
Reckless Need (Book Three)
Sweet Scandal (Book Four)
Restless Rake (Book Five)
Darling Duke (Book Six)
The Night Before Scandal (Book Seven)

Wicked Husbands
Her Errant Earl (Book One)
Her Lovestruck Lord (Book Two)
Her Reformed Rake (Book Three)
Her Deceptive Duke (Book Four)
Her Missing Marquess (Book Five)
Her Virtuous Viscount (Book Six)

DON'T MISS SCARLETT'S OTHER ROMANCES!

Wicked Dukes Society
Duke with a Reputation (Book One)
Duke with a Debt (Book Two)
Duke with a Secret (Book Three)
Duke with a Lie (Book Four)
Duke with a Duchess (Book Five)

Christmas Dukes
The Duke Who Despised Christmas (Book One)
The Duke Who Ruined Christmas (Book Two)

League of Dukes
Nobody's Duke (Book One)
Heartless Duke (Book Two)
Dangerous Duke (Book Three)
Shameless Duke (Book Four)
Scandalous Duke (Book Five)
Fearless Duke (Book Six)

Notorious Ladies of London
Lady Ruthless (Book One)
Lady Wallflower (Book Two)
Lady Reckless (Book Three)
Lady Wicked (Book Four)
Lady Lawless (Book Five)
Lady Brazen (Book 6)

Unexpected Lords
The Detective Duke (Book One)
The Playboy Peer (Book Two)
The Millionaire Marquess (Book Three)
The Goodbye Governess (Book Four)

Dukes Most Wanted

DON'T MISS SCARLETT'S OTHER ROMANCES!

Forever Her Duke (Book One)
Forever Her Marquess (Book Two)
Forever Her Rake (Book Three)
Forever Her Earl (Book Four)
Forever Her Viscount (Book Five)
Forever Her Scot (Book Six)

The Wicked Winters
Wicked in Winter (Book One)
Wedded in Winter (Book Two)
Wanton in Winter (Book Three)
Wishes in Winter (Book 3.5)
Willful in Winter (Book Four)
Wagered in Winter (Book Five)
Wild in Winter (Book Six)
Wooed in Winter (Book Seven)
Winter's Wallflower (Book Eight)
Winter's Woman (Book Nine)
Winter's Whispers (Book Ten)
Winter's Waltz (Book Eleven)
Winter's Widow (Book Twelve)
Winter's Warrior (Book Thirteen)
A Merry Wicked Winter (Book Fourteen)

The Sinful Suttons
Sutton's Spinster (Book One)
Sutton's Sins (Book Two)
Sutton's Surrender (Book Three)
Sutton's Seduction (Book Four)
Sutton's Scoundrel (Book Five)
Sutton's Scandal (Book Six)
Sutton's Secrets (Book Seven)

Rogue's Guild

DON'T MISS SCARLETT'S OTHER ROMANCES!

Her Ruthless Duke (Book One)
Her Dangerous Beast (Book Two)
Her Wicked Rogue (Book 3)

Royals and Renegades
How to Love a Dangerous Rogue (Book One)
How to Tame a Dissolute Prince (Book Two)

Sins and Scoundrels
Duke of Depravity
Prince of Persuasion
Marquess of Mayhem
Sarah
Earl of Every Sin
Duke of Debauchery
Viscount of Villainy

With *NYT* Bestselling Author Melanie Moreland
Maid for the Marquess

Sins and Scoundrels Box Set Collections
Volume 1
Volume 2

The Wicked Winters Box Set Collections
Collection 1
Collection 2
Collection 3
Collection 4

Wicked Husbands Box Set Collections
Volume 1
Volume 2

DON'T MISS SCARLETT'S OTHER ROMANCES!

Notorious Ladies of London Box Set Collections
Volume 1
Volume 2

The Sinful Suttons Box Set Collections
Volume 1
Volume 2

Stand-alone Novella
Lord of Pirates

CONTEMPORARY ROMANCE
Love's Second Chance
Reprieve (Book One)
Perfect Persuasion (Book Two)
Win My Love (Book Three)

Coastal Heat
Loved Up (Book One)

Writing as Lora Whitney

Mafia Romance
Andriani Brothers
Brutal Devil (Book One)
Cruel Sinner (Book Two)

ABOUT THE AUTHOR

USA Today and Amazon bestselling author Scarlett Scott™ writes steamy Victorian and Regency romance with strong, intelligent heroines and sexy alpha heroes. She lives in Pennsylvania and Maryland with her Canadian husband, their adorable identical twins, a demanding diva of a dog, and a zany cat who showed up one summer and never left.

A self-professed literary junkie and nerd, she loves reading anything, but especially romance novels and poetry. Catch up with her on her website https://scarlettscottauthor.com. Hearing from readers never fails to make her day.

Scarlett's complete book list and information about upcoming releases can be found at https://scarlettscottauthor.com.

Connect with Scarlett! You can find her here:
    Join Scarlett Scott's reader group on Facebook for early excerpts, giveaways, and a whole lot of fun!
    Sign up for her newsletter here
    https://www.tiktok.com/@authorscarlettscott

- facebook.com/AuthorScarlettScott
- x.com/scarscoromance
- instagram.com/scarlettscottauthor
- bookbub.com/authors/scarlett-scott
- amazon.com/Scarlett-Scott/e/B004NW8N2I
- pinterest.com/scarlettscott

Made in United States
Orlando, FL
13 December 2025